THE UNINVITED

JONATHAN DANIEL

Copyright © 2011 by Jonathan Daniel

All rights reserved.

No part of this book may be reproduced in any form or by any electronic or mechanical means, including information storage and retrieval systems, without written permission from the author, except for the use of brief quotations in a book review.

For my family. Thank you for your constant support, love and encouragement. I love you all.

AUTHOR'S NOTE

Hi! Jonathan here. I wanted to take a quick second to thank you for buying The Uninvited. Seriously, I know you have a lot of choices when it comes to horror fiction, and the fact that you made the decision to spend your money on my book means the world to me.

I had a lot of fun writing this. I genuinely hope you have a lot of fun reading it.

If you find yourself liking it (and even if you don't) I would love it (and I'm using 'love' in the strongest way possible...like bordering on creepy) if you took a moment to leave a review on whatever platform you purchased The Uninvited. As an indie author, I live and die by reviews. Seriously, it's that important.

Now, on to The Uninvited.

1

At ten minutes after eight in the morning, Sunday, March 18th, Owen Decker woke with a freight train careening through his skull and the overwhelming sense that he was drowning. The headache seemed to pulse, growing with every fluctuation like a cancerous tumor determined to occupy every crevice of his being.

With monumental effort, he threw the sheets off of him and rolled out of bed, standing on shaky legs all in one fluid motion. Before the roaring pain in his head could regain itself and communicate with the roiling nausea in his stomach, Owen threw on a pair of ragged cut off shorts, a patterned shirt that he had bought in Nassau the day before, and slipped on his shoes. Dressed, he walked determinedly across the room of the resort, ignoring completely its lavish décor and went into the hallway to find the other guests, coffee and– God help him–Advil.

He entered a hallway that, despite the lack of open windows, was breezy and full of the salty scent of the ocean. Another smell, slightly darker, wafted on the breeze, barely perceptible. The hallway was painted a muted yellow. Above an arched ceiling was painted a light sky blue. To his left a small decorative table sat against the wall at the end of the hallway. For a moment he stared at the table, his pain-riddled mind telling him something was wrong with it, but unable to comprehend what exactly that was. Then it came to him. On the floor in front of the table was a blue and white ceramic vase, shattered into dozens of irregular pieces. The dirt that had been contained within bulged from beneath the broken shards, like some organic brain matter peeking from behind a skull. Stems of what had once been flowers were pulverized as if a shoe had purposefully ground them into the stone floor. The sight of the upset vase among all the calm beauty disturbed Owen and he turned quickly away.

The hallway ended at a short flight of stairs that descended into a larger room with dark hardwood floors. Owen stopped at the bottom step and looked around. The room seemed to be some kind of open foyer, not really used for anything. Several more of the decorative tables lined the wall at intervals. Some held more plants, others nothing. Each wall held several original paintings. To his left was a large wooden door with ornate carvings in its surface. Across from him was an open doorway flanked by two large potted plants. Through the opening, a long hallway disappeared into the gloom. To his right was an open arched doorway that led to another room. Owen thought of calling out, but something about the silence was so oppressive that his mouth refused to open and create sound. The feeling of unease that he had experienced while looking at the destroyed flowers and vase returned, snaking a cold hand up the back of Owen's shirt.

"Get over it," he whispered. "You're hung over and everyone is outside enjoying the place." Owen shook his head and walked into the dining room. The dining room was empty of people. A long table filled the center of the large room, with benches to either side instead of individual chairs. A sideboard ran along the right hand wall, the top of it decorated with more plants. The walls were a muted golden yellow with a faux pattern, giving the walls a stony textured look. Owen let his eyes play over the polished surface of the table, the benches, and then the walls. Everything seemed to be holding its breath in anticipation.

Then he saw it. The wall opposite him, at the far end of the room.

A splash of deep crimson on the yellow wall. The pattern seemed much too random and irregular to be a form of artwork. Owen's tennis shoes made no sound on the floor as he crossed the room, his eyebrows furrowing at the marking. As he reached it and stretched his arm out to touch it, the toe of one of his shoes squeaked on the floor beneath him, then shifted slightly. He looked down and saw more of the deep crimson on the floor, pooled at his feet and leading away around the corner of the table like some oily carpet. In Owen's chest, his heart increased its speed. Someone had an accident. He followed the blood around the table and to the doorway leading to the kitchen. His mind reeled. What could have happened? Did someone cut themselves? Before he knew what was happening, his arm swung up and pushed the door to the kitchen open.

The bloody carpet continued into the room, the blood becoming brighter under the stark fluorescent lights mounted on rails along the ceiling. The floor was a muted grey tile, the walls white. Every table, appliance and utensil was brushed nickel. The blood trail wound between two tables and around a corner to Owen's left. He stared at it. If someone had been cut and rushed into the kitchen for a towel, they had certainly bled a lot. The trail he looked at resembled more a heavy flow from someone lying on the floor and being pulled into the room.

Something shifted in the recesses of the room. Somewhere off to his left, around the corner and in the direction of the blood, Owen heard a scuff of shoe on tile, then a soft grunt. Silence fell again. He opened his mouth to call out, thinking that the person may be laying against a freezer unit or other large appliance and unable to walk. However, his mouth refused to emit sound. He could feel his throat constrict against the will of words.

The clatter of a utensil on the metal surface of a table rocked the space. Owen flinched at the sound, his heart joining his constricting throat. He took a tentative step forward, eyes bouncing from tabletop to tabletop. Slowly, like a slug, Owen moved further into the room and cleared the corner. He turned left and let his eyes move along the trail of blood to where it stopped. The body lay prone in a massive pool of the red ichor. The person's upper body was coated in it, and through the red he could make out the white scraps of what looked like a staff's uniform. The chest was exposed and the flesh was torn horribly, exposing a gaping hole of gore.

Squatting over the body was another figure, wearing blood-stained shorts and an equally bloody white staff member's shirt. The staff member knelt and had his hands buried halfway up the forearms in the open chest cavity of the dead man. The arms moved in short motions, and the living man grunted softly with each movement. Likewise, the corpse jerked slightly as the hands within it worked. There was an almost quiet, wet, tearing sound then the staff member brought a hand out of his coworker. Owen noticed in growing horror that the hands of the living man were seemingly deformed, having become elongated somehow. The fingers were as long as rail spikes and ended in what looked like short claws. Dangling from between two of the appendages was a bloody scrap of meat. The man lifted his head and gazed at it. Owen couldn't stop the scream that rose from within him like a leviathan rushing to the surface of the ocean. The sight of the living man was almost more than he could bear.

The man's face resembled a human visage only in that the organs were still in generally the right area. The eyes were black with yellow pupils so bright they seemed to burn. The nose was flat, but the nostrils had turned upwards so that they almost resembled open pits carved in the front of the man's face. The lips were cracked and the color of liver, peeled back from a bloody mouth that, through the gore stains, flashed pointed teeth that looked as if they had been filed to the sharpness of needles.

Owen screamed.

The man-thing snapped its head around and stared at him, the yellow pits of its eyes narrowing then growing large as they focused and took in his image. It froze, one arm cocked in the air with the piece of human flesh dangling like a fish held by the tail. A deep rumbling filled the room and Owen didn't need any time to know that it came from the heaving chest of the thing in front of him. The creature—Owen couldn't bring himself to think of it as a man, as irrational as that was—flicked its wrist and tossed the scrap of meat into its mouth, then stood so swiftly that it was stepping over the body towards him before Owen knew what was happening.

It sprung forward with a growl, clawed hands hooked and grasping for Owen. Owen scrambled backwards and almost went down as his left foot dragged over the blood trail. The creature's feet connected with the slick floor and it went down hard on the tile. A howl of pain and anger erupted from its lips. The sound jarred Owen into action. He turned and sprinted from the kitchen, back into the dining room and into the foyer beyond. His momentum carried him directly to the large wooden door. With trembling hands that seemed filled with sand, Owen struggled to grip the round knob and pull the door open. As the door swung inward on quiet hinges, a thought sprinted across his mind.

He pulled the door fully open then turned on his heels and dashed to the right, heading down the dim hallway. A dozen yards ahead of him, he could see the corridor take a turn to the right. His breath coming in panicked gasps, Owen increased his speed. He had to reach the turn before the creature caught up to him.

He made it to the turn and bounced off the opposite wall, springing back with his hands. The hallway opened into a wide courtyard filled with greenery and metal benches. Grey stone statues peeked at him from between large tropical leaves as if they were playing a game of hide and seek with him. The walls of the house rose at the fringes of the space, arches beneath a balcony that encircled the courtyard. Owen couldn't see doorways on the second floor. The support beams ran from the floor to the glass ceiling overhead. In the center of the space, a large fountain shot a geyser of water several feet in the air, only to have it cascade down several levels of stone to a wide pool. The air was particularly thick and muggy here. Owen cut between two bushes and made toward the fountain. Maybe he could circle around in the plants and get back down the hallway and out the front door. The fountain would drown out the sounds of his progress.

But, he realized, it would also mask the sounds of his pursuer. The thought was hardly clear of his mind when he stopped short. A body lay at the edge of the large fountain. It was a man. That much Owen could tell from the legs and lower torso that protruded from the water and rested on the ground. Thick, hairy legs jutted from dark green shorts that were even darker from the water that splashed down on them. The water in the basin of the fountain was a cloudy red.

Owen set his jaw and continued moving, determined not to look back at the corpse. He angled around the fountain and started back toward the entrance. The bushes to his left began to shake violently, and instantly Owen crouched, his heart jack hammering in his throat. He twisted away and began to duck crawl in a new direction.

He moved toward one of the many arches. There had to be a way out of here, he thought. It surprised him only briefly that he was still capable of rational thought. It would seem that when a person was faced with impossible reality, being hunted by something that couldn't possibly exist yet somehow did, that all coherent thoughts and reasoning abilities would cease. However, as he moved through the thick foliage, Owen found himself thinking several steps ahead, trying to fight through the hangover and the steady pounding of his head and reclaim some memory from the night before. He was certain that during the party he would have come through here. This room was too spectacular for Donovan not to have shown it off to his guests.

The bushes thinned and through them he could see the pathway that encircled the garden. Across it was an arched doorway that led into a darker corridor. Owen risked a glance over his shoulder but saw nothing other than the leaves he had just crawled through. There was no sign of the thing that followed him, no rustle of greenery, no scuffing of its black shoe on the ground. Not that he would probably hear it, he thought. Even across the large courtyard the fountain was still loud.

That thought brought the flash of an image of the dead man sprawled in the water. Owen shivered, felt his throat tighten up in panic and swallowed hard. He had to keep moving. Moving slowly he edged closer to the cement path. At the fringes of the garden he paused again and peered along either side of the walkway. It was empty. Sweat that he hadn't noticed before dripped from his eyebrows and tickled his cheeks. He felt it now, coating his body in a slimy skin. He breathed once and moved quickly through the last of the bushes and across the path. He winced as he moved, anticipating the roar of the creature, the stinging pain of its bite, but nothing came. The hallway and the relative safety of its shadows swallowed him instead.

He ran on the balls of his feet, trying to keep as quiet as he could as he moved down the corridor. The walls were dark, painted a deep golden and felt rough under his palms. Dim amber light filled the area and Owen followed the path until it turned sharply to the right. He paused at the turn, risked a quick glance around the corner and breathed heavily when he saw a large open room that was well lit and furnished with plush furniture. There were voices coming from the room.

"Thank God," he whispered and moved around the corner. As he neared the doorway leading into the large room, he felt his gait slow and his shoulders relax. He hadn't noticed just how tense he had gotten until that moment. The voices continued a heated discussion regarding the current administration's newest policy. The debaters, two older men he could tell, were trying to be civil to one another but condescension and dislike ran thickly beneath their voices. Owen walked through the doorway and into the lighted room. It was a large entertainment room. Half a dozen thickly padded leather couches and chairs were strategically placed throughout. Next to each were dark wood end tables, some with plants on them, others with small lamps. To his left, the voices continued their argument. Owen looked that way, his mouth opening to interrupt their discussion.

A large flat screen television was mounted to the wall; the screen split into two halves each featuring the solemn faces of the debaters. Owen's shoulders slumped. He walked to the television and switched it off. The ensuing silence was loud in his ears. He turned around and surveyed the rest of the room. A dark mahogany bar lined one wall, its bottles filled with amber and clear liquids. To the right of the rows of bottles, mounted to the wall, was a large square pegboard from which dangled several sets of keys. Many of the keys had yellow foam bobs attached to them, and Owen assumed they were used for jet skis or boats. At the sight of them, Owen noticed a faint sour scent in the air. Frowning, he moved toward the bar, slid between two of the plush stools and leaned over. On the floor was a large pool of blood. Small chunks of flesh were stuck within it, like horrible islands in a terrible sea. The sour scent was stronger here and Owen winced as it stung his nostrils. He looked around and saw several feet to the right of the blood several broken bottles of liquor. The scene was a grim reminder of things.

Behind him he heard a noise and wheeled around. Nothing moved in the room. The sound came again, this time faint but clearly from the hallway he had arrived. Owen felt his knees grow weak at the sound. The creature was still back there. Christ, where was everyone else? Dead? How could it be that one thing killed everyone but him? He was drunk and passed out, but surely he would have heard carnage like that happening.

The sound came again, a soft scrape of footsteps on tile. The thing was moving down the hallway toward him. Owen's head swiveled crazily as he looked for a way out or suitable hiding place. Behind the bar he saw another door. Without thinking, he went to it. It swung inward noiselessly and Owen found himself standing in a small storage room filled with shelves and boxes full of liquor bottles and cases of beer. To one side of the door a large silver icemaker hummed softly.

"Shit," he whispered. He turned to leave and heard the creature enter the room.

Although Owen couldn't see it, he could picture it, crouched just inside the room, sniffing and scanning. Oh God, had it heard him turn off the television? Was it that stupid of a move that had him trapped now?

The room on the other side of the door was silent. Owen couldn't hear even the tiniest of sounds. He stood at the door, straining to hear anything. Before he knew what was happening, his hands reached forward and moved the door open a fraction of an inch. He peered through the crack, his heart hammering so loudly in his chest he was certain it would give him away. From his vantage, Owen could see the corner of the bar and a large chair in the middle of the floor. There was no sign of the creature at all. Had it gone? Surely it would have moved on, having determined that its quarry wasn't in the room.

Then it was in front of him, its grotesque face filling his vision before the creature turned away. The back of its skull looked sickly, large patches of hair were missing in random areas. Owen bit his lips together and felt the lower crack from the pressure of his tooth. Blood filled his mouth and he swallowed it down, wincing at the pain and the salty taste. The creature hadn't seen him yet; its back was to the door. It seemed to be leaning toward the bar, sniffing the coagulating blood on the floor. Owen eased the door closed and backed away. He knew it was a matter of time before the thing decided to check the storage closet. He would be trapped, then ripped to pieces. He would die among dusty boxes of Captain Morgan rum.

As he backed from the door, his heel bumped something hard. The ice chest. Owen looked at it, as if he had never seen one before in his life. It was a standard restaurant style ice chest, with a large lift up door that would allow the user access to the deep bin of frozen water. Owen's gaze shifted from the ice chest to the door, then back again.

He lifted the lid to the bin and found it only half full. Looking down at his shorts and thin shirt he frowned then climbed carefully into the ice, laying on his right side and closing the lid with his left hand. Enshrouded in blackness, Owen fought to hear the creature enter the storage closet. The ice was a solid wall of painful cold surrounding him. The air above him was frigid and seemed to push him down into the cubes below. He could feel them digging into his flesh, slipping into the legs of his shorts and trickling down to his buttocks. The urge to shift his position came strong, but Owen swatted it away like an annoying bee.

Then he heard it. A cough from outside the freezer. It was slight, almost imperceptible through the thick door of the ice chest and the hum of the freezer motor. But it came through all the same. Enough for him to know that the thing chasing him with animalistic intent was inside the storage room. Owen tensed, not feeling the cold anymore. He clenched his hands into fists and waited for the lid to the freezer to lift open. He would go down swinging, by God.

The cough came again, then silence. The deadness of sound stretched into long minutes. Owen pictured the storage room and tried to imagine the creature searching it. It couldn't take very long to inspect the entire area, he thought. The closet was nothing more than that, and filled with boxes of liquor and beer. Not many places for a man to hide. Why didn't it look in the freezer? he wondered. Maybe it couldn't smell him through the ice and the walls of the container. Maybe it didn't notice the freezer, or if it did, perhaps it didn't know what it was or that it could be used as a hideout. Owen didn't care about the answers to these questions, only considered them to distract himself from the fear and the returning feeling of cold. It now was deep into his body, burning his skin with a cold fire that wouldn't dissipate.

He waited several more minutes before deciding that he couldn't take lying on the ice any longer. With a numb hand he lifted the door and peered out. The storage room was empty. A large breath escaped his lips and he climbed carefully out onto the floor. As he stood rubbing his arms and legs, trying desperately to force feeling to return, he looked around again to confirm that he was alone in the closet.

Another quick peek out the main door revealed nothing in the larger room. Owen shut the door again and debated leaving the space. If the creature had already searched the closet and determined it was empty, it stood to reason that he could stay here and be relatively safe for as long as it took for help to arrive. There had to be others on the island; surely they would come looking for him. And if not, then people back in America would know when he had been missing for a length of time.

A new, more horrifying thought occurred to him. If there were more than just the one creature out there, chances were good that another one would find its way into the entertainment room and that would be the end of him. Owen had no reason to believe there were others out there, but he decided that he didn't want to take the chance. It would be better if he were out there, moving and maybe finding others who had survived whatever had happened than trapped in a small closet waiting to be rescued or eaten.

He opened the door again, slowly, and peered out into the room. It was empty. Owen took one small, tentative step out into the room and paused. His ears strained to hear evidence of the creature. There was nothing. He stepped further into the room, his skin still burning from the ice and his head still throbbing from the exertion and the hangover.

Owen allowed himself to relax slightly and walked slowly to the center of the room. He collapsed into one of the chairs and let out a sigh. What the hell would he do now? His eyes focused on the sole doorway to the room and he watched it with guarded caution.

Something shifted behind him and Owen started as the cold blade of a large kitchen knife came to rest on his throat.

"Are you normal?" a woman's voice demanded quietly. Owen found himself unable to answer. Fear coursed through him, a blinding tingle. What if he opened his mouth to speak and the action caused the blade to cut him? He'd bleed to death before he could do anything about it.

The pressure of the knife increased and now he felt it slice his skin. Hot blood ran down his neck to his shoulder, over his collarbone and down his chest. "Yes," he managed. His voice came out in a hoarse whisper.

"How do I know?" the woman asked.

To his surprise, Owen found his fear disappearing. The woman behind him was normal, a survivor like him. Otherwise she wouldn't have used a knife, and most likely wouldn't be asking him questions. She would have simply killed him. "Because I'm talking to you," he said.

Owen felt the knife pull away from his throat. He put a hand to his neck and turned to look at the woman. His breath caught in his throat. She was beautiful, even through her sweat soaked hair and tan complexion. Long red hair fell in wet clumps around her shoulders. She stared at him intently with deep brown eyes. She had moved back a step, but still held the knife ready in one hand. Owen noticed she wore a light green shirt and denim shorts. Despite the situation, he found himself noticing the curves of her body, the fullness of her breasts and the muscular legs that held her up.

"Where's the one chasing you?"

Owen shrugged. "I don't know. I hid in the ice chest in the storage closet over there and it left." He stood and walked to the bar, leaned over and found a small hand towel, which he used to press against his neck. "Where did you come from? That's the only doorway to the room and the creature had to have gone through it when it left."

The woman pointed with the knife over her shoulder. Owen looked and saw, next to a fake palm tree, a small doorway. He nodded. "I'm Owen Decker."

"Jessica Walters."

"Jessica, what ..." his voice died and he gestured weakly at the room around them.

She looked around the room like a sentry. "I don't know. I went to bed last night because I was bored at the party. I remember seeing you there. I woke up this morning to someone screaming outside my door. When the screaming stopped I looked out and found one of the staff members dead. He had been torn apart by something. I've been trying to find anyone else who may have survived and get the hell out of here, but you're the first person I've come across. But yes, there are others out there ... a lot of others."

A snarl sounded from the corridor. Owen gripped the bar and saw his pursuer standing in a half crouch. The thing filled the doorway. From where they stood, Owen could smell its fetid breath. It took a step into the room and Jessica brought the knife up. The thing looked at the weapon with its black and yellow eyes. It bared its teeth and for a moment Owen thought it was laughing at their attempts at a defense.

When it moved toward Jessica, it moved swiftly. Owen barely registered its motion. The woman screamed and slashed at the air in front of her with the knife. The creature dodged the blade and leapt onto her, sending her sprawling on the floor.

Owen grabbed a large square bottle of whiskey from the bar and rushed over. The creature raised one clawed hand to swipe at Jessica's head when Owen brought the bottle down on its skull with every ounce of strength he had. It connected with a wet thump and the creature went instantly limp. Blood sprayed from its skull and it fell to one side. Jessica scrambled to her feet and retrieved her knife.

"Is it dead?" Owen asked.

"I don't know." She looked at him and motioned to the door next to the palm tree. "Let's get the hell out of here." Owen took one last look at the motionless figure on the floor and then followed Jessica out of the room.

2

Three days ago ...

"How have you been?"

Owen looked up from his lap where his hands had been fidgeting. Doctor Sturn sat in his comfortable leather desk chair, legs crossed, notepad in his lap. He held a thin gold pen in his manicured fingers. The doctor's face was relaxed, a soft, expectant smile on his lips. Owen's eyes traced the doctor's lips, then worked their way outward along his beard and up past his thin, rimless glasses.

Owen shifted on the plush couch and cleared his throat. He shrugged. "I've had my good days and my bad. Probably more bad than good. That's how it seems, anyway."

Sturn scribbled quickly in the notebook, his soft green eyes darting down to the paper then back to meet his patient's face. "Bad in what way?"

Owen pulled his gaze away from the psychiatrist and forced himself to look around the small, cramped office. Nothing had changed over the numerous visits he had attended, but he looked at each item as if it were something new and undiscovered. Books lined double bookshelves that flanked the small wooden desk. Certificates hung on the wall between the shelves, as if they were there to reassure the mentally unstable that they were receiving only the highest quality of services. The only thing missing, Owen mused, was a health board rating. He looked at a small fern that hung from the ceiling and wondered what kind of rating Doctor Sturn would receive.

He sighed, moving his eyes suddenly across the framed picture of the doctor and his family that hung on another wall, above a small table that held a lamp, a box of tissue, and a bottle of water provided for the patients during a long-winded session. Owen looked back at the doctor, who hadn't changed his posture or expression in the slightest. "You know what one of the hardest things to deal with is?" Sturn didn't answer, simply waited for Owen to continue. "It's expecting her to be everywhere. If I go to the grocery store, I expect her to come walking around every corner, bringing me some random item that wasn't on our list. If I see a blonde woman along an aisle, for the briefest of moments I can see Heather's face, and I almost expect her to look at me and smile." Owen felt his throat tighten slightly as he spoke, and he swallowed hard against it. Goddamnit, he wouldn't cry at this session, too, he vowed.

"When I hear something, a bit of conversation between people, or if something I read online or heard on the radio earlier in the day pops into my head, if I see something on the shelf that gives me an idea or something, I find myself turning around to get her attention, to tell her about it." The tightness in his throat increased. "It's almost enough to make me stop going to the store."

"That's understandable, Owen. These feelings are completely normal. Some would say healthy, even."

Owen blinked away wetness that hadn't fully developed into tears. "Healthy? How the hell can you sit there and tell me that it's healthy? Missing my wife? Wishing that she were with me, that I could see the way her eyes danced when she smiled, that I could hear her laughter, or the way, when she was feeling goofy and playful, she would refer to shrimp as shromp? How is that healthy? I can't get it back. She's lost to me, forever."

"It's healthy that you keep her in your memories. That's all I meant. I don't want you to think that I'm suggesting that there will be a time when you forget her completely; I know that you never will. But what I mean to say is that your constant thoughts of her, your expecting her to come around the corner, that's all normal. It's the healthy part of you dealing with the loss and getting control of your situation. I would be concerned if you never thought about her, if you felt no remorse, no sense of loss."

Owen thought about how just the day before he had been in the grocery store, shopping for something to eat for dinner. A woman with shoulder length blonde hair approached his section of the aisle and for a moment he saw Heather's face in the woman's features. He had almost spoken to her, asked her if she had remembered to get the right kind of toothpaste since they were out. His mouth had been open to ask the question when the woman looked at him, smiled politely, and then walked away. Owen had stood there, holding a jar of spaghetti sauce and watching her walk away, thinking how even the way she moved looked like Heather's gait. He had managed to hold back the tears until he was in the car. That time.

"How's work?" Sturn asked, his voice brightening.

Owen looked back down at his hands for a moment, collecting himself. He cleared his throat and looked back up at the therapist. "It's good, actually. Our store was one of the three highest grossing locations across the country."

"Owen, that's wonderful. You must be very proud."

"I am." Owen felt a small surge of relief at the change of subject. His job was the one thing he had been able to cling to in the wake of losing Heather. As the store manager of Wee Lad Toys, he was in charge of one of the fastest growing and most popular toy stores in the nation. Founded in 1993 by Carlton Donovan, Wee Lad had grown exceedingly fast thanks largely to low prices, wide selection and customer-friendly stores. The fact that they always guaranteed items in stock helped as well. When the new Xbox 360s went on sale and every other store in the state sold out, Wee Lad had plenty. As store manager, it was Owen's duty to ensure that these things continued to happen. Not once in his eight years running the place had there ever been an instance of an item out of stock. Every day he verified the inventory lists, checked the shelves behind the stock clerks, and held impromptu meetings with the floor sales personnel to get the "view from the trenches" on what people were buying and what their needs were. He valued his employees almost as much as the customers who came in for the occasional Barbie or PlayStation game. Because of that attitude, his store had been number one in sales for the entire region.

"I'm sure that upper management is very pleased as well," Sturn said.

A slight twitch of panic coursed through Owen's chest. He looked up quickly and hoped that the doctor hadn't noticed his reaction. Sturn had. "What's wrong?"

"They are pleased. I've been invited to a thank you getaway by the president of the company. He and his board and the managers of the six top grossing stores in the country."

Sturn smiled and wrote again in his notebook. "You don't sound too happy about that. Surely you could use the break from the store. I know for a fact that a change of scenery can really help the healing process as well."

"Normally I'd agree with you. But this is to a small island in the south Atlantic." Owen dug in his back pocket and pulled out a folded piece of paper and handed it to the doctor.

Sturn opened it and read the letter out loud.

"Mr. Thompson,

On behalf of all employees of Wee Lad Toys, Inc., we would like to extend to you a most gracious thank you for all your hard work in the past fiscal year. Due to your diligence and professionalism, you have made store number 54 the highest grossing store within the Southeast Region. Congratulations, and thank you.

This year, as you may know, Wee Lad Toys, Inc. surpassed the competition and recorded record-breaking profits for a retail store.

You and store 54 were integral to that achievement. As a result I, Carlton Donovan, would like to personally extend an invitation to you to come celebrate with myself, my board members and the other six highest grossing store managers on Bezeten Island in the South Atlantic. This trip will be all-inclusive, your airfare, hotel and all personal needs will be taken care of by Wee Lad Toys, Inc. The trip will last one week, starting Saturday the eleventh through Saturday the eighteenth.

I hope you will join us for this celebration of our incredible success and again, I thank you for your help in achieving this.

Sincerely,

Carlton Donovan"

Sturn handed the letter back to Owen who returned it to his pocket. "The trip starts tomorrow. Are you going?"

Owen shook his head. "I can't. It's too soon. Me, on an island? It's not even that it's an island, but you know ... It's too soon. Besides, I don't like the thought of leaving the store. This is a critical time for us, we've got that new shipment of Fedor Dolls and you can guess how in demand they're going to be."

Doctor Sturn was quiet for a moment, looking down at his pad. Owen wasn't sure if he were thinking of something or waiting for Owen to say something more. Owen was just opening his mouth to offer more reasons why he couldn't go, no appropriate clothes, he wouldn't know anyone down there, the list went on and on, when Sturn spoke. "Could you take someone with you?"

Owen knew what the doctor was getting at, who he was referring to. "No. The letter doesn't invite me to bring a guest."

"She's an employee of the company; I'm sure they would make an exception."

Owen shook his head. "There'd be nobody left to manage the store while I was gone if she came with me. Besides, we don't have that kind of relationship."

Sturn sighed and placed his pad on the desk behind him. He removed his glasses and rubbed his face, then leaned forward in his chair. "Owen, it's been almost a year since Heather."

"Ten and a half months."

"Right. I'm not suggesting that you start a new relationship with Michelle, understand? I'm not saying that you jump into bed with her, or fly to Vegas and get married. What I'm saying is that the one constant in your life other than your work and myself, has been her. She's known you for years. Based on what you've told me, she has feelings for you. There's nothing wrong with you just spending time with a good friend, another adult, in a situation outside of the store. Changes of scenery are good, almost vital to the healing process. But at the same time, it's good to have a tether, a link back to what you consider the normal world. I think that Michelle could be that link for you. You've said yourself how she's helped you through a lot of rough times. If nothing else, you could think of this as a way for you to repay her, to thank her for always being there for you."

"It just wouldn't be right," Owen said in a voice that was just barely above a whisper.

"Owen, look at me." After several moments, Owen met the other man's gaze. "You don't have to love this woman. You don't have to date her. You don't have to kiss her or have sex with her. I've been doing this job for over thirty years. I've learned the pacing with which people heal from traumatic events. I'm not saying that you're healed. What I'm saying is that despite what you've told me a few minutes ago about seeing Heather's face, and expecting to see her at the store, you're at a place where you're ready to take a new step in your healing. You're ready to reach a new level. Sure it's going to be challenging. Nothing is ever easy in a situation like this. But you can't stay where you are and just hope and expect the pain to go away, for the feelings to fade and to be replaced by any sort of happiness. Happiness is something you have to go out and achieve. You have to work at it. You meet new people. You make new friends. You go on vacation, you go to concerts, and you learn new hobbies."

The room fell quiet. Owen could hear the soft whisper of the second hand on the clock that hung next to the door. He thought about Michelle, the assistant manager of his store. Michelle Piquot had been his assistant manager for almost five years. She was attractive, more so than any assistant manager of a toy store should be. Owen didn't think she would make it to a Victoria's Secret photo shoot anytime, but she had certainly turned heads on the floor.

"Does she know about the trip?"

Owen nodded. "Yeah. She was there when I got the letter."

"What did she have to say about it?"

"She told me that I should go, that I should move on, that Heather would have wanted me to."

"Do you agree with her?"

"I don't know. I told her I wasn't ready to date anyone. She told me that going on the trip wasn't a date with anyone, that the trip wasn't a singles meet and greet. Then she said," he smiled, remembering Michelle's words, "'Besides, you know damn good and well I'm the only one you're allowed to date once you get ready to.'"

Sturn smiled. "So why don't you take her?"

"I told you. I couldn't do that, even if I were on board with the idea. Someone has to stay and manage the store. That's probably why the letter didn't state 'you and your assistant manager can come to the island.'"

Sturn sat back in his chair. It reclined easily on well-oiled hinges. "Okay," he said. "So the subject of Heather aside, how do you feel about going?"

"I told you, I don't like the idea of going to an island."

"This could be a huge step toward you getting past some things. I really think that this is exactly what you need. In fact, as your doctor, I'm telling you to go on this trip. You'll benefit from the change of scenery, meeting some new people, and you'll be forced to get close to the ocean. All three are a perfect recipe for healing. And when you get back, we can talk more about Heather. Maybe you'll have a new, healthier outlook on things."

When Owen left Sturn's office, it had begun to rain. Fueled by his conversation with the therapist, Michelle's words echoed throughout his head. "You know damn well I'm the only one you're allowed to date once you get ready to." Had she really meant that she wanted to see him socially? He had worked with her for three years; they were close, especially after Heather; after the accident. But he never saw it as anything other than a close friend working to help another through an especially hard time. People who work together end up forming deep friendships sometimes. Hell, they spent as much time, if not more, with each other than they did with their respective families, it was only natural. But while most work friendships were relegated to only working hours, the occasional one would extend beyond that, each person finding something special within the other. He and Michelle had found that within each other quickly. She was lighthearted and funny, quick with a joke or serious debate topic that would last for days when the work was slow. He felt he brought a solid emotional state to the friendship.

The sky lit a sudden, erratic electric blue as lightning sheared the air overhead. Everything along McFarland was lit as if under the dancing strobe light of a nightclub. In that moment, Owen looked across his passenger seat to the near curb. A small glass bus vestibule stood near the corner. Standing within it was a person, their sex undeterminable. They wore dark clothes, soaked even darker by the storm. In the briefest of moments, he had the impression they were rags like the clothes worn by the area's homeless. But what held his attention, what captured his breath and for a split second arrested his heart were the two, shiny, feral eyes that gleamed back at him through the paused, electric air.

The moment passed, the air returned to its normal state and the person was swallowed by thick rain and distance as Owen's BMW moved slickly past. Owen returned his concentration to the road, but couldn't shake the feeling that he had just witnessed something unnatural. How could a person's eyes shine like that? He shook his head. Had to be the lightning. Does crazy stuff, that lightning. Once he was back at his condo, he paused long enough to listen to his messages. There were only two, one from a creditor asking him to call at his earliest convenience and the other from Michelle.

"Hey, just wanted to say goodbye again since I won't see you before you take off. You lucky bastard. I can't believe they won't let you take me. I still think you should hide me in your suitcase. I'll fit, you won't need clothes, trust me," she giggled. "Anyway, I hope you have a good flight and a great time. You really need to use this as a break, a time to get your head straight and reevaluate things." Her voice dropped to a softer tone. "I'll be here when you get back. I know it's just a week, but I'll miss your face, Owen. Come back soon." The message ended. He stared at the black machine for several seconds, a smile traced across his lips. Then he moved to the bedroom to pack.

The next morning, Owen caught the flight to Nassau International Airport. The flight was smooth and easy, and his nerves were aided by the $30 drink credit that Donovan had allowed for each of his guests. In Nassau, he was directed to a shuttle that sat parked in the thick, sweltering heat. The inside of the shuttle was as frigid as an icebox and the driver played Bob Marley tunes loudly, obviously to get his guests in the mood for some island fun. The shuttle took Owen to a small lake, ten minutes away from the airport terminal. There, he was directed to a pier, at the end of which sat his connecting flight.

The next airplane looked small and old. Owen didn't know much about aircraft, but the mere sight of the faded red paint and dark rust stains near some of the bolts in the airplane's skin caused him to grow more apprehensive with each step. He saw discoloration in the paint on the pontoons and hoped it was because of long years of exposure to salt water. The plane was a single engine propeller vehicle. Just behind the smoky glass of the cockpit was a doorway leading into the bowels of the craft. A small five-step staircase allowed entry for passengers.

Inside the belly of the plane, the heat seemed to change. Instead of dissipating, it instead seemed to contract, to tighten around him and make the very air thicker and hard to move through. Owen stole a quick look inside the cockpit, saw nobody sitting behind the controls that looked more simplistic than what he'd expected or hoped for in a plane, then turned to the aisle to find a seat.

There were seats for eight people, however only one other person occupied the space. He saw a thin, skeletal man with pale blond hair and sunken eyes lift his face high as if he had to stretch to see over the seats before him and waved to Owen.

"Here he is," the man said. "We were wondering when you'd show up. Thank God, now we can get the hell out of here." He indicated the open seats. "Have a seat anywhere, man. We'll see if we can't get the pilot in this bitch to get us out of here." Owen nodded, mumbled an apology and took a seat near the front.

Five minutes later, the pilot arrived wearing a white short-sleeved shirt and khaki pants. He nodded briefly to his passengers, then entered the cockpit and began manipulating the controls. The propeller, when it started, vibrated the entire plane.

"I don't know if I can take an hour and a half of this shit," a voice said next to him. Owen looked up, startled, and saw Skeleton man sitting across the aisle from him. Not having noticed the man changing seats, Owen stared at him momentarily.

"Hour and a half?" he said loudly. The man nodded.

"This will take us right up to Bezeten Island, but it takes a little while to get there." He extended his hand. "Gordon Dixon. I manage store thirty-five up in Denver. How about you?"

Owen shook his hand. The man's palm was tacky with sweat. "Store fifty four. Owen Thompson. You ever been to Bezeten before? I've never heard of it."

"Nope. Nobody's ever been there. Donovan bought it just a couple of months ago as sort of a reward to himself. I heard he spent like forty million for it, then another thirty million fixing it up with some little villas, houses and stuff. I'm stoked. It's going to be awesome."

"So what are we going to be doing here?" Owen asked.

The man's waxy lips peeled back to reveal crooked teeth, yellowed from too much coffee and—Owen could only speculate—cigarettes. "Party our asses off, my man. There's a staff that Donovan has for the island, they're going to cater to us hand and foot. Swear. Anything you need or could want. Drink, sir? Sure. Another plate of food, sir? Right there. Hand job, sir? Bam." Dixon laughed. "It's going to be great. He's supposed to be bringing a band out to play for us too. Not some cheesy ass local unit, but someone big. Don't know who. I plan on getting fucked up as soon as my feet touch the ground and I hope I don't come off my buzz until three days after I get home, except for when I'm going to be out hunting."

"But aren't Donovan and his board members going to be there?" Owen asked. He gripped the seat tightly as the small plane jostled for several seconds as they passed through a wave of turbulent air.

Dixon waved a frail hand dismissively. "So what? His board only consists of four other people, and from what I hear, Donovan likes to drink it up as much as your average college sophomore."

"What do you mean by hunting?"

Owen looked around as if there were others close by who would steal his thoughts. "You've never heard of Bezeten Island?" Owen shook his head. "Oh man. It's an old Dutch word meaning 'possessed.' I did some research on it a few days ago, right after I got my invitation. Dude, this place has got some serious history. At one point drug smugglers and rumrunners used it. But this place has history that goes even further back. It may be just legend, but back when there were pirates in the area and Spain was still exploring the islands pretty heavily, there was a lot of talk about this place. None of it good. Now, of course, these people back then still thought there were sea serpents and that the Earth was flat and all that. But from what I could read, there wasn't anyone who would actually land on this island. One diary entry said that the captain anchored the ship offshore and from the main deck he could see fires from torches dotting the trees. None of his men would go on the island, and throughout the night they heard people screaming on the land. The way the guy described it, they weren't screams of pain. He said it was as if the men on the shore had gone mad, or had been possessed by demons."

Owen looked at the man as the plane jostled through a rough patch of air. "Are you serious?"

Dixon's eyes were wide. "Oh yeah, man. The diary said that the captain tried to get a shore party or something to go to the island and see what was going on. He had to have the rest of his crew basically force them with guns and swords, but they finally went."

"What happened?" Owen thought it odd that he had become so wrapped up in the story.

Dixon shrugged. "Don't know. The diary didn't say. The next entry was dated a month later and they were down the coast of South America. But," Dixon stretched again and looked around. Owen wanted to slap him and remind him that they were alone on the plane. "I figure that at least there's got to be something there. Nothing horrible, but old artifacts. Helmets, swords, maybe even one of those old ass muskets that they used to use back then. I figure that if I can find some of that stuff, even if it's in a cave and rusted, I can sell it for a shitload of money on eBay." He grinned again, that toothy, Cheshire cat grin.

Owen shook his head in amusement and looked at his watch. They had been airborne for thirty minutes. Another hour to go. Less if the pilot managed to catch a tailwind. He felt the tickle of panic at the fringes of his thoughts and remembered what Michelle had said. He needed this trip, to move on. He needed to relax. Well, he didn't know about moving on, but relaxing sounded good. If the island was large enough, he'd try to find a secluded area and hole up there during the day, sleeping and trying to let the salty air clear his head.

Not that he liked the idea of going near the ocean, let alone on a small island several hundred miles out in the ocean. But there was nothing he could do about that now. He laid his head back against the seat and closed his eyes, hopeful that Dixon wouldn't start talking again. He wondered what Michelle was doing, how the store was.

Unbidden sleep took him. He fell through the darkness into a swirling chaos of wind, rain and debris. Pieces of a large house flew around him, chunks of wood and siding pinwheeling through the air. Glass shards stung his body, peppered his skin with tiny bloody cuts. His hair fluttered wildly as if trying to pull itself free from his scalp. The water stung his eyes, forced them closed.

From beneath him something shifted, the floor buckled and split open. A long jagged crack ripped through the wood floor and splinters took to the air as the wood slats broke apart. Water and sand rushed up from the crack, piling into the room. It pooled around his feet, the sludge cloudy and swirling as it rose higher and higher. With effort, he managed to pull his feet free of the morass and began running. He ran through what became rooms, the walls forming from the gloom at the extent of his vision. Holes ripped in walls, crown molding struggled to remain in place but was torn free by the relentless wind.

From somewhere above he heard his name being called. Screamed, as if the person were in mortal danger and desperate for his help. He looked right and saw a shifting staircase, each step undulating under the pressure of the wind and rain. The water and sand had risen to the third step and steadily climbed to the fourth. Owen raced through it and up the buckling stairs. Twice he slipped, the second time reaching out for the handrail only to have it snap off and tumble to the blackness below. For a long moment he teetered on the brink of his balance, looking down into the dark swirling mass of water and sand. Then he regained his footing and continued up the stairs.

On the second floor landing, he moved back against the wall, toward the only room visible to him. The door had swung outward into the hallway and hung by one weak hinge. A large crack extended halfway down the center of it. His name was called again, from inside the room. Owen reached the doorway and stopped. There, inside the room was Heather. She floated in water that Owen's mind couldn't comprehend. Where had the water come from? Why was it only at floor level, yet she was clearly drowning? From beneath the water she reached out a hand to him and he could see the white tips of her manicured nails. Her blue eyes pleaded with him. Her blond hair was dirty from the water and floated in the water around her head. The water was to her chin, and seemed to rise with every breath he took.

"Owen, please!" He took a step forward and fell forward into the water. The shock of it hit him like a truck. One hand found Heather's wrist and he pulled her close as his head broke the surface and he struggled to clear his eyes. When he did, he looked at her.

Her face had changed. It now was vicious, feral. Her eyes were black and yellow and her teeth were elongated and sharp. From her throat emanated deep animalistic growls. "Ooowwweeen," she grumbled and lunged for him, her mouth yawning wide as she came for his face.

A rough hand on his arm brought him sharply from sleep. Owen sat up and whipped his head around, disoriented. The plane was a solid, buzzing hornet around him. The air inside the cabin had grown even more sweltering than it had been when they had first boarded.

"Owen, man you alright?" Dixon's voice cut through the haze surrounding Owen's brain. Slowly things solidified in his mind and he nodded.

"Yeah, sorry. Bad dream." Owen rubbed his face and tried to ignore the man staring at him as if he were a child who had just wet himself in public. "Where are we?"

Dixon, who was seated next to the window, leaned back some and pointed out the small glass port. "Island is down there. Lean over man, you got to see this." Owen leaned forward until his forehead almost touched the glass. Below them was a massive stretch of blue-green water. Tiny ripples on its surface gave it the only definition. Just in Owen's field of vision was a light green patch that faded to a dull yellow.

"What is that?"

"Sandbar. You may not be able to see it, we changed positions just before you woke up, but the island is probably two or three hundred yards away from that sandbar. But look just to the right of it. Where the water is still that jade color. See it?"

Owen did, although at first he didn't know what he was looking at. "What is that?" he asked again.

"Sharks. A whole shitload of them by the look of it. I grew up in the panhandle of Florida. Trust me, that's a common thing, them all grouped like that. Probably some tiger sharks, maybe a bull or two. Point is, you don't want to go out there at all."

Owen refocused on the dark splinters in the water. With concentration he could make out their motion, how they angled sharply one way then another. Then the plane was passing over the large sandbar and into very shallow water. Owen leaned back in his seat just as the pilot dropped them sharply and angled to the left for a landing.

The plane jolted on the water, a rough, wrenching motion that almost threw Owen from his seat.

"Bloody hell, man. That fucker needs to learn how to fly. You alright?" Dixon asked.

"Yeah," Owen gasped.

"That was the kind of landing that only a drink can cure." Dixon stood up and stretched. "Come on. Let's go get started on forgetting." He started toward the front of the plane despite it still moving toward what Owen could only assume—though he couldn't see—was a dock. His suspicions were confirmed when the plane stopped moving and the engine cut off. In the ensuing silence—his ears still buzzed slightly from the absent noise—Owen could hear ropes being tied down and a door from below his feet opening. Owen unbuckled his seatbelt and joined Gordon Dixon at the door of the plane. Within moments, the pilot opened it. Owen detected the strong scent of vodka on the man as he brushed past to open it.

But the thought was shoved aside immediately by the smell of brine, water and good old clean air that wafted in on a warm breeze. Owen heard water lapping against the plane, the gentle rocking sound of the waves against the shore as he stepped out into the warmth. On the dock, dressed in khaki shorts and a white, short-sleeved collared shirt, a large cigar smoking in one hand and a bottle of beer in the other, was Carlton Donovan, president and CEO of Wee Lad Toys, Inc. And behind him, bathed in golden sunlight, was the most beautiful piece of land Owen had ever seen in his entire life.

3

They ran blindly into the darkened hallway, Jessica leading the way. Owen struggled to keep up. Several yards in and his chest began to tighten and burn from the exertion he had already endured. His skin tingled still from his time in the ice chest. Jessica seemed to have no problems setting a steady pace, her sleek body moving fluidly through the dim light.

They passed doors to other bedrooms. As the doors slid by on either side, Owen spared a brief wonder if they housed anyone dead or otherwise. "Hold up," he panted. Jessica ran on for several more feet then jogged to a stop. She turned and bent at the waist, her hands on her hips. Owen held onto the wall for support and noticed her breathing. "Where the hell does this lead?" he gasped.

Jessica swallowed hard and stood. "More guest rooms, then I think there's an exit to the beach."

"You think?" Owen asked. "What do you mean, you think? You came from this hall."

"I ran in here earlier and ducked into one of the rooms to hide from one of those things. My room is actually down next to yours."

Owen thought about what she had said. "How many more of those things do you think there are?"

She shrugged and stared down the direction they had come. "Not sure, but I'm guessing most everyone."

"Most ..." Owen couldn't bring his mind to comprehend. "What do you mean most everyone?"

Jessica glared at him, her eyes a mixture of fear and irritation. "You're really not this stupid, are you, Owen?" Her voice cut through the air and dug into him.

"Look," he said. "I don't mean to offend your superior intellect, but I don't remember shit about last night, and when I woke up this morning, the first thing I saw was some creature eating the stomach of one of the staff members. You're the first person I've seen in the last hour or so and I'm a little freaked out. So give me a break, will you?" He blinked, surprised at himself. Normally not driven to outbursts or staunchly defending himself, Owen found his heart racing. But his reaction got through to the beautiful woman in front of him, because her eyes softened and she sighed slightly.

"Sorry," she said. "Look, we can talk about this later. Would you mind if we got going again? I don't like the idea of sitting here in this hallway when that thing wakes up, or if another one comes along. But for now, yes, there are more out there. A lot more." She stared at him for a moment, waiting for some reaction. Finally Owen nodded. Jessica turned and started down the hallway again, moving at a steady walk.

Owen followed. His breath came more easily now, but his heart continued to race, whether from the run, the fear, or as a reaction to his self-defense, he wasn't sure. They moved quickly but quietly through the hallway, both turning to look behind them periodically. The corridor ran for about thirty more yards then ended at a thick metal door with a glowing red EXIT sign above it. Jessica paused at the door, one hand on the metal bar and looked back at Owen. Owen glanced behind him, strained to hear sounds of pursuit, then turned and nodded to her. "Go for it." As she pushed the door, he thought that the right thing to do would be for him to go first; that would be the manly thing to do. But the door swung outward with a slight moan and click of the bar depressing and then Jessica was through it into blinding sunlight. Owen followed her, stepping through the opening and squinting as the brightness and warm salt air rushed over him.

His feet continued along a concrete path for a few steps, then there was a lurch as he came abruptly to the end and plunged into thick sand. A loud report sounded behind him and Owen cried out despite himself. He looked wildly around and saw that the metal door had closed itself. He shook his head and looked around as he plodded through the sand to catch up with the quickly moving Jessica. She walked through the sand as if she had spent her entire life in it, her tan, muscular legs pumping steadily.

The path they were on ran thinly between thick foliage and disappeared over a small hill several yards in front of them. Owen could hear the sound of the waves further ahead, slapping the beach like a relaxing siren song. Owen's breath seemed amplified and he closed his mouth and tried to draw air through his nose. Ahead of him, Jessica had reached the crest of the hill and crouched in the sand on one side of the trail. Owen reached her and knelt beside her. "What is it? Are there more of them?" Jessica didn't answer at first, instead keeping her gaze further down the beach.

"I saw something cross the path as I came up. It wasn't an animal." Owen felt a tickle of fear race through his chest.

"See it now?" She shook her head.

"No. Whatever it was, it went into the bushes and hasn't come back out. I haven't heard it moving either, so I don't know if it's still there or not." She looked at him and he could see the fear and indecision in her gaze. Somehow, seeing that made him feel better.

"Want to keep going?" he asked. Jessica stared down the trail and chewed her lower lip. Owen followed the trail with his eyes. It was empty, no sign of life anywhere. The plants to either side of the sand stood motionless as if they were sentries guarding a sacred temple. The trail stretched for several dozen yards before widening to the beach. To the right of the mouth of the path, he could see a section of a volleyball net. The ocean beyond was a clear aqua blue. He looked back at Jessica. "Look, we have two choices. We can either go ahead and chance that whatever it was is gone now, or we can go back inside and face, at the very least, the thing I cold cocked with that bottle. Personally, I would rather take my chances out in the open. We have the beach, the ocean and all these woods or jungle, or whatever the hell you'd call it. Inside, we can be trapped a lot more easily." Jessica continued to stare down the path, seemingly unable to either decide or act. Owen sighed and said, "Okay. I'll go first. Stay right behind me. Alright?" She turned and looked at him, then slowly nodded.

He stood slowly, feeling his knees pop. As he started down the trail he became aware of just how tired he already was, the muscles in his legs felt weak as he walked. His eyes shifted constantly, from the bushes to the trail ahead to the bushes again, intently searching for the slightest indication of movement. Jessica was almost immediately behind him. He could hear her steps shuffling in the sand, could feel her warm presence near him.

They reached the halfway point of the trail.

Owen's heart increased its rhythm, as if it were trying to punch through his chest to escape the certain mutilation that would come at the hands of one of the creatures. Creatures, he thought. Plural. Jessica had been firm that there had been more than just the one he had encountered. How many more? And what the hell were they, exactly? Where had they come from? The silence around him, save for the ocean, begged another question. Where were they now?

Twelve yards before the mouth of the path.

Something rattled the leaves to his right and as Owen turned to it, a large figure erupted from the bushes. It collided with him and they both went down in a spray of sand. Owen slapped and punched at the attacker. Jessica was on both of them immediately, punching and trying to rip the assailant off of Owen.

"Fucking quit!" Owen hesitated, one fist cocked above the other person's rib cage. He knew the voice. And it sounded normal.

Jessica continued to slap at the man and he protested again. "Goddamnit, Jessica! I said quit fucking hitting me!"

Jessica gasped, "Dixon?" Owen felt the larger man peel himself off and stand. Owen looked up at Dixon. The man's clothing was ripped and he sported a large scrape on one cheek but otherwise seemed normal and unharmed.

"What the hell are you doing?" Owen demanded. Dixon took in deep breaths and looked down at the man he had tackled.

"Thought for a minute you were one of them. I killed one with a rock a while back, so I figured I could take you out. I didn't plan on Joan of friggin' Arc here." He extended his hand. "Get up, man." Owen realized he still lay on the sand, one fist cocked to hit a target no longer available, and took Dixon's hand.

"You killed one?" he asked. Dixon nodded.

"Yeah. Couple of hours ago, down on the beach where we had the bonfire last night. I used one of the rocks from the fire pit and cracked his head open. That's how I got scraped." He pointed to his cheek. "Bastards are fast and vicious, but they go down like a normal person."

Owen felt reasoning beginning to shut down on him. He held out a hand. "Wait. You two seem to be in the know about what's going on. All I know is that I woke up and started getting chased by one of those things after finding it eating one of the servant's guts for breakfast. Could you please let me in on this?"

"It is the servants," Dixon said. "Not all but most of them; it's some of the board members, and it's a few of the other employees that came here. I don't know how or why, but somehow overnight they became those ... things. It's like night of the living dead or some shit, but they're not dead. They've mutated. Turned nasty."

"There's one inside," Jessica said. "Back there. Owen knocked it out with a liquor bottle."

"You didn't spill the liquor, did you?" Dixon asked. Owen shook his head. Dixon smiled. "Good. Otherwise, it's a damned waste of alcohol. I'd have to kick your ass for alcohol abuse." He chuckled at his own joke.

"We need to get off this island," Owen said. The phrase sounded like a cliché from a cheap horror movie, he thought. But then, he was living one. And living one was infinitely worse than watching.

"How do you suppose we do that?" Jessica asked. The trio fell silent. Owen tried to remember if there were other boats on the island. He was certain that he had been told, or taken a tour or something yesterday, but all of it had been washed away in a tide of liquor and beer. They hadn't come in by boat, instead—

"The plane," he said. "It is probably still here, don't you think? I mean, the pilot would have most likely stuck around to have a few drinks, to enjoy Donnavon's hospitality. So the plane would still be there." He paused. "I just don't remember where 'there' is."

"Yeah, you got quite friggin' wasted last night, my man," Dixon said. "You were quite the animal."

Owen felt his cheeks flush. "Sorry. I sometimes can't stop myself once I get started."

"Don't have to apologize to me, man."

Jessica stepped forward, putting her body between the two men. "I don't mean to sound like a prude, guys, but do you think we could get moving? Just like Owen, I don't like the idea of just sitting here. We need to move. The plane was docked on the other side of the island. Probably a quarter of a mile from here, I guess."

"That's if we take the trails," Dixon said. "If we take the trails, we could make that in about thirty minutes, maybe less. But taking the trials also means that anything looking for us has a better chance of seeing and getting to us."

"But," Owen said, "if we take the woods we'll move slower and it will be harder to get away from one if we come across it." Jessica agreed.

"Okay. We'll take the trail," Dixon said. "But do either of you know how to fly a plane?" Owen pushed past the man, starting toward the beach.

"I'll figure it out if I have to. Nothing better than OJT, and it beats hanging around here waiting for the alternative."

"Wait," Dixon said. Owen stopped and turned. "You were wasted last night. Do you have any idea where the hell you're going?" Owen didn't answer. "I thought so." Dixon walked forward. "Better let me lead."

They exited the trail and stopped at the edge of the beach,

studying the sand in every direction. The volleyball net stood unmolested, a depressing reminder of what only a few hours before had been a normal world. Beyond it were several beach chairs and umbrellas for guests to lounge in. Owen looked at them and felt a welling of sadness in his chest. Why the hell had he come? Why had he let Michelle talk him into it? He would have been better off at home with a bottle of Jack Daniel's.

"Since you've lost most of your short term memory," Dixon said over his shoulder, "let me lay it out for you. The island is basically a crescent. We're on the large bowl section. The plane landed on the hump, in a small inlet there. The building you guys came out of is the main guesthouse and is the largest. There are two other guest quarters, but none were occupied, since this was such a small group. However, Donovan said he had the entire staff on hand to cater to any and all desires we had. So there was about five to one staff to guests. I don't know how many of them became those things, but I'm betting more than those that didn't. Anyway, small sand trails litter the place. They lead everywhere; the other side of the island, both ends of the place, the tennis courts, the servants' quarters, everywhere. Somewhere there are electric golf carts but I haven't come across them yet. I don't know where the staff keeps them stored. One would sure as hell come in handy right now though."

"The noise would attract any of those things nearby," said Jessica.

"Yeah," Dixon countered, "but we could outrun it."

"In a golf cart? Are you retarded?" Dixon didn't respond. Instead he stopped walking and pointed. Owen followed his finger and saw another trail opening just a few yards ahead. The sand disappeared into the thick vegetation. The mouth of the trail yawned open, leading into the darkness of the woods. Torches mounted on thin bamboo poles flanked the opening, the flames extinguished. As they moved toward it, Owen felt a rising sense of dread, a sudden unwillingness to leave the open safety of the beach. At least out there, they could see if one of those things was coming, or—better yet—they could see a ship or airplane that passed by, signal for help or something.

The thought trailed out of his mind as he took the first step into the shaded canopy of the woods. Instantly he felt the temperature around him drop several degrees as the shadows enveloped him. He noticed that along the path, spaced evenly, were more of the unlit bamboo torches. Thin shafts of light penetrated the tall trees, spearing toward the ground like holy golden lances from on high. Somehow seeing them made Owen relax. Several steps into the forest, the thickness of the trees blocked all sound of the ocean. Owen stopped and turned, looking back at the opening of the trail. He could see the sliver of blue that was the ocean just beyond a tiny slice of white beach. Seeing it made his heart ache with a sharp pang of fear. Even at this distance, the sight of the water made him think of Heather.

He felt a tightening in his chest at the memory and quickly turned away from it. Jessica and Dixon were a dozen yards ahead of him, each looking from side to side as they moved carefully along the dirt path.

Owen moved to catch up, his own eyes employed as vigilant sentries against the mutated creatures. The jungle around him was silent. No birds sang their songs, no insects buzzed irritably. The only sounds were those of the three people's footfalls on dirt and the rustle of their clothes.

Dixon stopped after a few minutes. Owen and Jessica gathered around him. "Why aren't any birds singing?" Dixon asked.

Owen shrugged. "Maybe they're too scared to make noise."

Jessica thought about it, her vision moving among the trees around them. "I don't know. Now that I think about it, I don't think there were birds singing yesterday when we got here either. I can't be certain, but I don't think I've seen or heard one animal on this entire island."

Owen sniffed. "That's got to be paranoia. It's impossible for a place like this to be completely devoid of wildlife. It's the damned Bahamas. There are birds and snakes and small mammals everywhere." He looked behind them, down the path then shook his head.

"No. No, it's got to be that they sense something wrong and are keeping their traps shut. That makes the most sense."

"Not if you knew the history of this place," Dixon mumbled.

"What's that mean?" Jessica asked. Dixon shook his head dismissively and started back down the path.

Despite the lowered temperature beneath the canopy's shadows, the air was thicker and muggy in the forest. It clung to them as if it were a soup trapped within a leafy bowl. Minutes had passed since their entering the woods and Owen found his shirt now to be completely soaked with perspiration. The others had similar dark stains on their clothing and as they passed through a patch of sunlight, he noticed that Jessica's tan skin had a sheen of sweat on it. Her hair hung in thick wet clumps along her shirt collar.

They trudged on, and Owen's eyes struggled to take in everything around them. The trees—what kind he had no clue, although he could see an occasional palm tree—rose out of the ground like self important giants, each vying with the others for coveted sunlight. Beneath them, carpeting the ground like humbled subjects before their kings, was a thick, tangled mass of lesser bushes and trees. He recognized ground ferns but couldn't identify any of the other greenery or small bunches of colorful flowers.

Within a matter of minutes, he thought, he had been plunged into an alien world, a landscape so foreign to him that human eyes may not have ever witnessed it. It seemed incomprehensible to him that they were on a privately owned island that was only an hour and a half flight away from Grand Bahama Island. Only ninety minutes away from thousands of people, buildings, shops, boats, cars, tourists, police and local inhabitants. The world's largest civilization compared to the place he marched through now in fear for his life.

His life. What did that mean anymore? he wondered. Widowed, depressed and working a job that to most should be manned by a high school graduate, not a thirty-eight-year-old man. He had nobody; he had nothing rewarding or fulfilling in his life. He had Michelle to speak to from time to time when he was at the office, but otherwise there was nothing. He should have stayed home yesterday like he had planned. Should have stayed home, drank himself stupid and then found a gun. That would have saved him the trouble of coming all the way here only to fight to keep from being ripped apart while still alive.

His headache flared again at the sudden cerebral activity. Owen winced, placed a hand to the top of his head and increased his speed. He caught up with the others, not having realized just how far back he had fallen, just as they were cresting a small hill. At the summit, Dixon paused so everyone could catch their breath.

"Damn air is thicker than water," Jessica gasped.

"You're not used to the humidity?" Owen asked.

"No shit," she muttered. "Sorry. No, I'm from Seattle."

Owen waved the rudeness off. "It's okay. It's just that people from up north aren't used to the heat and humidity. I'm from Alabama. It's like this all the time. We're used to the humidity from the time we're a fetus."

The redhead wiped sweat from her face with both hands, flicking her wrists and sending the drops of water to the dirt. "How do you people stand it? How do you not go crazy and kill yourselves? This is insane."

"You don't have humidity up in Seattle?"

"Not like this. We have wet, sure. We call it rain. But the air is never like this."

Owen smiled. "Well, to be honest, this place is a bit worse than Alabama. Ocean, closer to the equator, all that." He turned to Dixon. "Any idea how much further it is?"

The tall man was bent at the waist, his cheeks flushed and hair soaked through with sweat. He ran a hand through his hair and stood up, exhaling as he did. He swallowed hard and pointed in the direction they were traveling. "Not positive, but I'm guessing it's a few hundred yards more. The island can't be that large and we've been walking for close to half an hour now."

"Yeah, but we've been going pretty slow, looking out for those things, too," Owen said.

Dixon shook his head. "Not that slow. Not slow enough. We

should have been more careful, gone more slowly. You know we've been making a shitload of noise and haven't been paying attention worth a damn. I knew it all along but have been so anxious to get to the plane that I didn't really give a shit." He sighed. "You guys ready? I think we can get there quick if we step it up some." Jessica and Owen took a few deep breaths and nodded. The three moved further down the path.

After what seemed another hour, they reached the end of the wooded trail. The path opened to a planked boardwalk that bent to the left and out of sight behind the trees. The opening was bright and Owen squinted reflexively against the light. They paused again, half a dozen yards from the beach.

"Okay," Dixon said. "The plane should be just down that path about thirty or forty yards, if I remember correctly. This should be the path that leads directly to it. If not, then we're not too far to one side of the dock. Either way, we need to move slow until we know that the area is clear." Owen nodded in agreement. Jessica continued to look past them at the beach and the boardwalk.

"We should take weapons," she said softly. Dixon looked at her as if she were speaking Latin.

"Weapons? Are you nuts? Where the hell do you think we're going to get those? We've been walking through the woods for two hours. There are no weapons other than a tree branch. Besides, we're just going to run down the beach, get in the plane and take the fuck off. It's not like we're doing Butch and Sundance's last stand."

Jessica ignored the comment. Instead she stood up and moved off the path several feet. She placed her hands on her hips and looked around, her gaze directed upwards. Owen couldn't help but notice how attractive she was, standing with her hips cocked to one side, sweat plastering her shirt to her body. His momentary lapse was broken by the sharp cracking sound of Jessica tearing a branch off of a nearby tree. She hefted the branch as she walked back to the men. "Do you feel better?" Dixon asked. Jessica just smiled, a gesture that in the dim light looked more like a grimace.

Again, the three moved down the trail. The air became filled with a low buzzing, a droning that sounded like waves of insects approaching through the trees. Owen strained to see through the foliage, but saw no swarms bearing down on them. However, as they walked, the noise became louder. This time they didn't stop until they were well down the boardwalk and could see the pier. The trail they had been following had been, as Dixon had guessed, off to the left side of the dock. They stopped near the end of the wooden pathway and stared at what was before them.

The dock seemed vaguely familiar to Owen as he stared at it. He seemed to recall through the fuzziness that was the night before the long centerpiece of the dock and the three small arms that jutted out to either side. The seaplane, however, was not tethered to the pier. Instead, it was moving quickly out to sea, heading directly away from them, its engine providing the buzzing sound they had heard.

"Oh Christ," Jessica whispered. Owen felt his heart sink at her words. They seemed to put the finishing touches on everything he had experienced up to that point. Then motion on the plane caught his attention and he moved forward two steps. There were figures on the plane, standing on the pontoons and holding onto the struts. The mutant creatures pounded on the fuselage with their free hands, trying desperately to break into the cabin. The plane turned to the left, and seemed to pick up speed as it moved toward lift off. Owen could see the silhouette of a lone pilot in the cockpit. If anyone else sat in the rear seats, he couldn't see them.

"Is it just one guy?" he asked.

"I think so," Dixon said. "I don't see anyone else."

"There's four of them," Jessica said. Her voice quavered slightly as she watched the creatures fight to break through the metal skin of the plane. Across the distance and despite the buzzing of the propeller, the three on the beach could hear the tiny sound of glass shattering as the creatures broke the windows on the plane. The pilot gunned the engine and pulled the stick back and the seaplane began to nose out of the water, streams of the ocean trailing from the pontoons. The plane rocked crazily as the pilot fought the groping arms that extended through the shattered windows. One of the creatures lost its footing and tumbled into the ocean. Owen saw it flail helplessly for a brief moment, then it was gone beneath the choppy sea.

The engine began to sputter, short farting sounds that echoed across the bay. "It's going down," Dixon said in almost a whisper. The crash, when it came, was larger than Owen would have thought. The right wing of the plane dropped sharply and sliced into the water. That act began a pinwheel of the aircraft. The propeller slammed into the surf, chopping it up into large geysers, the white froth shooting skyward several feet. Then a sickening crunch as the nose of the plane impacted with the water. The creatures that had maintained their grip on the aircraft were flung away. Owen barked a grunt of horror as he saw one pass through the moving propeller a split second before the prop submerged. The creature erupted into a large ball of red mist that was instantly obscured by the body of the plane as it upended then flipped over. The fuselage separated from the wings and broke in half as the force of its movement carried it around.

Within moments it was over, the water continuing to churn around the sinking body of the aircraft as it rushed in to fill the gaps within the fuselage. From where he stood, Owen couldn't see any of the creatures that had caused the crash, nor could he see evidence of any human survivors. He stood, staring in disbelief and drained horror as the last pieces of the seaplane slipped quietly beneath the waves.

To his right, Jessica shifted. He felt her stiffen. He looked at her, saw she was turned to look further down the beach to the right of where they stood. Her face was drained and her mouth hung slack. Watering eyes reflected the terror that her face couldn't express.

Owen looked down the beach, following her gaze. What he saw was inconceivable.

"Holy God," he whispered.

4

Several dozen yards down the beach a mass of the creatures had gathered. From where he crouched, Owen could make out the tattered clothing they wore; remnants of uniforms or of vacation wear. A couple wore what appeared to be pajamas. The group had gathered closely together and seemed to be focusing on something in the center of their mass.

"What the hell are they doing?" Dixon wondered. Owen shook his head in response.

Jessica's head bobbed up and down as she tried to focus on what she was seeing. "They're digging," she said. Owen looked at her, unsure he had heard her correctly. Then he turned his gaze down the beach and saw that the bulk of the creatures massed on the sand were in fact on their hands and knees, digging a large hole in the sand. Plumes of sand flew behind them as they clawed deeper and deeper into the earth.

After several minutes, the hole was deep enough that only the tops of the creatures' heads were visible when they stood inside it. They crawled out and stood waiting, watching the forest. Owen heard the sounds of branches snapping. Then the source of the sound was revealed. A group of creatures pushed a massive, jagged boulder from the woods onto the sand. When the rock hit the beach, the slow momentum they had stopped. All the creatures on the beach gathered around the large stone and together they pushed it into the hole.

The rock extended only a few feet above the sand and had a large, flat surface on the top.

"Should we get out of here?" Jessica asked. "I mean, that down there has to be most all of them, right? So we should get away while they're all in one place, focused on whatever the hell they're doing."

"Where would we go?" asked Owen, not taking his eyes off the construction on the sand. "We came here because we didn't know where else to go; because the plane was supposed to be our way out of here. There isn't a boat that I know of. Do either of you know where a boat is?" Neither of his companions offered an answer.

"Owen's right," Dixon said. "Yeah, most all of them are down there, but we don't know where the others are, if there are more. We don't know of any other way to get off the island right now, so why don't we rest a while here and keep an eye on them? As long as they're down there, we're safe. If they leave, we know we're in trouble." Owen looked at Jessica; saw that her beautiful face was pale from fear. He could see the horror in her eyes, the look of a frightened little girl hidden behind them. At that moment, he wanted to run onto the beach and slaughter all of the creatures, just so he could reassure Jessica that she was safe and that everything would be all right. Instead, he continued to look at her, almost mesmerized by her beauty.

Jessica nodded, a reluctant gesture. "Okay," she whispered, and settled back against a large tree. "As long as they can't see us, we can stay here. I need to catch my breath anyway. Maybe we can figure out what they are and where they came from."

"I told you that already," Dixon said with a grunt as he moved to a tree not far from Jessica. He kept his voice low. "It's the servants. It's Donovan and most of his board. It's pretty much every person that was on this island last night but us. How we managed to not become like them I have no idea. But ..." his voice trailed off. Owen could hear the weariness in his words.

"That's crazy," Jessica snapped. "How could people, normal, sane and nice people—"

"I wouldn't call most of them nice," Dixon cut in. "Donovan himself is the biggest piece of shit this side of Kim Jong Il."

"You know what I mean. They were normal people. Like us. Just regular people. What would change them like that? What would mutate them, make their teeth grow like that, or their skin change to that color? Their eyes; Jesus, did you see their eyes?"

"Only time I've seen eyes anything like that was when my dad took me hunting bobcats when I was eleven," Owen said. "And even then they were nothing really like those things down there. The black and yellow ..." He had finally turned away from the creatures, but felt a tugging at the back of his mind, a need to raise up on one knee to watch them, to not let them out of his sight. Partially for the protection of the group and partially for his own morbid curiosity. Exactly what was that damn thing they were building?

"Yeah," Dixon said, his eyes lighting up. "They do look like inverse cat's eyes, all black with a yellow vertical pupil. And the speed that they move with, Christ Almighty, those things are as fast as cats."

Owen felt a question rise to the surface of his mind, but recoiled at asking it. He wasn't about to ask such an absurd thing in front of two rational people. Even with all the insanity going on around them, he wouldn't ask something that outlandish.

Jessica did it for him.

"Cats. Do you think they were infected with some kind of cat-like disease? Or something like a virus that would have turned them into those things? Like maybe they were bitten by something and this is what they became?"

"You mean like werewolves?" Dixon asked. To Owen's surprise, there wasn't even a hint of mockery in the man's voice. "I don't think so."

"Then how do you explain this?" Jessica snapped, her hand

flinging outward to point in the direction of the beach. "How do you explain people who, regardless of their personalities and what you thought of them, were normal yesterday—hell, a few hours ago—and now have been literally physically changed into beasts?"

"First of all, I'm not denying that something got inside them and changed them. I just don't see how it could have been a creature biting them. I mean, first of all, you'd have to be talking about a creature with the ability to go around and bite everyone in the resort without causing alarm, which couldn't be done. Most people were in groups or gathered around that bonfire most all night. So one creature couldn't do it alone. Not to that many people at once. Second, if it wasn't just one creature but a pack of them, don't you think they would have been seen before this excursion? And if they hadn't been spotted before this trip, I think that they most certainly would have been seen last night by one of us. You can't imagine that an entire pack of monstrous creatures would be able to enter a resort, bite everyone in it but us, and not be seen by us. Well, by you and me, at least. Owen there was so drunk that he wouldn't have heard a shotgun going off next to his head." Owen smiled a sarcastic smile of thanks to which Dixon winked in reply.

"Also," Owen added, "it couldn't have been a werewolf, or werecat or were-anything."

"Why not?" Jessica asked.

Owen pointed upwards toward the sky. "It's daytime. Those creatures aren't supposed to be able to do anything during the day. It's only a full moon or something that brings them out and makes them change."

Jessica sat quiet, seeming to digest the information. She stared at the ground between her and Owen. Finally, her voice small and child like, "I want to go home."

The trio fell into silence, weariness overtaking them suddenly, wrapping around them like a blanket on a frosty winter day. Owen felt himself being lulled into sleep by the soft rhythm of the ocean's waves cresting and breaking on the sandy shore. Although the thought of being so close to the ocean still caused him to be nervous, the sound relaxed him in the way that rocking and soft humming will calm an upset child. His eyes grew heavy and the heat of the day, the humidity in the air, pressed down on them and forced them closed. In seconds he was asleep, his chin drooping against his chest.

A hand on his shoulder, gentle but firm, ripped him from sleep. There was a moment of jolting panic, sour adrenaline in his mouth and his heart thundering in his chest. His eyes snapped open, the fragments of the distorted dream he had been engulfed in blowing away on the ocean breeze. Owen looked up sharply and saw Dixon kneeling beside him, one hand still on Owen's shoulder, but his gaze fixed at a point behind Owen.

"What?" Owen whispered. He looked at Jessica and saw that she was awake already, crouching behind her tree and staring in the same direction as Dixon. Then he remembered. The beach. The large rock, like a stone stage the creatures had placed on the beach. Owen wiped sleep from his eyes and turned around to kneel next to Dixon. His head felt heavy from the nap, and his back was stiff from leaning against the tree. Overhead the sky had begun to darken slightly, the sun starting its descent in the east. Have we really slept here most of the day? he wondered. The terrifying acts of earlier in the morning seemed so far removed now that their memories stirred nothing within his mind. It was as if he had watched them all on a television before entering the forest.

He fixed his eyes on the large black shape that was the rock.

The fear that sliced through him made his gut knot and his testicles contract. They made that for us, he thought. They plan on hunting us down and spreading us out on it to kill us and then to eat us. He felt a muscle spasm in his upper back as he thought of being dragged down the beach, lifted by several rough and clawed hands and placed on the surface of the rock. What would happen next, he didn't want to imagine.

"Shit," Jessica hissed. Owen's heart took off again, as he snapped his head around, thinking that they had been spotted, or that the woman had seen a band of the creatures sneaking up on them. Instead, her eyes were locked to sea, in the direction of the pier.

The ocean had returned to its normal, almost placid state just inside the sandbar after the incident with the airplane. Owen couldn't even see a single trace of the aircraft or where it had gone down. It had vanished entirely beneath the surface, the pilot's body either still trapped within his seat or devoured by some ocean creature. But what Owen did see, further out past the sandbar, caused a mixture of feelings to surge within him.

A large yacht was moored just on the opposite side of the sandbar. It was big, with a giant housing for the crew and guests. Owen guessed it to be at least forty feet long. Antennas bristled from the pilot box and even from this distance Owen could make out the bustling movement on deck. People were lowering boxes and dark objects onto a smaller boat with a motor mounted on the rear.

"Who are they?" he whispered.

"The band, I'm guessing," Dixon said. His tone was flat, as if he had already dismissed this as an opportunity to escape.

Jessica said, "If they can get here, maybe we can warn them, get to them first and get in that boat. They're going to come to the pier to offload their equipment. Maybe we can get down there before those things see them and convince them to take us back to the yacht."

"I think those things down there already knew the band was coming. What do you think that rock is for?" Owen said. "Besides. Look." He pointed to the right, toward the rock. The others turned their heads and watched as half of the creatures broke away from the larger group and trudged down the beach toward the pier. Their clawed feet kicked up large sprays of sand as they walked. "So much for beating them down there." The group made it to the pier, walked to the end of it and began waving at the smaller boat that now approached, laden with at least ten or eleven people and several black cases. "I'm going to guess that this is the band coming now, probably most everyone on board, since I don't see any other movement right now."

"What are those cases?" Jessica asked.

Owen shrugged. "Either some of their equipment or their luggage, or could just be booze. Who knows? I would think that they'd want to come ashore, meet everyone and see where they'd be playing before lugging all their equipment over here."

"Maybe they'll see that it isn't people waving to them on that pier and they won't come ashore," said Dixon. Owen nodded but doubted it. By the time the boat got close enough to determine that what waited for them on the pier wasn't human, it would be too late. The creatures were too fast for the people in the boat. They'd be able to leap off the pier and into the boat before anyone else could react. Owen's only hope of getting himself, Dixon and Jessica off the island would be if the creatures left the smaller boat intact and unguarded after ravaging the members on board.

"We can't just let them walk into this," Jessica protested suddenly. "We can't just let them come up to that pier to get slaughtered."

"What do you suggest we do?" Dixon said through a tight jaw as he watched the boat pull to within fifteen feet of the pier. Owen couldn't see the expressions on the boaters' faces, but could begin to hear the sounds as they called to the things on the dock. There was some laughter; probably a drunken band member thinking the people on the island had put on costumes to greet them.

Dixon continued, "If we make noise, one, they won't understand us and the things will kill them before the guys in the boat figure out what we're trying to say, and two, the creatures will know we're here and that'll be it for us too. I, personally, am not willing to die just so I can save a drunk bass player."

Jessica started to reply, to argue the point but was interrupted by screams. Instead of speaking, she closed her mouth slowly and shut her eyes in a gesture of resigned sorrow. Against his better judgment, Owen turned to watch. The boat had made it fully to the pier and the creatures had attacked. They pulled from the boat the band members and what Owen could only assume were people who served double duty as crew for the boat and stagehands for the band.

Everyone was taken toward the large rock, where the remainder of the group of creatures stood in a loose grouping, their hands slack by their sides, a hungry look in their eyes that was visible even to Owen and his companions at this distance. A few began to work their jaws, the enlarged and sharp teeth clicking against each other.

When the welcoming party had arrived with their captives, they quickly began to work. One of the band members was selected at random, a tall skinny man with dark hair that cascaded down his back. He wore black jeans and a black shirt that had some sort of logo on it, but Owen couldn't make it out. He was pulled by his hair to the center of the boulder then held in place by creatures positioned at each of his arms and legs. The man screamed, his voice rising to the pitch of a woman's. The creatures surrounding the rock quickly moved in, stripping the man's clothes off. Within seconds he hung naked, tattoos dotting his upper and lower body. His screams continued, the man struggling to form words. All that spilled from his mouth, however, were garbled gibberish; the words were broken apart by his pain.

Owen looked to the rest of the band and saw that they were still held fast by some of the creatures. The guards seemed to be disappointed that they weren't able to participate in what was coming up, that they had to stand fast and watch over the captives. Owen could see their anger and hunger on their faces, in the way they stomped their feet and occasionally tugged or slapped one of the captive people. Eventually, one managed to land a blow that rendered his victim unconscious. The woman fell to the sand, limp. Quickly the other creatures followed suit, each hitting their respective captive until he or she was unconscious. The band and crew out of commission, the creatures moved forward eagerly.

The dark haired man continued to struggle against his captors but with less enthusiasm as before. The creatures stood still, watching him, their eyes dancing across his naked flesh. Finally, deciding that it had waited long enough, one of the creatures moved forward and grasped the man by one knee. It raised one claw to his leg and pushed it into the calf muscle. The man's head rose and he screamed with fresh pain. The creature pulled its claw downward, in slow and jerky motions, opening a large wound on the outer side of the man's leg. When it had reached the ankle it stopped and reached across the man so that it could repeat the procedure on the other side of his leg. The blood that poured from the wounds stained the boulder and ran down the jagged edges of the rock.

With a fast, hard motion, the creature pulled the entire calf muscle away from the man's leg. His screams reached a pitch that bordered on inhuman. Owen stared in horror at the leg that was now nothing more than a bone with a foot at the bottom. Behind him, he heard Jessica gasp. He realized that she no longer displayed the cold indifference and survivalist attitude that she had shown in the resort that morning when he had met her. Then she had seemed like a strong soldier, doing her duty to survive. Now she seemed more like a helpless little girl, disgusted by the carnage she witnessed. The creature stared at the large hung of flesh in its hands and then reached out its tongue and lapped at it. Satisfied, it bit into the meat and chewed. Another creature approached and repeated the same procedure with the man's other leg. Another came forward and tore off one of the man's feet. There was no cutting, nothing of the sort. It simply grabbed the foot, twisted it until the anklebone snapped so loudly that Owen almost felt it in his own body and then pulled it forcibly away.

"What's the status of the boat?" he asked, unable to take his eyes away from the mutilations occurring on the beach. Another creature had approached and using a claw had slit open the man's abdomen and was chewing on the mottled pink and red intestines that had spilled out.

"Huh?" Dixon asked in almost a grunt.

Owen looked at him. "The boat these poor bastards came in. What's the status of it? Is it still there?" Dixon tore his gaze away and looked back at the pier.

"Yeah. Damn, it is still there."

"Okay. We have to get to it. If we don't, we won't get off this island."

"How are we going to do that?" Jessica asked.

"Easy. Those things are pretty much occupied for a while. Considering they have about ten more people to dismember and eat, they're going to be occupied for a long time. We're going to sneak down there and get in that boat and ride it out to the larger yacht."

"But what about those people? What about the ones that they haven't killed yet?"

"Those people are dead already. They just haven't stopped breathing yet. We can't go down there and save them, not a single one. To even try would be suicide. You know how those things are. Come on, Jessica, you fought with them this morning. Remember?" Owen watched her eyes solidify, remembering what she had been through that morning, only hours earlier. "There's no way we can get down there and save any of them. I don't like it anymore than you do, but that's the truth of it. Those people are dead. We're not. We're still alive and we're going to stay that way by getting to the boat and getting the hell off this island."

Jessica nodded. "I know. I'm sorry. I seem to have lost it for a while there. It's just that seeing—"

"I know," Owen reassured her. "Believe me, I know. And you can fall all to pieces, you can scream and cry and beat the hell out of something, once we're on that boat. Until then, I'm going to keep you alive and safe." Her eyes met his, held his gaze. A smile twitched at the corner of her mouth, her sensuous lips moving slightly.

"Get a fucking room, you two," Dixon groaned softly. "If we're going to go, let's go already. I'm not going to sit here anymore and watch these goddamn things eat long pork sushi."

The trio moved slowly in a crouch to the edge of the forest. Before them lay close to thirty yards of open beach, all flat with nothing to hide behind. It would be an all out sprint for the pier, then a mad dash along the wooden planks to the boat. Owen stared at the boat, bobbing with the motion of the waves. "Okay, ready?" he asked.

Dixon rose up and peered over the bushes to where the carnage was taking place. "They should be pretty well distracted right now."

"What are they doing?" Jessica asked.

Dixon's face was devoid of emotion. "You don't want to know." He turned to Owen. "We going to sprint this or go slow?"

"I'm not sure. What do you think? If we sprint, then when we hit that dock, everything down there will know we're here. But if we go slow, we extend the length of time we're exposed."

"Let's sprint to the dock, then take it slowly once we're there."

"No," Jessica cut in. "We sprint to the dock. We get in the water, putting the pier between them and us. The water will mask the sounds of us moving and we can just wade around to the front of the dock, climb into the boat and they won't know we're there until the motor is cranked and we're racing away." The men looked at each other, then smiled.

"The lady has a point," Dixon said. Owen agreed. They gathered themselves up, and when Owen counted to three, all sprang from the bushes and raced along the sand to the ocean. With every step, Owen felt his chest tightening up, the water looming before him and getting larger and closer with each step. At the same time, his ears strained to hear any sound that would indicate they had been spotted and that a pursuit was ensuing. There was nothing but the sound of the ocean, the rushing of blood in his ears and the occasional grunt from the creatures down the beach from them.

The trio was ten yards away from the water when the first scream sounded. A vicious roar filled with surprise and rage rocketed across the expanse of the beach. It scared Owen so much that he lost his footing and plowed forward in a spray of sand. As he landed, the breath was knocked from his body, and he lay on the beach trying desperately to suck in a single life giving breath.

"Oh Jesus," cried Dixon. "Let's go!" Owen managed to draw in a single, weak breath, then another. He pulled himself to his feet, still struggling to suck in larger amounts of air. Down the beach, a group of five creatures had left the festivities and were racing toward them, their hungry grunts plowing through the air in front of them. Damn they're fast, Owen thought. He looked forward to the pier and the boat and saw instantly that there was no way they could all three make it to the boat before the creatures were upon them.

"Back to the woods!" he yelled. Jessica was already moving past him, sand flying behind her as she sprinted the way they had come.

Dixon grabbed Owen by the arm and helped pull him along. Stumbling, they ran for the relative safety of the trees and bushes. As they plunged into the green gloom, Owen looked back over his shoulder. He saw the creatures at the pier and moving up the beach toward them. Their eyes glowed a preternatural yellow in the rapidly dimming light, focusing intently on Owen as he turned and ran into the bushes.

5

The forest swallowed them. Owen raced blindly through the brush, his hands raised in a weak attempt to fend off the branches and leaves that groped for him, as if they were minions of the creatures and were desperately trying to help their masters. Ahead of him, Jessica and Dixon ran in leaping gaits as they hurdled logs and low bushes. His breath still coming in tortured gasps and his chest burning from the exertion, Owen seemed to lack the coordination to dodge most of the natural obstacles that the other two avoided.

He wanted to look back, to see how close their pursuers were, but knew that as soon as he did, he'd see them mere inches away from him, their black eyes burning with hate and hunger. He thought for a moment that he could feel their hot, stinking breath on his back, rustling his shirt. With a gasp of terror, Owen plunged forward.

They ran for what seemed like hours. Night was settling in well by now, the trees surrounding them melting into the dark shadows like wraiths reclaimed by death. The air had cooled slightly with the dusk but the three people still had a thick coat of sweat on their bodies. Dixon slowed, and then brought the group to a halt. They crouched near a large tree with rough bark. Owen tried to calm his breathing, or at least to quiet it, but felt as if he were thirty feet below the surface and couldn't draw in enough oxygen.

They huddled together, as much for comfort as for the dying of visibility. In the murky light, Owen saw Jessica's hair clumped to her skull in dripping strands. Her head moved slightly from side to side as she tried to watch out for the creatures.

"Think we lost them?" Owen asked, hoping his voice was low enough. A soft rustling crept through the air as Dixon shifted his position.

"Don't know," he said. "It's possible, but then again, we don't know how well those things see in the dark, or how quickly they get tired. I mean, they used to be people. Still are in a way, I think."

"How can you say that those things are still human?" Owen asked, incredulous. "Didn't you see how they looked? How their teeth and eyes changed? Did you see what they were doing to that man? Christ Almighty, they were eating him alive, piece by piece."

"Can we talk about this later?" Jessica snapped. Her eyes continued to scan the darkness around them. "I don't think we need to be talking too much, and I don't like sitting here in the dark like this. We have to assume they can see in the dark, and we need to get the hell out of here."

"We need weapons," Dixon said. "If we're going to survive, we can't keep doing it by always running. Pretty soon, they'll probably corner us and we'll have to fight."

"Where are we going to find any?" Owen asked. "You think Donovan kept any guns here?"

Dixon shook his head. "No, Donovan was a firm believer in gun control. He hated them. Didn't you know that?"

"Guess I never cared too much about the man who owned the company," Owen said with a shrug.

"Guys," Jessica hissed. "Will you two please shut the fuck up? Those things are still out there."

"Well, where the hell do you suggest we go to find weapons?" Dixon shot back.

Jessica sighed. "The main house," she said. "The kitchen will have knives. And there's bound to be a maintenance shed somewhere near the complex; we can find axes or something there."

Dixon started to say something in protest, something Owen could probably guess. There were creatures back at the house most likely, and neither he, Jessica, nor Owen knew exactly where the main house was in relation to where they sat now. They had run blindly into the woods, avoiding the trail in their panic. Now, after crashing though the forest, none of them had any clue as to where they were.

Dixon rubbed his face with both hands, then brushed back his hair. "Alright. She's got a point. Besides, anything is better than sitting here. At least moving we have a chance of avoiding them." He looked over his shoulder in the direction they had been traveling. He nodded toward the dark forest. "I'm guessing that if we continue straight that way like we were, we'll run into either the house, or the other side of the island. It's not that huge. So if we hit the beach, we'll know to start moving to one side or the other." Owen didn't bother asking how they would determine which direction the resort was.

They gathered themselves and rose from their position. The dark was almost complete now, the only light coming in faint shafts through the canopy overhead. As usual, no wildlife sounded around them. The only sounds were their own labored breathing, the soft rustle and crackling of their movements, and—very faintly—the sound of waves lapping the shores of the island.

Owen trailed behind, keeping Jessica in view. He hated that he had to keep his eyes on her as he walked, feeling the need instead to scan the surrounding woods for any sign of their pursuers. Yet another part of his brain informed him in a very matter-of-fact tone that there was no way in hell he was going to be able to catch a glimpse of the creatures in the surrounding darkness. He wouldn't even know they were there until he felt one's hot breath on his neck.

Panicked, Owen whipped around and in doing so got his feet tangled together. He landed on his back with a leafy thump. Pain flared up his body to his skull and he groaned. Jessica and Dixon stopped, each crouching and making their way quickly back to him.

"You alright?" Jessica whispered. Owen nodded, then when she repeated the question he realized she couldn't see him. He whispered his confirmation. Embarrassment flooded through him, filling his limbs and causing his cheeks to flush. Without warning, he felt Jessica slip her hands under his arms—her grip was amazingly strong and at the same time gentle—and help him to his feet. His back and rear rumbled painfully at the movement, and Owen tried to mask his discomfort by brushing the dirt and leaves from his clothes.

"Thanks," he mumbled to Jessica. She didn't reply, only turned and whispered to Dixon that everything was fine and they could continue. The trio began walking again, Owen a little slower than he had been. With every step he winced, feeling sharp stabs of pain from where his coccyx was. God, please don't let me have broken my ass, he prayed. It's bad enough I'm on this island; please don't give me a broken butt bone, too.

It was the first time he had thought about the island in a while. He could feel the ocean around them, pressing in on the tiny strip of land as if the sand and trees were merely a single mouse, trapped in the corner by a larger cat. The ocean toyed with the land, allowed it to develop a false sense of security about its continued existence. In truth, the depths could surge forward with simplistic ease and swallow the entire island. It would require no more warning or effort than it took Owen to blink. The ocean around him, as he trudged painfully through blackened woods, pressed on every side like a slowly tightening vice.

Owen's breath became more labored as his mind wandered. If he started to sweat more due to the panicked thoughts that rumbled through his head, he couldn't tell, for he was already thoroughly saturated.

The pitch black around him acted as an extension of the ocean. Deep and enveloping, it covered him and threatened to drown him if he panicked.

Dixon slowed his pace, bringing the small group to a stop. The three crouched next to a large bush full of small berries. The leaves of the bush danced erratically in the wind that gusted through the forest. Owen's ears were assaulted by sound. All around him, the forest had seemed to come alive. Trees moved back and forth, while the smaller saplings and underbrush seemed to dance about the bases of their trunks like hungry minions. Interspersed with the slithering sounds of leaves in motion were the sporadic complaints of the storm; thunder peeling across the sky only to roll off into the blackness over the ocean. Owen could picture the ocean itself, inky water churning as the waves raced for shore and broke upon the sand. The scene could be something out of a horror movie.

He pushed the thoughts away. If he allowed himself to dwell on those fears, then he may as well walk back to the beach and let the creatures tie him up and begin to carve him apart. Instead, he peered through the undulating shadows around him and tried to see what Dixon and Jessica appeared to be staring at so intently.

"Doesn't look like anybody's there," Jessica whispered.

"Some of the lights are on inside. But none of the exterior ones are lit," Dixon added.

Owen squinted and managed to, after several seconds of focusing, see the outline of the main house several dozen yards away. Sure enough, he could see the faint amber glow of an interior light through what he assumed was a window. From where he crouched, it was impossible to determine what room or hallway the light illuminated.

Owen heard breathing, hard and loud, and felt his heart respond. He spun on his toes, keeping in a crouch. His mind's eye conjured images of the creatures right behind him, their enlarged teeth angling toward him as their mouths groped for his throat …

The breathing was his own. Nothing crept behind him. Around him were only the whispering woods, leaves stirred even more angrily now by winds that served as the leading edge of the storm they had seen hinting at itself offshore. Slowly, willing his heart to return to a semi-normal pace, Owen turned back to the others and the main house.

"What now?" he asked.

Jessica answered, keeping her eyes glued forward. "We need to get in there, find some weapons. Maybe we can even find a radio, or someone's cell phone."

"You really think a cell phone will work way out here?" Dixon hissed. "Get real. A radio, maybe. But I wouldn't count on it. My guess is that Donovan didn't want anything like that within his guest quarters. Wouldn't want anything to spoil the illusion of pure isolation and relaxation. No, if there's going to be a radio, it'll be in the staff's quarters, or a maintenance building. But," he turned his eyes back to the lone window through the trees, "there's bound to be some kind of weapon in there."

"So let's go get it and stop talking about it," suggested Owen. "I don't know about those things, but I don't like the idea of trudging around the woods in a rainstorm. But, if they don't either, they may come back here for the night."

"Owen's right," Jessica said. "They may come back here and eat the dead that are still in there. I'd rather be out here than in there. So let's get in, find something and get the hell out."

Dixon looked back at the house for a long moment. For a moment Owen felt certain that the other man would suggest that only one of them go in, that way if there was danger in there, all three of them didn't risk being killed. And he knew in his heart of hearts who would be volunteered for the duty. Instead, Dixon stood up and led them quietly through the bushes, their passage masked by the rustling from the wind.

They approached the house at a speed that to Owen felt so slow it threatened his very sanity. With every step he found his eyes darting to a million different places. Every shadow became a creature, ready to leap at them. Every darkened corner of the large house became a den, housing some horrible tentacled creature. And every step away from the shelter of the trees made them even larger targets to the hordes of bloodthirsty mutants his fellow islanders had become.

When they reached the house, they found themselves at the small window through which they had seen the light. Owen had to stand on his toes to see inside, and was rewarded with a view of a guest's bedroom. He could see the bed, the open door to the bathroom and a few scattered clothes on the floor. He stretched his memory, tried to identify the occupant by the clothing but found only a black fuzzy mass where his memory of his fellow guests would have been.

Dixon tried the sash and mumbled a victory curse when it slid up noiselessly. Owen and Jessica stood behind him as he worked, their eyes glued to the looming night around them. Owen could no longer see the trees of the woods, but could still hear them. Occasionally the sky to his right would illuminate from the lightning high in the clouds, soft seizures of light muted by the clouds.

"Okay," Dixon breathed. "It's open. I'll go in first. Jessica, you come second." Owen almost protested, but then realized why he got last billing. Chances were better that he'd be able to boost himself up rather than her. The ledge of the window was at least a foot and a half over her head. Dixon jumped, grabbed hold and pulled himself up. Loud scrapings of his shoes on the side of the house and his grunts of exertion accompanied his climb. Each noise sounded like a gunshot to Owen.

With effort, all three made it inside. They crouched in the room, letting their eyes adjust to the brightness. Dixon went quickly to the bathroom and then the closet, clearing them. Then he opened the door to the hallway and peered out. He stood still for several seconds, and then looked back in at the others.

"It's clear. This looks like the hallway that leads down to the kitchen."

"My room is on this hall," said Owen.

"Got anything for a weapon in there?" Jessica asked. Her hands moved at the back of her head, securing her hair in a ponytail.

Owen thought. He had barely come on the trip as it was, only boarding the plane at the urging of Michelle and his therapist. He hadn't packed much more than a few items of clothing and a couple of paperback novels. He shook his head. "No. Nothing. I didn't expect to be fighting for my life."

As a group, they moved out of the bedroom and into the darkened hallway. Owen looked behind him and saw the smashed flower vase on the table that he had encountered as he had exited his room hours before. Its pieces no longer looked helpless and terrified like they did when he first saw them, not understanding why they had shattered. Instead, now they just looked cold and dead, the victim of sudden violence.

The hallway led them, as they knew it would, to the dining room and the kitchen. The blood was still visible on the carpet of the dining room, only now it appeared almost black, having soaked into the fibers of the carpet. They hesitated outside of the kitchen doorway, peering into the large room. It was still brightly lit and full of stainless steel tables and implements. Owen remembered seeing the mutant with its face buried in one of the staff, one of the unfortunates that somehow hadn't been affected by whatever had changed the others. Suddenly he didn't want to go into the room. He felt himself backing away, creeping backwards into the hallway. As he moved, Jessica turned.

"What?" she asked, her voice barely audible. Owen just shook his head. She stared at him for a moment longer then turned back to the kitchen. Without a glance back, she and Dixon walked into the room, each moving incredibly slowly, making each step as quiet as humanly possible. Owen stood inside the hallway, leaning against the doorjamb of the dining room and watched them. Within seconds they were gone from sight, having moved around a corner.

Owen was alone. For the second time that day, he found himself alone in the hallway outside the dining room. A shiver tore through his body as he turned and looked behind him. The hallway was empty, but seemed threatening, almost like it was holding its breath, waiting for the creatures to pour from the rooms like ants from an overturned hill. Each one would race for him, their guttural growls preceding them, their rancid breath hot on his flesh as they bit deep into his neck.

In an instant, Owen spun on his heel and walked into the kitchen. He searched to the right of the door first, not wanting to move to the left side where the servant had been. There he found Dixon, the man working to dismantle what looked like an industrial sized paper cutter. The arm of the instrument was a single curved blade with a handle at one end. The cutting edge reflected the fluorescent lighting with cold indifference. Dixon popped the final pin and removed the arm. He held it up, turning it back and forth in the light and smiled.

"This'll work," he whispered.

"Got anything for me?" Owen asked. Dixon nodded.

"Yeah man. There are about two hundred knives over on the other side where Jessica is. Plus I'm sure there's a cleaver or something." They walked to the other side of the kitchen, Owen's eyes staying on the doorway as they passed. Nothing stirred in the dining room and the shadows beyond.

Jessica emerged from a massive pantry. Owen gaped at her. She had tucked her shirt into her pants, and slipped at least half a dozen long bladed knives into her belt. In each hand she held a meat cleaver. "How's this?" she asked.

"You look like you belong on Kung Fu Theater," Owen said. Jessica smiled.

"I was going for 'tough and don't fuck with me.'"

"I think you've pulled it off," Owen admitted. "What about me? Find anything I can use?"

"Lots of things." Jessica led him to a counter tucked into the wall near the large gas stoves. Affixed to the wall were three large black strips from which hung dozens of razor sharp knives. Owen selected a few, plucking them from what he discovered was a magnetic strip. "What else?" he asked. He didn't want to admit it, but down inside he wanted something cool like what Dixon carried. He couldn't be just another knife wielder like Jessica. Jessica opened a drawer and pulled out a large metal spike and a thick, heavy two-pronged fork. The fork was similar to ones Owen had used before in cookouts, but was much larger, the tines and shaft at least half an inch in diameter.

"I don't even want to know what kind of thing they had to use that on," Dixon said.

Owen started to laugh, but felt the emotion die within his chest. His eyes had shifted and stopped, focusing on something behind Dixon. The tall man turned to follow the gaze and Owen's heart leapt to his throat as he fully took in the creature standing less than six feet away from them.

"Fuckers are quiet," Jessica said. Owen couldn't bring himself to move. The creature—he couldn't even begin to tell where it had been at one time human—stood staring at them with its black and yellow, hate-filled eyes. Its chest heaved as it breathed, and now Owen could smell the offal that was its breath. The thing's claws dangled at its side and flexed slightly with each breath.

"There's only one of them," Dixon said. "We can take it." The final syllable left his mouth at the same time that a second, then third creature stepped into view from around the corner. Owen felt his world shrink. He looked around them. They were trapped in the kitchen, having let themselves linger in the dead end that was the knife corner. The only way out was through the three mutants that stared at them as if they were some alien display in a museum. One of the things cocked its head to the side, reminding Owen of a dog who was seeing or hearing something completely baffling.

The lead creature took a step forward, its clawed foot loud against the tile floor. Owen stared at it. Whatever clothes it had worn when human had long ago been shed. Patches of coarse fur coated its body. But it was the teeth that held his attention. Each was pointed and appeared as sharp as the knives Jessica held.

When it attacked, it did so with a speed that Owen hadn't seen before. It launched itself directly at him. Owen had no time to react. He screamed as the claws of the creature ripped open his left shoulder, raked down his chest. The blow of the impact knocked him backwards into the counter, and he saw bright fireworks of pain as his lower back collided with the leading edge of the counter.

Then, as suddenly as the thing had attacked him, its head was falling away and the body crumbled to the floor. Blood—red to his surprise—pumped from the stump. Owen looked up, pain clouding his eyes. Dixon stared down at the body, his blade coated in gore.

The other two creatures didn't hesitate. Seeing their leader dead, they attacked. Later, Owen wouldn't be able to determine if it they had attacked out of hunger, rage at their leader's death or in a desperate bid for dominance over the other. Whoever could kill the normal people first became the leader of this squad.

Jessica engaged one, driving her cleaver deep into its forehead as it rushed forward. The two collapsed in a bloody heap on the floor, and Owen managed to see Jessica swing her other cleaver into the creature's side before his attention was ripped away. Dixon had stepped in front of the other survivor, and waved his blade back and forth, back and forth as if it were a torch and the creature afraid of fire.

"Come on, you toothy son of a bitch," he taunted it. "Come get me. Maybe I'll take your fucking head, too, you prick." The creature stared at Dixon with a malice and hatred that Owen felt sure would have rivaled Satan's contempt for the world. Dixon crouched and waved the creature forward with one hand, holding his blade high with the other. "That's right. Come eat me. Come on. I taste better than chicken. Come on, fuckstain."

The creature moved, but not for Dixon. Instead, it had caught sight of Jessica struggling to stand after killing its comrade. She was off balance, trying to push the corpse off of her. The last creature sprinted forward, ducking beneath Dixon's blade as it ripped through the air inches above the mutant's head.

The jaws opened, aiming for Jessica's head which now stared at the attack in pure blinded terror. Owen felt his body move. He gripped the fork and slid along the floor toward Jessica. With every ounce of strength he had, he thrust the fork at the creature and watched the tines sink deep into its chin. Almost as if he had flipped off a light switch, Owen saw something go out in the black eyes. He let go of the fork and the attacker fell to the floor, its blood mingling with that which had already pooled on the tiles.

The three survivors stood panting, staring at the corpses in near disbelief. Owen pulled his fork free of the skull and wiped it off on the creature's body. "We better get out of here," he said. "If those three found us, you can be damn sure that others will too. There's probably more in the building now."

Jessica and Dixon agreed, and the three left as quickly as they could. Jessica wanted to look at Owen's wound, but he pushed her away, telling her that she could look at it all night, long after they were away from the house and hidden in the woods again.

"Don't you want to look for a radio?" she asked.

"Not now. Not after that run in. If the others find us, we may not be so lucky. Let's get out of here first, find someplace to hole up and patch up some of these cuts. We can try for a radio again in a few hours." Reluctantly she agreed.

Dixon led them down yet another corridor and, after checking the exit, out into the night. Instantly the wind assaulted them, pushing and pulling at their hair and clothes, buffeting their bodies as if to punish them for ever having gone inside. Owen looked around, his teeth gritted against the pain in his shoulder and chest. The blackness around them was near absolute. They had exited the house on one side that was well away from the front door. Again the shadows looked threatening, full of hidden dangers.

And once again, the trio melted into the darkness of the woods.

6

The rain came down, spilling from the clouds in the night sky as if they were torrents of blood pouring from a torn artery. The jungle around them became a cacophony of sound. Water pounded the leaves and branches of the trees and bushes as Jessica ran ahead of the group, leading them deeper into the jungle and angling them away from the path they had arrived on.

Owen ran behind her, lagging only by five or six steps, the pain from his wounds a constant fire. Behind him he knew Dixon ran, but couldn't hear the man for the crashing sound of the rain assaulting the forest. The very world around them had become one giant auditorium filled with a million deafening handclaps. However, for all the water that dumped on them, they stayed relatively dry. The canopy of the forest was thick enough in the area they traveled that it deterred most of the moisture from seeping through. Water did reach them, warm yet unsoothing as it saturated their clothing further. Owen scrambled over a fallen tree and marveled that he still seemed to be getting more and more wet. Didn't think it was possible, he mumbled silently.

He slid to a halt, his shoes scraping the ground and almost losing traction. He heard and felt Dixon at the same time, the large man running squarely into his back. Dixon grabbed Owen to keep both of them from going down.

"The hell did you stop for?" Dixon breathed.

Owen stared ahead. The trees around them had finally melted away completely into shadows. "I lost Jessica. I don't know where she went. We went over that tree and when I started to refocus I realized she was gone."

Dixon grumbled an obscenity that was lost in the din. "What now?"

Owen shrugged and took a small step forward. "I guess we're going to have to keep moving forward and hope that she realizes that we're not behind her. Maybe she'll stop and wait for us, or start back."

"Maybe one of—"

"Don't say it. Even if it's true." Owen was surprised to discover that he felt a genuine sense of dread at the prospect of losing Jessica. He had only known her for less than twenty-four hours and already he felt a connection to her, a bond. In his mind he saw her face appear, and with it brought a determination to find her. He had to know that she was okay. He didn't understand why now, when they were simply running through the woods, not being chased, that he felt this chivalric notion toward her. But it was there nonetheless.

"Let's get going," Dixon urged. "I don't want to be out in this rain any longer than I have to. Can't hear those fuckers coming with this noise around us. Owen nodded, not sure that the other man could see the gesture.

They moved forward, Dixon remaining behind Owen but keeping one hand on Owen's shoulder. As they stumbled through the forest Owen was reminded of the haunted houses he used to go to as a young kid. Every Halloween his dad would take him and some of his buddies to the local haunts. Charity groups who donated all the proceeds put on most all of them, but a few, the ones that were really good, were straight for profit. In the best of them, small groups were sent in single file into the houses or tunnels or mazes made of plywood and draped with black plastic sheeting. Every person had to put their hand on the shoulder of the guest in front of them, to ensure that everyone stayed together and came out safely. But that rarely worked. The groups always got separated, people in front being scared by a certain monster and sprinting forward, leaving the rest to flounder their way forward.

Owen felt like that now. Jessica had moved forward on her own, leaving him and Dixon to the mercy of the creatures that were somewhere in the woods around them. And how many of them were there? he wondered. How many of them filtered through the greenery, moving as quick and silent as shadows in a vacuum? And what the hell were they? Owen found the question just as daunting now as he had twelve hours ago when it had first been posed.

He pushed it from his mind. He'd worry about the whys later. Now he had to concentrate on getting to shelter safely without breaking his ankle or worse. As if to drive the point home, his foot slipped on a tree root and he tumbled down. Pain flared in his shoulder and chest where the creature's claws had penetrated him. They hadn't even had time to address his wounds, feeling that flight was the best option after the encounter back at the main house. Owen grimaced against the pain and regained his footing. His ankle seemed fine so he began moving again. As he walked, his eyes traced a constant pattern around him. First down the dark path, in an attempt to see obstacles or some discernable path. Then to either side, hoping to catch movement that would signal the creatures or Jessica.

Nothing around them other than the wind and leaves moved. Together the two men, store owners of Wee Lad toys, crept through the darkness, oblivious to the dangers around them.

They had traveled for what seemed to be a mile or more, but Owen knew that in reality it was probably only a few hundred yards when Dixon hissed in his ear, "There. To the right." Owen froze, his heart jack hammering in his chest. He strained his eyes to the right, focusing only on the thick gloom around him.

"What?" he asked back over his shoulder.

Dixon didn't answer, but instead moved around to take the lead. "Put your finger through my belt loop," he whispered. Owen hooked his index finger through a belt loop at the rear of Dixon's pants and felt them pull as Dixon began to walk. Having decided that it couldn't be danger, otherwise they wouldn't have engaged in a walk toward it, he allowed himself to be led.

Finding himself in the rear of the party again, Owen couldn't help but feel exposed and in danger of imminent attack. He swiveled his head around, but gave up after a few moments. The motion of looking behind him was fruitless, the dark was too complete. And looking away from Dixon's shade enshrouded back disoriented Owen and caused him to stumble more than once. Around him the rain continued to punish the forest for providing shelter to the fugitives.

Dixon slowed his pace once again and finally halted. Owen stood with his finger hooked into Dixon's pants and waited, trying to control his breath. "What is it?" he asked impatiently.

"I think I see something; someplace where we can hide out, get out of the rain."

"Do you see Jessica?"

"No." Owen cursed.

Dixon started forward before Owen could ask him if he had seen any of the creatures. The path Dixon led them on was directly through the foliage that had been around them. Owen knew immediately that they had managed to stay on some kind of trail through most of their flight. However, now he felt the sodden branches and leaves scraping against his exposed skin, leaving tentacles of water to crawl along his body as he passed.

The forest gave way to a large mound of rocks. Dixon walked slowly along the face of them, the boulders extending well over his head. There were no trees by the rocks and Owen felt the full force of the storm lash down at him. He risked a glance upward, only for a moment, and saw lightning rip apart the sky, illuminating clouds that looked as if they had escaped from Hell itself.

"I don't see an opening or anything," Dixon said loudly. Owen looked to his right just as another streak of lightning lanced overhead. In the split second of illumination, he saw a turn in the rocks.

He motioned for Dixon to follow and together they made their way around the stones.

A natural path had been eroded in the rocks. It was narrow, in one place almost too narrow for the men to pass through, but they managed by turning to one side. When they cleared the path they found themselves on a natural rock shelf with ample overhang from the boulders to shelter them from the storm.

Owen's breath caught as his eyes took in the rest of the scene. The shelf was but one side of a natural grotto in the island's shore. Mere feet below the edge of the shelf the ocean boiled, black and hateful. Even in the night, Owen could see the water's fury, could see clearly the whitecaps as waves broke and reformed, wrestling with one another as if they were two rabid dogs fighting over the last piece of maggot-infested meat.

As he stared, he felt his entire world drain away. Every fear he had lived with since Heather's death rushed in to fill the void in his soul. He felt himself begin to tremble, and jerked violently when Dixon touched his elbow.

"Hey, man," Dixon cried. "The hell's gotten into you?" He studied Owen's face. The fear was clear; Owen knew it but didn't care. Couldn't care. His mind was preoccupied with other things, worse thoughts. Water receding quickly, so quickly that if you blinked you would miss it. But coming back. The water came back, and when it did, Hell followed with it.

Dixon's face softened in the rain. His short hair was plastered in chunks along his forehead. He reached out a hand again and touched Owen, this time on the shoulder. His grip was soft but unyielding. "Come on, Owen. Let's get under that overhang and out of this damned rain." His eyes tugging back to the raging water only feet from him, Owen allowed himself to be led further away from the edge and under the overhang. Once out of the rain, the air turned chilly. A soft breeze pushed through the space, and the two men began to shiver. Owen faintly noticed that his wounds had ceased to hurt, the pain replaced by the thick numbness brought by the cold. They sat, keeping close to one another for warmth. Around them, the rain increased its intensity, angered that the men had escaped its wrath again.

Dixon rubbed his hands together and blew onto them. "I guess a fire is out of the question," he snorted. Owen didn't answer, his eyes locked on the dimness beyond the portion of the rock shelf that he could see in the sporadic lightning bursts.

A noise, a scrambling and tumbling of small rocks, jerked the men to their feet. He strained to see what had caused the disturbance.

Another flash of lightning.

In the light, he saw a small pile of dirt and rocks only feet from where he stood. He knew it hadn't been there before. He scanned the surroundings. Nothing moved, only the wind and rain roared.

Another scrambling sound, this time louder and closer. Owen tensed, crouching as he readied himself for an attack. His hands found the fork and the spike tucked into his belt. His eyes cut to the side and he saw Dixon raising the long blade he had armed himself with. Together the men stood, shoulder to shoulder, their chests moving in almost perfect synchronization, and they waited.

When the dark form moved toward them, it did so quickly. Owen raised the fork and was ready to throw it at the creature when lightning split the night again and his eyes found Jessica's terrified face. Then shadows closed around her and he lowered his weapon.

"Where the fuck have you been?" she demanded.

"Us?" Owen asked, incredulous. "What do you mean, where have we been? We never fucking left you. You took off on us!"

Jessica moved closer and the trio sank down together. In the dim light of the shelter, Owen could see her features as if they were through a kaleidoscope. "I didn't leave," she said. "We got separated. All I know is that we're hauling ass through the woods. I'm looking all over for a place to hole up, or at least pause so we can get our breath. When I look back, you guys were gone. I doubled back but didn't see you, couldn't hear you. Nothing. So I started to look for you, figuring you had strayed off the trail. That's when I found this thing." She pointed to the overhang. "I must have been right behind you the entire time. When I realized that this was some kind of shelter, I figured you may have found it and gone in. At the very least I was going to use it as a place to rest before looking for you guys again."

"Bullshit," Dixon coughed. Owen saw Jessica's shadowy head turn toward the man.

"What?"

"I said 'bullshit'. I think you were going to leave us to whatever. You found this place, but finding us was purely accidental. Hell, I bet you'd even have stayed here all night and the next couple of days without ever leaving to come find us. Just figured we were gone and left us to those things."

Jessica was silent. Finally she said, "You stupid son of a bitch. Do you really think that I'm so heartless that I'd leave you assholes alone?" As she spoke, her voice rose in volume. Owen looked around, seeing only darkness. He didn't know if the walls of the shelter would cause an echo, but he didn't want the creatures to be nearby and have any chance of hearing them. He held out his hands, gently touching both of his companions.

"Guys, let's calm down, alright? I'm positive that Jessica wasn't going to leave us."

"How the fuck do you know?" Dixon demanded. Owen winced at the harshness of the words coming from a man who was normally so jovial.

"I feel like I know Jessica and that doesn't sound like something she'd do to us. I think she needs us just as much as we need her if we're going to get out of here."

Dixon coughed. "Just because you want to fuck her, doesn't mean she wouldn't leave us at the drop of a hat if it meant she could save her own ass."

"Dixon," Jessica cut in, "why don't you go fuck yourself, okay? If you have that big of a problem with me, either come get you some or get the fuck out of here. But if you come get some, keep in mind that I don't have a problem with sticking one of these knives into your ass." They stared at each other through the night, a close-quarters standoff.

Finally he heard Dixon mumble, "Fuck it." The tension between the group slowly dissolved but never fully left. They listened to the storm surge around them. Owen looked out into the twilight, feeling the tension creep back into him at the knowledge that the ocean was that close.

"How did we get here?" Jessica asked.

Owen shook his head, despite knowing that nobody could see the movement. "I don't know." He chuckled softly, "I don't remember much. I remember being on the plane with Dixon, I remember landing and meeting Donovan on the dock and then the next thing I clearly remember is waking up this morning with a hangover that would make even the worst alcoholic repent."

"Yeah," Dixon said. "I crashed after the party and woke up to one of those things coming into my room. It had on the uniform of one of the servants."

Jessica shifted, the movement making soft scratching noises on the rock. "I was the manager of the best selling store in all of Washington. I had a boyfriend who would have done anything for me. I had a cat." At the mention of the animal, her voice became pinched.

"You still have those things," Owen said. "Nothing's changed; we're just here and they're there."

"No. I am still the manager, and I do still have the cat. That is if he hasn't starved to death because my dumb ass neighbor didn't feed him. But the boyfriend is history. He left me a week and a half ago. Said he had to move to New York to pursue his dream of being an artist."

"I know the feeling," Dixon said. "My wife left me for a twenty-two year old personal trainer. This was two years ago, of course, but still. It still stings."

"You ever talk to her?" Owen asked. "Or see them out in public? That's got to sting, seeing her with him."

"Actually I do see them, but it's not so bad. And the trainer ... is a female."

Jessica whistled. "Damn."

"Yeah. Just a little bruise to the old ego, but nothing irreparable." Dixon turned to Owen. "What about you? Married, single?"

Owen's chest constricted and he felt sweat pour from every gland, soaking his already waterlogged body. Could he really talk about it? It had been almost impossible to open up to his therapist; what made him think he could do it now?

"I was married," he said, surprised at the words. He felt his throat beginning to constrict, to choke off the flow of speech. He swallowed hard and pressed on. "My wife died when we were on vacation. She ... drowned."

The others were silent. Finally, after what seemed an eternity broken only by thunder, Jessica said, "I'm sorry." Dixon added his condolences.

"Yeah, well. I've managed," Owen said. "Work has kept me occupied. And I do have some truly great people at the store." His mind conjured up an image of Michelle, smiling at him and chiding him for his reluctance to take this trip. "Besides, my therapist told me that it would be a good idea to come here, to get away from my problems and to relax a little. Get some perspective on the whole thing. He thinks I will be able to move on after this trip."

The admission felt good, and was met initially with silence. The only sound was the storm. Finally a cough from Dixon followed by a snort from Jessica. Within seconds the two were bursting with laughter. Owen stared at them. What in the hell were they laughing at?

Finally Jessica composed herself enough to speak. "Get away from your problems. Come to Bezeten Island, where all the natives are raving monstrosities."

Dixon chimed in. "Come to Bezeten Island, where all your problems will be eaten away, along with your small intestine." The two disintegrated into uncontrollable laughter. Jessica fell over on her side and continued to laugh, her voice musical and lilting. Owen found himself laughing with them, small chuckles at first, then a full-blown laughter, his stomach hurting with the exertion and tears running down his face. It was wonderful, being in that moment. For a few seconds, he truly found release from the fears and doubts that had plagued him in the past year.

Slowly the group regained their composure. Their thoughts turned to other things, primarily food. Dixon was the first to admit that he was starving. He looked at Jessica and announced that if he had to, she'd be the first person they'd eat. She replied to this with a promise to shove the blade of her knife deep into his scrotum. Nobody had anything worth eating on them, and they all assumed that finding anything to eat within the forest at night during a storm would be just beyond impossible. Going back to the resort buildings was out of the question, at least for the night. To combat the hunger, the three drank water from a shallow pool of rainwater that had collected in a natural depression near where they sat. Then they lay down and went to sleep.

A gentle licking on Owen's arm tried to coax him from sleep. He fought against it, rolling slightly away from the sensation. Whatever animal was licking at him would have to wait. However, by the time that thought had finished in his mind, his brain was coming online, rising from the depths of slumber like a hulking beast.

The licking moved down his back, and lapped at him through his shirt. Instantly Owen's eyes were open, his senses fully awake. He rolled over and sat up quickly. The platform upon which they had camped was visible through the dim morning light. The continued rain muddied the sun that crept into the horizon somewhere beyond his vision under the alcove. Owen felt the licking at his ankles and along his leg and looked down. What he saw froze his blood.

The ocean had risen, whether from the storm or from the tide, he didn't know or care. But it covered the rock where the group lay. Yards away he could see the edge of the rock, could see the ocean still boiling from the storm. With every wave, more water flooded the area and lapped against him and his companions. Panic seized Owen's brain, screaming at him to run, to get anywhere but there.

"What the fuck?" he heard Dixon swear from behind him. With effort, Owen pulled his eyes away from the rising ocean and stared through the gloom at his companion.

"We're flooding," he whispered. Jessica came awake with a grunt and her own vulgarity.

"Let's get the hell out of here before we drown," Dixon said. Owen couldn't help but feel a sharp pain of loss and sadness at the phrase. He cut a glance at Dixon, saw that the man had no idea what he had just said but instead was gathering himself to vacate. Jessica brushed against Owen as she stood. The water now had risen to her ankles; it pulsed and undulated against her shoes as if it were a living entity, a creature mindlessly trying to gain access so that it could murder everything inside.

Owen found himself unable to move. He sat up, one hand on the ground as a prop, his hand invisible beneath the dark water. The ocean felt alive against him. He could sense its malice, its desire to take him into its bosom, to suffocate him and to reunite him with all the other rotting souls it had claimed over the eons.

Then Dixon's hands were under his own arms, pulling Owen up and getting him on his feet. Dixon's face swam into view. "Dude, we have to get out of here. Are you okay to go?" Numb and never taking his eyes from the surging water, Owen nodded. Dixon turned, said something to Jessica, and then started for the path back up and over the rocks. Jessica moved behind Owen and put a hand on his shoulder.

"Come on," she said. "I'll be right behind you." She gave him a soft push and, to his surprise, Owen began walking. He sloshed carefully through the dark water, his gaze returning to the water around him. It had now risen to a midpoint on his calves. As he moved clear of their sleeping area, the wind whipped and clawed at him.

Dixon had moved ahead, picking his way carefully but quickly up the rocks toward the small path that led to the jungle. Owen had to squint through the rain and wind to catch glimpses of his shirt as he slipped through the narrow crevasse.

Behind him, he heard a scuffling through the rain. Owen turned and saw Jessica climbing onto the first rock. She reached forward, her hands slipping as they grasped for purchase. Owen stood where he was, watching, until she had secured her hold and began to straighten. She looked up at him, met his gaze and smiled. "Piece of cake," she said, but her words were all but drowned by the roar of the ocean behind her.

Then she was gone. As quickly as a blink, Owen watched Jessica's face turn from a smile to a mask of terror as her balance tipped the wrong way. Her feet slipped on the rock, and she pinwheeled her arms almost comically as she desperately struggled to grasp a handhold. Owen reached forward, stretching out his own hand, but was too far away. Jessica toppled backwards, landed on her feet on the platform, then slipped again and fell into the ocean.

Owen cried out, scanned the surface of the hateful water for any sign of her. Nothing broke the surface. He looked back up the trail to where Dixon should have been, but saw nobody. The other man had moved beyond sight and sound of them, oblivious to the tragedy behind him. Owen's mouth worked silently, forming words that couldn't be heard by anyone.

He looked back to the ocean and saw her, bobbing along the surface almost a dozen yards further out toward the open sea. Jessica shouted at him, thrust one arm toward him as if he could actually grasp it. Then her head was covered by a large wave. She reappeared moments later, sputtering and coughing, but keeping her eyes on his. As he watched, helpless, her face changed. What appeared in its place was his ex-wife's face, Heather's beautiful visage bleached pale and riddled with abject terror.

Owen's heart twisted painfully even more in his chest. Heather, his wife of fourteen years who had died in the Tsunami on their vacation to Thailand. Through the storm, through his attempts to repress it, he heard her screams as they ran from the rushing water. The wall of it surged forward as if it were a starving beast from the depths of Hell and could smell their souls. In the rush, in the stampede, Heather was separated from him, her hand torn from his grip. He caught a glimpse of her through a platoon of people all scrambling for their lives, then he was pulled along with the crowd. He ended up on the roof of a building with fifteen other people.

Heather's body had been recovered four days later. Owen,

standing now on the rain soaked rock and staring at Jessica as she drifted further and further away, struggled to push aside the images of his wife's pale, bloated and broken body. Reluctantly the visions of Heather left, slipping beneath the waves of his thoughts with whispered promises of their return.

Owen blinked rain from his eyes. Jessica bobbed in the surf, her arm still outstretched. Owen stared at her, focused on her. His mind raged against the terror and the memories. He couldn't let another woman in his life suffer the same fate as Heather, could he? Could he really just turn and follow the path up to the forest, knowing he had left Jessica to drown and then later be bashed against the rocks? As he warred with himself, he watched her float farther and farther out.

Before he could think again, Owen stepped off of the rock and back down to the platform. The water now was above his knees, and it leapt hungrily up at his thighs and crotch. Owen looked down at it then back out to Jessica. She stared at him between waves that crashed over her head. If she made any other gesture, he couldn't tell from where he stood. But he knew that he couldn't let her die, couldn't let the ocean have her like it had Heather.

He jumped forward and entered the swirling water with a crash.

7

Images dance before his eyes, fluttering in from one side—Mister Demille, I'm ready for my close up—and swirling out the opposite side. Faces of people he knew, friends from high school that he hadn't seen in over twenty years, their visages the same as they had been they day they graduated. The guy he sat next to in three classes his senior year, Rob Danyik; killed in a car crash three days before graduation. Rob swims out of the blackness, his head a concave shape where the impact of the dashboard collapsed his skull. Owen sees the bone fragments jutting from the skin; he can see the fractures of Rob's cheekbones beneath the sallow skin, warping the flesh.

Rob's eyes are hollow, having long ago been chewed out by maggots and other parasites. Yet, somehow Rob stares at Owen knowingly, and Owen is certain that Rob cannot only see Owen, but can see deep into Owen's thoughts. Rob opens his mouth to speak, and for a moment Owen thinks that if he hears Rob's favorite expression, "What's up, doc?" that he will die. But Rob doesn't say anything. He can't. As his jaw lowers, revealing shattered teeth and a broken gum line, something black and viscous flows from between his swollen lips. Owen recoils against the sight and Rob sinks down into the cold that surrounds Owen.

Movement now, pushing and pulling against Owen, as if he were being pulled back and forth, a prize to be won between images of unspeakable horror and unimaginable terror. From the gloom another face rises, swimming up to Owen even as he shifts, back and forth, back and forth. He knows who it is even before they reach him. Heather's blonde hair precedes her face. It reaches forward in thin, wispy tendrils, seeming to grasp through the emptiness for him. Owen finds himself petrified with fear of what will happen if her hair touches him.

She hesitates in her ascent (or is it descent? He doesn't know) toward him and turns her face to him. Her face is sunken, battered and bruised from the collision with the water and other debris from the tsunami. One eye has ruptured and a grayish, golden jelly runs down her cheek. For a fleeting moment, Owen wonders what it would be like to spread the substance on a cracker and eat it. But his repulsion overtakes the curiosity and he stares at his dead wife. Her lips do not move, yet he hears her voice just as clearly as if it were whispering in his ear as they lay in bed watching Letterman.

"Get out of the water, Owen." Owen blinks in disbelief. As his vision clears and focuses, Heather's face changes. Her features grow sharp, more defined. He can feel her inches away from him, staring at him with her one good eye and waiting as if for him to say something. However, he can't speak; he can't do anything other than move back and forth as the forces pull and tug on him.

"Get out of the water, Owen," she says again. As his name rings in his ears, Owen watches Heather's face change. It's almost instantaneous, the difference happening in the blink of an eye. Her remaining eye burns a muddy yellow through the gloom around her. Her teeth become elongated and her fingers—usually carefully manicured—wicked claws. Owen feels the panic surge through his chest as he recognizes the creature she has become. He struggles against the ebb and flow of his body, struggles against the darkness that surrounds him, until he feels her beneath him, strong and hard against the skin of his hands.

Owen opened his eyes and immediately shut them against the burning. In that instant he became aware of himself, of where he was, and just as quickly as the burning had invaded his eyes, the suffocating invaded his lungs. He pushed against the rocks and felt his head break the surface of the water. Air, pure and moist, rushed into his lungs. With it came a certain amount of seawater. Just as quickly as he had been relieved to draw a breath, Owen found himself coughing and gagging violently in an attempt to expel the salt water from his throat and lungs.

A wave broke near him, pushing him violently to one side. He rode the wave limply, without attempts to fight the force or to maneuver through it. The water boiled around his face, causing him to squeeze his eyes shut tight as he continued to hack and cough. He became aware of something brushing against his feet and his mind instantly lit up brightly with panic. Shark. Oh dear Christ in Heaven, please don't let that be a shark that's beneath me.

The sensation continued along the toe of his right shoe, and after several long moments Owen realized that it wasn't a living creature preparing to devour him kicking and screaming all the way down its throat, but rather sand of the encroaching beach. The sun, despite the rain that had now tapered to a slow, steady drizzle, gave him sufficient light to see that he was now only twenty yards or less from the beach. A figure lay prone on the sand; its legs still in the undulating surf.

Jessica lay on one side, a single foot rocking back and forth as the water crashed upon the beach and then retreated. Owen searched his mind for logic, desperate to remember what had happened, but couldn't. Only fragments of ghostly sounds—mostly dull roars pinpricked by cries of people in distress—were found in the dregs of his mind.

Another wave broke behind him and forced his head under the surface of the water at the same time that it pushed him forward as if the he had overstayed his welcome and the ocean was eager to be rid of him. His lungs burned from lack of oxygen, but Owen didn't panic. Instead, he pushed his head back upright and inhaled deeply, this time managing to draw in the air and keep the salt water out. His feet —he noticed that a shoe was missing—dragged deeper into the sand below him, and with the force of the water behind him, Owen was pushed to his knees in the surf.

He crawled on his knees for a bit, gritting his teeth against the burning of his flesh where the sand and saltwater had washed into his open wounds, then fell forward and crawled on all fours until he was free of the waves and next to Jessica. Her eyes were closed and Owen saw no sign of breath; no rising of her chest. A new wave of panic surged over him like the waves he had just escaped. Quickly he rolled her over to her back and placed an ear on her sodden shirt, just above her left breast. He heard nothing. He put a finger on her neck, but knew as he did it that he hadn't the slightest clue as to where to position his digit to feel for a pulse.

"Jessica?" he said loudly. His voice was much louder than he had expected and the sound of it drew his eyes up from the woman and over to the jungle nearby. He scanned the foliage anticipating seeing one or more of the creatures peering back at him, yet saw nothing. In front of him, Jessica remained motionless. He returned to her and bent close to her face, placing his cheek near her nose. He thought for a moment that he felt a breath tickle his skin, but couldn't be certain. After all, it could have been wishful thinking. Not wanting to take a chance, he tilted her head back, parted her lips and bent over them.

"What are you doing?" Jessica whispered just as Owen's lips were to touch hers. The movement of her lips brushed against his skin ever so softly before Owen, who leapt back from her, broke the contact.

He sighed heavily, relief entering into him with a hollow feeling. "Thank God you're alive," he said.

Jessica swallowed hard, winced at some pain and said, "Isn't that what people always say when someone wakes up? 'Thank God you're alive.' I hate that phrase. Of course I'm alive. You saved me out there."

"What happened out there? I don't remember anything before waking up in the ocean and being washed up here."

The woman pushed herself up onto her elbows and brushed the rain from her face. "Do you remember us staying on that ledge?" Owen nodded. Instantly it came back.

"That's right. We woke up and the ledge was flooding because the water was rising with the storm. We went to climb out and you fell in."

"And you jumped in after me. To save me." She looked up at Owen, her eyes locking onto his and holding his gaze. Her face seemed softer, the hardness brought on by the stress of their situation having melted away momentarily.

Owen felt his cheeks burn under her stare, and with effort tore his vision away. "Yeah, I couldn't let you drown. My wife ..."

She nodded, the hardness returned instantly and she looked out to the ocean. "Anyway, when we were out there, you managed to get to me and together we swam in the direction of shore."

"How long were we out there?" Owen asked, looking back over his shoulder to the waves. The ocean was now a deep green under the new morning's sun.

"Not long. Once you got to me and we started to the beach, a mother of a wave came and separated us. I got pushed almost all the way in." She looked at him. "We weren't out long, but we were a good ways out. Friggin' currents. When I finally got all the way in, I crawled here before I passed out." She shook her head. "I had no idea where you were. I wanted to find you, but I just didn't have the strength."

Owen looked around to the jungle again. The trees and brush seemed to be sitting still, hanging on every word of the recounting of events. "We'd better get going."

Jessica sat up fully and brushed sand from her elbows. "Where do you think we should go?"

Owen thought back over the past hours. They had gone into the kitchen of the main house and found weapons. His hand went to his belt. His weapons were gone, the knives and large metal spike that he had armed himself with earlier. He raised his hand to his shirt and pulled it gingerly away from his body. It protested; it was soaked thoroughly and clung to his skin like a wet napkin.

Beneath the cloth the wound was visible. It wasn't nearly as bad as he had originally thought. The blood it had produced had been considerable, but now the gash that scarred his left shoulder and pectoral muscle was about five inches long and maybe half an inch wide. The flesh around the wound was a pale white and the meat inside seemed almost surreal. That can't really be me in there, he thought.

A shadow fell across his chest and he felt Jessica's face close to his as she leaned close to peer at the injury. "Doesn't look so bad now," she said quietly. Owen shook his head.

"No. I guess the salt water did it some good." He shrugged and winced at the pain that the movement caused. He released his shirt and let it fall back against his body. Jessica was on her knees and still leaning forward, her face close to him. He looked at her, and she returned his gaze. The sound of the pulsating waves diminished behind him, the beach and forest melted into nothingness. In that moment, all Owen could see or hear was Jessica, her face inches from his, her eyes intense and commanding of his own gaze.

Without thinking, without even knowing he was doing it, Owen leaned forward to kiss her. His lips brushed hers and for the most fleeting of moment he felt hers pucker and part slightly in welcoming response. A shock of electricity burned through him. However, no sooner had he registered the physicalness of the touch, Jessica had pulled away slightly.

"I'm hungry," she said, as she pulled her eyes away from his surprised face. She leaned back farther on her haunches, then rocked back and up to stand. The wind tossed her hair about, and she pushed it behind one ear with the casualness that all women seem inherently capable of. Owen stared up at her, dumbfounded. Had she kissed him back? Had she started to? If so, what happened? Why did she pull away? Oh God, he thought. I've blown it. I made a move and she's disgusted by me and now I'm in that horrible barren no man's land where I have to constantly beg her for forgiveness.

To his surprise, he felt her hand reach for his, grasp it and pull upward. The rest of his body followed and soon he was standing. Jessica faced him, her brown eyes dancing in the morning sun. She slapped at his arms and sides, knocking the sand from him. "Come on," she said and winked. "I'm hungry." Without waiting for him to reply, she turned around and began marching toward the jungle, her bare feet kicking up small tufts of sand as she walked. Owen watched her leave, his eyes seeing her shapely legs and firm ass moving, yet not registering it. He was stunned by what had just happened, his brain scrambling madly to make sense of it all.

"Are you coming, or are you going to stand on the beach all day?" she called over her shoulder. Her voice spurred Owen into action. He darted across the sand, kicking off his remaining shoe as he walked. He caught up with her a few feet inside the canopy of the forest.

"Where are you going?" he whispered.

She answered without looking back at him. "To find food. Aren't you starving?"

"Yes, of course I am." In fact, Owen hadn't realized just how hungry he was until she mentioned food. All the atrocities and the horror of having to run for his life had quashed all thoughts of food. But now that they were safe—for the moment, it seemed—he found the idea of anything edible to be the greatest thought in the world. Other than actually getting to kiss Jessica, he corrected himself.

"Then let's find something to eat. We're in the Caribbean, after all. It's not like there's no fruit or things on these trees."

They walked silently for several minutes, Jessica seemingly leading them in a random pattern. Finally she stopped and pointed to the right. "There. That looks good, doesn't it?" Owen followed her gesture and saw that she was pointing to what looked like a magnolia tree. He noticed dozens of small dark brown bulbs hanging from the branches between the thick, wide leaves.

"What is it?"

Jessica shrugged. "Hell if I know. But I'm going to eat it." She started forward and plucked a bulb from the tree. In her hand it looked like a baseball that had been dropped in the mud. A thick, short stem protruded from the top of it. Jessica lifted it to her mouth and bit into it.

"Jess."

She looked down at the item, then at him. "It's too hard to bite into. Oh what, what's that look for?"

"How do you know it isn't poisonous?"

She dropped her eyes to the item, then back at Owen. "Well, it's the only thing there is so far to eat. If we don't try it, we could starve unless we luck up on something. The only other alternative is to go all the way back to the main house, back into the kitchen and hope that there's still food in there and that those things aren't hanging around."

The mention of the creatures brought a sense of foreboding reality back to Owen. He blinked and gestured at the fruit. "Here. Let me see if I can crack it open with a rock."

Ten minutes later they were sitting at the base of the tree, a large rock between them serving as a makeshift table. The surface of the rock was littered with pulp and juice of what, to Owen's surprise, turned out to be an incredibly delicious fruit. His hunger had awakened with a ferocity he had never known after he devoured the first one, and he found himself having to concentrate on eating slowly, lest he risk making himself sick.

"Can I ask you something?" Jessica said quietly around a mouthful. Owen grabbed a smaller rock she had found and used it to crack open another of the baseballs against the table.

"Sure."

She hesitated a moment then said, "Since all of this started, you've mentioned your wife twice. You said she drowned." Owen's hands slowed as he peeled the rind away from the pulp. He felt his body grow slightly tense, yet he said nothing. "What happened to her? If you don't mind me asking."

He stopped fumbling with the fruit and let his fingers fall to his lap. His eyes remained locked on the rock between them. "We were on vacation in Thailand in 2004. It was the first vacation we had taken in over five years. It cost a lot, so we had to save for a while, stop taking short trips to the gulf during the summer, you know, that kind of thing. Anyway, we were there and were staying in a hotel in Ao Nang, on the coast." Why are you telling her this? his brain screamed. You haven't told anyone other than Doctor Sturn. Yet despite his mental protestations, his mouth continued to vomit the memories.

"We had gotten up early that day to go to the shore. There was a food stand down there that Heather had fallen in love with, and she made me go at least twice a day. We had gotten our food and moved to the edge of the water to eat when ..." His voice trailed off, the images moving before his mind's eye like the tidal wave he had experienced.

Jessica's hand found his, her touch soft and gentle, yet humming with strong reassurance. "Owen, if you can't, or don't want to talk about it ..."

"The ocean pulled away from the beach. I know you've heard or read statements like that, that the water just receded, but it's true. It didn't drift away slowly, creeping away like it didn't want to go but was being forced. No, it pulled away as if it was eager to go, like it knew what was coming and either wanted the hell out of the way, or wanted to join in as quickly as possible. I'd never seen that much water move that quickly before in my life. It ... it looked like someone had sucked it away with a giant straw.

"When the wave itself came in, it wasn't massive like the books and movies would have you think. No, it was small and low, but you could tell it had depth, that it had the whole of the ocean behind it. In movies, they make you think that the tsunami is a giant wave, dozens of stories high, taller than skyscrapers, and it crashes down on everything. But it's not. It's just a wave that never crests, never breaks. It looks like a huge lump, a massive swell in the water that just keeps coming forward, pushing toward you like it personally hates you and wants to tear you apart for something you did. We saw it coming in through the inlet, and knew what was happening. Most of the people just stood around, watching it, as if it were going to stop short of them, like it was just a normal wave that they could laugh about afterwards. But Heather and I, we saw what was in that wave, the force, the," he searched for the words, "the hatred in it."

Jessica's hand remained a hot, comforting presence on his own, and Owen was inwardly thankful she was there. The flood of emotions and memories was almost impossible to stop, the fierceness of them terrifying to him. "We ran between the buildings and down a street. I stopped once to look back at the wave and saw it hit the land. There are pictures on the internet, I'm sure you've seen them, of the wave hitting someplace and the water looks like the smoke from an explosion that happened just as the photographer snapped the shot. That's what it looked like. The water, when it hit the trees and rocks and things on the beach seemed to blow up, but it didn't slow down. There were several dozen people there. Most tried to run, but none of them escaped it. I saw people swallowed up by that thing, picked up and thrown into buildings or slammed down onto the street before falling under it.

"We managed to get two blocks away when the flood of people running away caught up with us. We got separated in the stampede. I couldn't fight the rush of people, and was forced to one side and up onto a low building, then I was pushed by several people up onto another, taller building. I saw Heather briefly; she had gotten caught up in another group that had turned opposite the way I had gone. But the water caught up with them. It ... it swallowed them up. Just covered them up like a blanket. She was there one minute, running in the middle of twenty or thirty people, then ..."

He stopped, unable to finish, unable to convey to the woman across from him the infinite sadness and terror of having to watch Heather's blond hair flowing behind her as she ran, seeing her face turn back one last time, seeing the panic and mind numbing horror on her face as she saw the giant wall of water only feet behind her; then, Heather was gone, covered by the wave. Owen felt the tears on his cheeks but made no move to wipe them away. His chest felt tight and his stomach was a hot, sputtering wire.

Jessica shifted across from him, moving around the rock and coming to sit next to him. She wrapped her arms around him and pulled him close to her. He let himself be enveloped in her embrace. He folded into her, putting his head on her chest and closed his eyes. She held him for a while, letting the moment pass. Finally she said, "That is why you've been skittish around the water. That's why you almost panicked last night at the ledge." Against her chest, Owen nodded. She pushed him away gently, not a rejection but a movement to position him so she could look him in the face. "And despite that, you jumped into the ocean after me."

Again, Owen nodded. "I couldn't let it get you. Not like it got her. I couldn't save her, I've come to realize and accept that. But I knew I could save you. So I had to."

Jessica stared at him, the intense look back in her eyes. Before Owen knew it, she leaned forward and kissed him. The kiss wasn't furious or filled with lust, but there was something behind it more than just a thank you. Owen let it come, his mind spinning uncontrollably in the wake of the rescue attempt, the near kiss on the beach, his recounting of Heather's death and the intoxicating feeling of Jessica's tongue in his mouth.

She pulled away and whispered, "I didn't do that because of what you told me or because you tried to save me. Well, maybe a little because you tried to save me. But—"

This time, Owen didn't let her finish. He grabbed her face in both hands and kissed her again. She responded by grabbing his waist and pulling him forward as she lay back, positioning her legs so that he could lay between them comfortably. Her hands roamed his back, up his neck and through his hair. Owen let his fingers trace along her cheeks, down her shoulders and around the firm mounds of her breasts. She responded by kissing along his check and nibbling on his earlobe, breathing heavily into his ear and whispering a moan as he increased the pressure of his grip on her breast. He felt himself straining against his pants, bulging against her body. Jessica could feel it, too, and wriggled her hips slightly to encourage and tease him. He slid one hand under her shirt and began to move it up along her smooth stomach toward the flesh of her chest.

A twig snapped off to the left of where they lay. Instantly they stopped, each bringing their head up and around to stare in the direction of the sound. Owen's heartbeat increased more than it already was and he began to slowly back off of Jessica. She moved with him, sliding backwards and rolling up to a sitting position, then to a crouch. Neither spoke, neither took their eyes from the forest around them. Owen reached backwards and found the smaller rock they had used to break open the fruit. He gripped it, ready to hurl it and at the same time knowing it would be a pitiful excuse for a weapon.

Silence settled across the wooded area; everything seemed to be holding its breath, waiting for something else to make the first move. Owen's heart beat so loudly he was certain that Jessica would tell him to be quiet.

"What the hell did you guys stop for?" a voice called out from ahead of them. "Christ, that was turning out to be one friggin' nice show. Owen, my man, you got some serious moves with those hands." The leaves of a bush ten yards in front of them and slightly to Owen's left shook and Gordon Dixon stood from behind it and began picking his way toward them.

8

Dixon walked toward them with an expression of mingled shock and humor. His lips pulled back in a half grin as he approached. "I didn't mean for you guys to stop. Hell, I'm sorry I lost my balance and broke that stick." He stopped and gestured with his hands, a rotation of the wrist. "Please, continue. If you want, I can always go back to the bush." He grinned fully.

"What the hell are you doing here?" Owen asked. His brain was swimming with the shock of sudden lust for Jessica and the surprise of seeing Dixon. "I didn't think we'd find you again." He cut a look over at Jessica who was sitting up, a leaf protruding from her hair like a fly caught in a spider's web. Her look at Dixon's beaming face was contemptuous. Maybe she's really pissed that he stopped us, Owen thought. God, did she really want to have sex here in the middle of the jungle? The prospect of the thought sent a ripple of pleasure down through him that centered in his groin.

"I told you I could leave again," Dixon stated. "It's really not a problem. But I heard your voices and when I got close enough to see you, you guys were already, well ... I didn't want to interrupt. But damn, Owen, I never figured you for a jungle love kind of guy. Risking bug bites on your 'nads and all that. Takes balls dude."

"Shut the hell up," Jessica snapped. She stood up and brushed herself off. "How did you find us?"

Dixon's smile faded only slightly. "Luck, really. I got to the top of the ledge before I realized that you guys weren't there anymore. I looked back and didn't see you. So I had to climb back down. The water was getting pretty high by then and I assumed you had fallen into the water. I climbed back up and walked the length of the shore for a ways in both directions, hoping to see you but the storm made it pretty hard to see anything. Hell, I ran into a couple of trees a few times." He pointed to a purple lump on the side of his forehead.

Jessica mumbled something about how it served him right but Dixon didn't hear it. Instead he walked to the tree and plucked a piece of fruit from a branch. "You guys eating these things? Are they good?" Owen told him they were and showed him how they had used the rocks to break open the rind to get at the pulp. Dixon ate it and smiled. "Fuck that's good." He sat down and sighed. "Okay. What now?"

Owen sat down next to Jessica and was happy when she didn't move away or give him a dirty look. He looked down at his feet, both of them, caked with dirt, scratches covering the once smooth pale skin. He saw that one of his toenails had broken almost to the nail bed. As he waited for someone else to answer Dixon's question, he busied himself with picking at and cleaning off his feet.

Nobody answered the question. The only sounds were of the wind passing through the trees and in the distance, the whisper of waves. An idea crept into Owen's consciousness. He frowned, furrowing his brow as he thought about it, turning it over and over. What the hell, he thought. "Have we discussed finding a radio?"

"I don't feel much like dancing, man," Dixon mumbled. Owen ignored the joke.

"All this running around, all I can think of that we've discussed was finding a way off the island. A plane or, after we saw it, the boat that the band arrived in. But I seriously doubt that this place, this resort that Donovan built, would have really been operational without a radio. Storms come through all the time when hurricane season is ripe. It only makes sense that the place has some means of communicating with other islands, even America, if the phones go down. And," he said, his voice growing faster as the idea poured into him like gasoline to a brush fire, "if they have that in anticipation of hurricane season, I bet they have shelters, bunkers or something with food and supplies."

Jessica looked over at him. Gone was the lustful gleam he had fallen into earlier. In its place was a tired sadness brought on by a reminder of their situation. "Do you have any idea where they are, these bunkers?"

"No. But they're going to be someplace close to the main houses, most likely underground beneath the houses themselves. That way the guests wouldn't even have to leave the building to be safe." He looked at them eagerly, but they didn't seem to return his enthusiasm. "Don't you see? If we can find those bunkers and a radio, we can call for help, tell whoever answers that we've been attacked, or something, and then hole up in the shelter with food and water until help comes."

"That means we have to go back to the main house," Dixon said. Like Jessica's lustful stare, Dixon's humor seemed drained away with the resettling of the situation.

"Yeah," Owen answered, "but don't you think that the chances are pretty good that they've moved on? That they're not in the houses anymore? I mean, hell, we saw most of them on the beach yesterday. I'd be willing to bet that they're still there." Eating the rest of the band, he thought but refused to say. And if they're not there, Owen my boy, they're here in the jungle, hunting for us. Hunting for you. Wanting to eat you, to pull your muscles from your legs with their teeth, as their black, devilish eyes stare up at you, watching you writhe in excruciating pain the way a woman looks up at her lover as she's going down on him.

"I don't know," said Jessica. "I don't want to go back to the houses. I'd rather find someplace and sit tight and wait for help."

"How will anyone know to come help us?" Dixon snapped. "Anyone back in the States won't realize we're missing and need help for, what, six, seven more days, at least? Do you want to sit somewhere and wait for another week, hoping these things don't find you?"

"It beats the hell out of walking back into the one place that we know they are. If you two want to sacrifice yourselves, serve each other up on a fucking buffet for those things, go right ahead. I'm not doing it. Alive, out here, there's a chance for me to live. Going to that compound and into those buildings takes away that chance." She folded her arms across her chest and looked off into the distance.

Owen sighed softly and moved closer to Jessica. He placed a hand on her back and began to rub softly. She didn't pull away, but stiffened up slightly at his touch. Owen continued rubbing as he leaned close to her. "I agree with you, you know. You're right. Going back there gives us a good chance of running into those things and getting killed. But tell me this; how long do you think we'll last, how long do you think we'll be safe and avoid them if we stay out here?" He hastened his words as she opened her mouth to rebut his point of view. "If we stay here, nobody will know we need help, nobody will know we're in danger. Not for a week or more like he said. The people back at the store, my assistant Michelle, she won't think anything's up for several days after I'm supposed to be back. We're down here with the owner and president of the company. It would probably be natural for us to stay longer at his behest.

"But going back there, if we're smart and careful, can give us a better chance of letting someone know we need help. Then, once we call for help and know it's on its way, then we can come back out here, or wherever you want to go and will feel safer. I promise." Jessica turned her head slightly and glanced at him out of the corner of her eye.

"You're just telling me this because you think it'll help you get into my pants," she mumbled. Owen grinned.

"Will it?"

Jessica shot a halfhearted elbow toward him. "Maybe." Owen felt his face grow flush and quickly stood.

He looked at Dixon who was cracking open another piece of fruit. "Alright. Let's get back to the houses."

The trip back to the resort took over two hours. Nobody was certain of the direction they needed to go, and when they settled on a direction, they proceeded very slowly, creeping through the forest. They stopped several times every minute to pause and listen, scouring the foliage with their eyes as they did, hoping to catch a glimpse of danger and praying they wouldn't.

As the forest began to thin, Owen felt his apprehension grow exponentially. This is stupid, he thought, and looked at Jessica. Her face was a sweat-sheeted mask of concentration. It seemed every fiber of her being was tuned into her surroundings and the landscape ahead of her. She didn't meet his glance. Owen looked to his other side where Dixon stood behind a tree, in a half crouch. Dixon glanced over, saw Owen looking and flashed a grin.

They moved forward, reaching the edge of the trees within seconds. As they had done the day before, they crouched behind the protective veil of brush and surveyed the buildings. Owen noticed that they had arrived on the flank of one of the smaller guesthouses; the one to the left of the main house it seemed. The sun was high overhead by now, its warmth beating down through the canopy of the forest and heating the moisture in the air. The humidity was almost staggering. Being from the south, Owen wasn't as affected as his companions, but still found it difficult to breathe from time to time.

Without waiting for an agreement from the group as to the best way to proceed, Dixon moved from behind the tree and crept forward toward the building. He moved slowly but deliberately toward the left side of the wall that faced them. Owen watched him walk and saw that he was moving toward a single metal exit door. The door was closed, but as Owen looked at it he thought that it may actually be open, just resting on the doorjamb. He strained to hear through the pounding of blood in his ears, listening for any sign of their detection by the creatures. He inhaled slowly and deeply, trying to catch the scent of any of the mutated party guests. There was none.

Dixon reached the door and paused, one hand re

silver handle. Owen saw the man look around, then glance back over his shoulder at the forest where Owen and Jessica hid. Then, with a grim look on his face, Dixon pulled the door open. It swung outward easily and soundlessly. Owen breathed a sigh of relief and thought he could actually feel Jessica relax somewhat.

Dixon stepped inside the building, but didn't tread too far; Owen could see the door propped open and he doubted it stood on its own. He held his breath as he waited for the man to reappear. When Dixon did, Owen let out yet another breath and smiled as Dixon waved them forward. Together he and Jessica stepped out of the woods and jogged quickly to the doorway.

"It's silent in there," Dixon said as he wiped sweat from his face. "I think this is one of the guest houses, so if we can find a bedroom we should be able to get inside and get to a phone." He turned and once again went inside. Owen let Jessica follow Dixon, and then took a last look around to ensure nobody had spotted them. Sure that the area was deserted, he went inside and gently closed the door behind him.

They were in a hallway almost identical to the others he had been in before. Dark colored ceramic tile lined the floor while rich colors adorned the walls. The hall was dark, the wall-mounted lights muted. In the deep gloom of the hall, Owen could make out the dim outlines of paintings and, at a lower height, small decorative tables.

They moved slowly, each walking inches behind the others, lest they lose sight of one another. Owen shot glances behind him, scolding himself each time. The hallway behind him was too dark to see if anything crept behind them. Besides, he thought, I'd see the outer door open. That's the only way in here.

Quickly the passage turned to the right and opened slightly. There was more light in the new hall, a weak illumination that seemed to come from nowhere and everywhere at once. It filled the hall with no discernable source and provided them just enough visibility to make out doors to guest bedrooms.

led them to the first one. They paused as they hovered near on glanced back at his two companions and then tried the knob. The silver handle didn't turn. Owen heard Jessica breathe a quiet curse, then they moved to the next room.

Of the eight doorways Owen could see along the hall, the fifth one was unlocked. The room inside was identical to the room he had woken up in the day before. Blinds were drawn behind curtains, effectively closing off the room to any light coming in from the lone window opposite the door. Owen shut the door behind them, keeping the knob turned until the door was completely closed. He then reached over and flipped on the light switch. Nothing happened.

"None of us were staying in this building," Dixon said. "They probably cut the power to it to save on energy."

"So the phones won't work?" asked Jessica.

"Maybe, but I think they may. If they're corded phones, they will. Only the cordless phones need electricity to function." He walked to the side of the bed and sat down, giving a weary sigh. Owen and Jessica remained at the door, each of them holding their breath in anticipation as Dixon looked over at the phone on the nightstand. It sat there, mute, fat and squat, like a large plastic toad. Owen wondered why Donovan would have installed the unattractive, slightly out of date phones rather than give his guests sleek new cordless phones.

Dixon reached over, plucked the tan receiver from the cradle and held it to his ear. Owen felt like he was waiting for the announcement of the winner for a major contest as he stared at the man's face. Dixon cut his eyes up to the others and shook his head. This time both Owen and Jessica breathed curses. Dixon replaced the receiver and lay back on the bed. He brought his hands to his face and rubbed his eyes.

"Fucking thing is dead. No dial tone." Owen peeled himself away from the door and moved to one of the plush chairs between the bed and the window. Jessica engaged both the deadbolt and chain locks on the door, then sat on the bed.

"So what now?" Owen asked as he peered around the corner of the curtains and blinds. The window gave him a view of the woods from which they had arrived. The trees were still. Not even the leaves fluttered in the breeze. It looked as if the entire island had been encased in a vacuum. The sight was unsettling, but Owen forced himself to watch.

"Maybe we need to go into the main house and try those phones," Jessica suggested. "If they cut the power here, wouldn't they have cut the phones, too? I mean, if nobody was staying here."

"Possible," Dixon said. "But I'm betting that the phones were all on the same system. It wouldn't make sense to have them on separate systems. That would be a pretty high expense."

Owen chuckled. "Donovan bought an island, man. Do you really think expense was a forefront consideration?"

"Do you really want to go back into that building?"

Owen replaced the blinds and slouched in the chair. "Not really. But if it's the only way we're going to get to a phone ..."

"And what if we get there and the phones are really dead, whether the storm last night knocked them out or those whatever-they-are's did it?"

Owen didn't answer. Instead he stared ahead, looking into the bathroom. From his seat he could see a corner of the counter next to the sink. There was a small object, the details of which he couldn't make out. He assumed it was a toothbrush holder. At the sight of it, Owen felt his heart wrench. That something so simplistic, so normal could be there, unmolested and removed from all of the horror surrounding it while he and the others were steeped in the ongoing nightmare seemed horrible to him. Why couldn't he be that holder? Why did he have to come on this damn trip? Why did he have to let Michelle talk him into it?

Owen blinked. Again he thought of his friend back home. He saw her face swim to the surface of his mind's waters, shimmering just beneath the undulating liquid of memory. He wondered what she was doing, if she were at the store. His brow furrowed as he tried to remember the day. It had to be a weekend, right? He shook the uncertainty away. It didn't matter what day it was. The fact remained that Michelle was home or in the store, or out having fun like she always did, and he was stuck here hundreds of miles away fighting to stay alive. Fighting to keep from being mutilated and eaten by abominations that used to be his fellow human beings, professional colleagues.

He missed Michelle, he thought. Missed seeing her smile, the way her eyes danced when she laughed—usually at something self-depreciating he did. He actually found himself missing the way she constantly scolded him for not moving on, for not getting out of the house, for not living his life.

Another thought intruded on his ruminations of Michelle. This one was of a bottle of whiskey sitting next to a pistol. Beside the gun lay a razor blade, and beside that were several white sleeping pills scattered across the tabletop. Owen marveled at how close to suicide he had come on more than one occasion, how often he had thought about it and wished for the strength to actually go through with it. The fact seemed completely stupid now, sitting in the abandoned room on an island populated with murderous mutants. That he could have wanted nothing more than to end his own life seemed now despicable. He cursed softly in anger, frustrated at how completely stupid he had been, and even more frustrated that he had seen the folly of his ways now, when his own death was possible at any given second.

"Holy Christ," Jessica whispered. She sat up straight on the bed. Owen and Dixon both leapt from their seats and spun around, looking for the source of her concern. The room was empty save for the three of them, but Owen felt as if they were being attacked by unseen phantoms. His heart wrenched in his chest and beat loudly against his ribs.

"What?" Dixon hissed. "For fuck's sake, there's nothing here. Calm down before you give us heart attacks."

"The boat," Jessica said, and looked directly at Owen.

"The boat?"

She nodded. "The boat that the band came in. The boat was still there, docked at the pier. They didn't do anything to it."

"Not then," Dixon snorted.

"And maybe not after, either. Remember, they were pretty occupied with killing those guys and then there were those few that came after us. That's it. I'm betting that the ones that stayed on the beach forgot or didn't even know we were there, and the ones that chased us probably forgot about us as soon as they realized we were gone and they had gotten back to where the kills were. Hell, even if they're really that intelligent they would have realized that we weren't getting off the island regardless, so they could take their time and hunt us down later."

"So you think the boat is still there, tied to the dock and waiting for us to come get it?" Owen asked. Jessica looked at him. From her expression he could see that she wasn't sure if he were just curious or doubted her the way that Dixon did. He tried to smile, to relax his features, something to give her the indication that he was on her side. For a moment he wanted to walk across the room and kiss her, push her back on the bed and finish what they started in the woods.

"I think so, yeah. I think that we should get out of here and get to the boat. If there aren't keys, we hotwire it."

"You know how to hotwire a boat?" Dixon said, sarcasm oozing on his words.

Jessica flashed a heated look at him. "Sure. I just cram that pin you call a dick into the ignition slot then stick my fist up your ass. That should do it."

Despite himself, Owen began to laugh. Dixon shifted his gaze to the giggling man and stared, incredulous. He opened his mouth to spew forth some barbed retort but nothing came out. Instead he threw his hands in the air and said, "Fuck it. I got nothing for that."

"So how soon do you want to leave?" Owen asked when he could finally speak without laughing.

Jessica lay back on the bed and stretched her arms out to either side. She breathed in deeply, held it, then let it out in a long controlled sigh. "Not just yet. Let's clean up and dress your cuts, and I'd like to feel the bed under me for a little while longer."

9

They left the room over an hour later. Jessica had dressed Owen's wounds using strips of bed sheets, then fallen asleep on the bed, arms thrown over her head and her hair fanned out beneath her. Dixon and Owen had looked down at her, silently admiring the curves of her body, the mounds beneath her shirt as her chest rose and fell with her deep breath. They decided to let her sleep, agreeing that they all needed a respite from the events surrounding them. Dixon had stated that it was highly unlikely that the creatures would come looking for them in the rooms. Owen didn't seem to agree with that line of reasoning. He felt that with the level of intelligence they had shown so far—they were highly intelligent humans before the transformation, after all—it would be only a matter of time before they conducted a thorough search of all the buildings and rooms therein.

When an hour had passed, Owen could take it no longer. His body had slowly increased in tension until he felt like his entire muscular structure had been replaced with concrete. He found his eyes constantly darting from the window to the door leading to the hallway, and then back again. He was certain that they'd be discovered at any moment.

Finally he stood, shook Jessica awake and nudged Dixon—who had dozed off twenty minutes prior—with his toe. The two rose slowly, complaining softly about having to get up and move. Jessica admitted that she could use another ten hours on the bed, and that it was unlikely that they'd be discovered at all.

"I'll buy you a king sized bed when we get out of here," Owen said as he looked again outside the window, his eyes scouring the surrounding woods. His companions grumbled more but rubbed their faces and gathered themselves to leave.

The hallway outside was just as dark and quiet as it had been when they entered the building. Owen led the way this time, followed by Jessica then Dixon. As Owen stepped into the hallway, he felt his pulse quicken and the hairs on the back of his neck stand up. Being in front of the group, leading them through the resort teeming with murderous creatures that had once been their companions, left him feeling naked and exposed. He darted a glance behind him, confirmed that the others were in fact present and hadn't been silently disposed of by an ambush, then moved quickly to the door.

As when they had entered, the door swung easily on quiet hinges. The land outside was painfully bright, their eyes weakened by the time spent in the gloom of the guest room. Owen stumbled forward, one hand shielding his eyes the other held before him lest he fall. He heard Jessica whisper a curse as she stepped into the blinding sunlight.

Owen continued forward several steps and paused, standing just inside a shadow cast by a large palm tree. In the shadow he found his eyes were able to adjust more easily. He stood, blinking, as the others joined him. The land around them was silent. He had long since gotten used to the absence of birds overhead or the rustle of other fauna through the thick underbrush of the forest. Now he stood, looking from side to side along the grassy path that encircled the building.

Where could the things be? he wondered. It had been hours since they'd come in contact with any of the creatures. Had they all gone away? Had they turned on one another and killed each other? Owen stared at the landscape around him but the only answer he got was the grass and the trees rustling in a soft breeze.

"Mind if we go?" Dixon whispered to him. Owen blinked out of his momentary fugue and nodded. Together they melted into the foliage and joined Jessica who crouched by a tree several yards in. As they approached, she turned her head quickly toward them. Owen saw the warning in her eyes and immediately stopped walking.

"How many?" he mouthed. Jessica shook her head, she wasn't sure. They waited. Owen strained his ears, desperate for any sound that would give him a location on the creatures. Finally he heard it. A soft rustling of leaves and then a sharp crack as a branch broke. The sounds came from his right, in the direction they needed to travel to get to the pier and the boat.

With agonizing slowness, he walked forward to Jessica and crouched next to her. Dixon remained where he was, one hand resting on the trunk of a large tree, his face impassive as he studied the forest around them. "Sounds like they're in the direction we have to go," he whispered. She nodded. Sweat trickled down her face, trailing a thin sheen along her cheek and finally her neck.

"What do you want to do?" he asked.

Her eyes never wavered from the sounds. "We don't have the weapons or strength to fight them." She looked at him and, despite the circumstances, Owen felt his heart race. "Think we can go around?"

"Don't think we have much choice. I sure as hell don't feel like fighting them. I just don't have it in me. Besides, if there's more than one of them, we're toast." He twisted and caught Dixon's attention. The man had been staring in the direction of the noises, and when he approached Owen, his eyes darted from the deeper forest to the path before him then back again.

"Jessica and I think we should try to skirt around them, circle wide left and avoid them completely."

Dixon nodded almost imperceptibly. "Good." Together the three stood and began to slowly and quietly pick their way through the forest. Jessica took the lead and guided them in a weaving trail as she took care to avoid thick brush or patches of ground littered with sticks. Although he was certain their progress was producing a minimal level of noise, Owen's ears picked up on every tiny crunch or scrape they made. The sounds seemed amplified to him, as if they weren't made by a person's feet but rather by some massive instrument wielded by a giant rock and roll god.

The path they traveled on led them up a steep incline. The brush thinned slightly as they fought to gain the precipice, but when the weeds and bushes receded, the rocks moved in. Owen found the footing poor at best and on several occasions they crawled with both feet and hands on the ground, their backs and rears hunched high in the air.

Owen had long since given up noticing the sweat that poured from his body. His throat burned with thirst and as he climbed his muscles felt weaker and weaker. His wounds burned and itched and spots of blood were appearing on his shirt. The rocks were loose and jagged beneath his feet and hands. Above him, through the thinning trees, the midday sun blasted the small island with every ounce of energy it could muster. Owen had the feeling of being an ant trapped beneath a large magnifying glass, waiting for his body to erupt in flames as some larger, cosmic child laughed at his pain.

Behind him, Dixon plodded along, his face showing the strain and weakness of his dehydration. As the man scrambled over and around rocks, he made soft panting sounds. Finally, as they neared the top of the hill, Jessica stopped and sat down, her strong, dirt smeared legs folding beneath her. Owen stumbled to a halt next to her, and then lowered himself to the ground. He sat with his knees bent slightly and his head hanging between them. The sun seared into his exposed neck. Next to him he heard Jessica's heavy breathing. He looked up as he heard Dixon scuffling past.

"Where are you going?" he asked, the words coming out slow and breathy.

Dixon slowed but continued walking the last few feet to the crest of the hill. Owen looked back down the way they had come. The climb wasn't massive by any means, but the heat and the terrain coupled with their wounds and lack of water had made the trek seem twice as difficult.

"Just going to see what's on the other side," Dixon mumbled. Owen watched him approach the top of the hill, then disappear as he crested it.

"I guess we'll hear him scream if something happens," he said. "Christ, I need some—

"Water!" Owen looked up quickly, his head whipping around to find the source of the word. Along the rise of the hill several feet away, he could see the top of Dixon's head.

"Did he say water?" he asked Jessica as he slowly got to his feet. When he was standing he could see more of Dixon, and the man's face was animated and full of excitement.

The man gestured behind him. "Water! There's a stream down here. Come on!" Then he turned and began running down the opposite side of the hill. Owen looked at Jessica, who hadn't gotten up. Her hair hung in ruins and her cheeks were flushed from the heat. She turned her head and squinted up at him.

"Think we should follow him?" she asked. Owen's response was to hold out a hand and pull her to her feet. She stood close to him for a moment, one hand resting on his shoulder. "Sorry," she said. "Head rush." She blinked and shook her head then looked at him and smiled. "What?"

Owen, not realizing he had been staring at her intently, said, "Oh, nothing. Sorry. Had a little head rush, too." He wanted to kiss her, wanted to wrap his arms around her and pull her even closer. He thought she wanted it, too, and before he knew it, he was leaning in as he snaked one hand around her sweaty waist. She allowed him to kiss her, even returned the gesture half-heartedly but the exhaustion and dehydration overwhelmed both of them and they parted with apologetic smiles.

Together they walked the rest of the distance to the top of the hill. The landscape leveled out and the vegetation returned somewhat more than it had on the upper slope. When they arrived, Dixon had already put a good bit of distance between them and Owen could see the man half jogging, half stumbling down the hill toward a thin blue tear in the forest growth.

Owen paused before starting down. The island's forest stretched before him for quite a distance. From his perspective, the ocean began just above the trees and rushed off into the horizon in a soft tableau of blues, greens and muted whites. He looked to the right, hoping to catch a glimpse of the pier and the boat, but the trees obscured that portion of the beach. He could, however, see the larger yacht that had brought the ill-fated band. Seeing it floating, pristine and unoccupied, several hundred yards away made him scowl in frustration and anger. He was looking at safety, a way back home. On board that boat were comfortable couches and beds, food and drink galore. But more importantly there was a radio, and an engine that worked.

"Seems so close, yet so far away," Jessica said beside him. Then her tone changed. "How does he know that the water he's running to isn't salt water?"

Owen shrugged, finally tearing his eyes away from the mocking safety of the yacht. "Don't know. I guess he doesn't. Probably doesn't care. Come on. Let's get down there before he drinks all of it."

Together they picked their way down the hill. Owen held her arm in some places to help her. They moved steadily and quickly, hardly keeping their eyes off of Dixon who was now halfway between them and the water. Owen watched as the man reached the stream and fell to his knees. Dixon pitched forward, practically slamming his entire head into the water. For a second Owen thought something was wrong, that his friend had gotten hurt, but then he saw Dixon moving, raking the water over his head as he drank heavily.

Dixon sat up and ran his hands over his head then rubbed his face. He brought handfuls of water up to his neck and dumped it down his back. Owen and Jessica moved to within fifteen yards of him and they could hear his cooing and laughing as he reveled in the liquid.

"Save some for us, man!" Owen called out.

Dixon laughed, a sharp, barking sound that cut through the air with alien clarity. "It's fresh water! I don't know how, must be an underground spring or something. But it's great! I've never tasted anything like it!" He bent forward and plunged his face under the water again. He stayed that way until Owen and Jessica were almost on him. Then he pushed up from the water in a quick, powerful motion. Water sprayed from his head as he whipped it up and turned to face them.

Jessica's scream mirrored the one Owen felt boiling up from his guts. Dixon's face had changed. His eyes had narrowed and darkened, the centers of them burned a deep yellow. His teeth had elongated and protruded like giant spears set into his gums. Owen stared at the man in horror. Dixon had turned into one of the mutants that Donovan and the others had. Somehow in the span of a few seconds, Dixon had mutated and now he crouched at the water's edge and glared at his two former companions with hatred and hunger in his eyes.

"What the fuck?" was all Owen could muster, and then he was tumbling backwards from Dixon's heavy form as it charged into him. Dixon rained blows from his heavily clawed hands, pummeling and cutting into Owen's skin. Deep, throaty and feral growls poured out of the creature's mouth as it beat Owen.

On the ground, Owen could only hold his arms up in a weak defense. He felt each blow, winced as the claws rent through his clothing and scored his flesh. His mind raced, fighting incomprehension. How had Dixon become infected? How had he turned into one of them? What had caused it? The questions tumbled over one another, vying for position with feelings of pain and terror.

There was a howl above him, a burst of noise filled with pain and rage. He opened his eyes and saw Dixon, still straddling him, holding one of his arms. Owen saw a flash of movement to his right and cut his eyes over. Jessica stood there, a thick, heavy tree branch in one hand.

"Get off of him, you worthless fuck," she growled. Dixon didn't move to relinquish Owen and instead hit Owen across the cheek with his unwounded hand. The blow felt as if it had come from a sledgehammer. Owen screamed in pain. The weight of the beast suddenly disappeared from his chest as the thing that had once been Dixon got up and rushed Jessica. Owen scrambled to his feet, his questions about the situation forgotten for the moment. All that mattered now was Jessica and getting away as fast as they could.

Dixon charged Jessica, but she had been ready for him. Owen watched as she crouched, branch held ready. Dixon closed the gap with a speed that shocked Owen to see. Dixon raked one clawed hand through the air, the pointed talons slicing down toward Jessica's upturned face. Just as they were on her, Owen watched as she dropped to the ground and rolled out of the path of the charging creature. With a surprising speed of her own, she leapt to her feet and drove a foot deep into the ribs and belly of Dixon.

The creature grunted, its breath rushing out of him in a quick "Oomph!" Owen heard the unmistakable sound of a rib breaking, and then Dixon hit the ground. Not wanting to hesitate any longer, Owen ran forward and grabbed Jessica's hand. "Come on, we have to get out of here."

She resisted. "We need to finish him."

Owen looked down at Dixon who was beginning to gather himself. "We don't have time. Come on." He pulled her again and this time she came with him. Together they sprinted into the forest, running parallel to the hill that bisected the island.

They ran, Owen still holding Jessica's hand, crashing blindly through the brush, veering around trees at random turns. Neither knew where they were going, only that they were trying to put as much distance between them and Dixon as they could.

It wasn't long before they heard the screams and crashing as he gained in pursuit of them. Jessica cursed as a large snapping sound erupted behind them. Owen risked a look backwards and saw a slender tree crash to the ground. Dixon peered from around the splintered base and grinned, his new teeth clicking against one another as he did.

They ran faster, angling away from the hill. Owen pushed branches and leaves aside as he ran. He threw a quick glance over his shoulder in time to see Dixon change his angle and disappear deeper into the trees. Confused but relieved the creature was no longer directly behind them, Owen continued to plunge forward.

Within moments the forest thinned as it gave way to the sandy beach. When they burst free of the trees and tumbled face first into the sand Owen noticed that they were well to the right of the pier that had been their initial target. His chest heaved with relief as his gaze fell on the small boat still tied to the dock.

"Come on!" he said and dragged Jessica to her feet. She resisted, not seeing the boat at first but rather the large killing platform they had watched the creatures create. Owen saw it too, and it took a moment for his eyes to focus on the half masticated corpse spread out on the sunken boulder. When the wind shifted, Owen recoiled at the stench that carried with it.

"Fuck, I'm going to be sick," Jessica said. She doubled over and vomited into the sand. Owen was surprised she had anything to purge, but remembered the fruits they had eaten earlier. He knelt by her with one hand on her back until she was finished spasming. Finally she tucked her hair behind her ears and looked at him, wiping a hand across her mouth. "Want to kiss me now?"

"We get to that boat and I'll do more than that. Come on." He stood and helped her to her feet.

"It can't be this easy," she said as they started jogging across the sand. Owen ran next to her and said nothing. He scanned from the white hull of the boat bobbing in the surf to the trees on their left.

They passed the rock with the rotting corpse. As they cleared it and the wind continued to carry the smell behind them, Owen felt his resolve strengthen. The air blowing in off of the water brought with it a briny, clean smell that infused him with a sudden burst of joy. They were going to be alright. The boat was thirty yards away from them and from what he could tell it looked alright.

"What if there aren't any keys?" Jessica breathed.

"Baby, where we're going, we don't need keys," Owen said. The joke took him by surprise and he began laughing uncontrollably as he ran.

His humor died instantly as he heard the thrashing sound of leaves and branches being ripped apart mixed with the throaty growl of one of the creatures. Both Owen and Jessica slowed and looked over their shoulders. Not far from where they had entered the beach stood five of the creatures, Dixon at the head of the group. Dixon's shirt now hung in wet tatters about his body. A few of the pieces fluttered in the breeze as if they were desperate to be rid of the horrible master they were forced to travel with.

Two of the other creatures were female. One, with short black hair, wore yellow bikini bottoms and no top; her pale breasts almost glowed in the sunlight. Owen could see scratches across her chest. The other wore what had at one time been khaki shorts and a blue bikini top. The shorts were stained in blood but the top was surprisingly intact.

"Holy Shit, that's Elaine Richards. She's one of Donovan's board members, head of marketing. And look to the right of Dixon. See the guy with the cuts on his body and the Speedo? That's Mitch Berger. He's the head of research and development," Jessica said.

Owen looked across the beach to the group. He felt an overwhelming sense of déjà vu. It had been almost twenty-four hours ago when they had been in almost this same spot facing a group of the creatures. He cast a glance behind them at the boat. If they got on it and didn't have keys, they were screwed. The creatures would cover the ground before he had time to find the keys. And he couldn't shove off from the pier; he'd seen the damn things leap.

"What are you thinking?" asked Jessica.

"I'm thinking that we're fucked. We can't make it to the boat, and running out into the ocean isn't a good idea."

"Why not?"

"Sharks. There are a lot of them out there. I remember seeing them on my flight in on the seaplane."

"So that leaves the woods again. Fuck." Her voice turned into a helpless whimper on the last word. He could hear her breathing fast and knew that she was on the verge of tears. Not waiting a second more to think about it, he grabbed her hand, gave it a quick squeeze and pulled her as fast as he could sprint into the woods.

As they entered the trees, he heard the creatures roar in unison. From the corner of his eye he saw them slip back into the woods themselves, not bothering to run the length of the beach, but rather to travel through the forest and cut them off at an angle. He mustered speed from his legs and pulled Jessica along.

Then his blood ran cold and he faltered in his run, his feet catching on vines and roots. Another set of howls and growls had sifted through the trees to his right. There are more of them, he thought. They've organized a party, and now both groups are coming after us. Jessica had moved ahead of him and he could tell by the way her head whipped from side to side as she sprinted that she heard the second group.

The path led them up a small rise and Owen saw the cart path to his left at the same time that Jessica turned for it. He didn't want to have to take the path because he was certain the creatures would be on it at some point, but he also knew that he and Jessica would make much better time and speed running on the smooth surface.

Around them, the sounds of growls and brush being plunged through filled the air. It seemed to increase in volume, and Owen wondered if the creatures had added to their numbers. Owen's feet pounded on the paved cart path. Sweat ran into his eyes and he blinked it away, too intent on running away from the oncoming slaughter to raise his arms and brush the stinging water aside.

They rounded a curve to the left and he heard Jessica gasp his name. He looked beyond her and saw what had caused her reaction. To the right of the trail, surrounded by a lawn of flat and well-manicured grass, stood a house. It was a single story and reminded him of the guesthouse they had rested in briefly before making their way to the beach. The house was tan stucco with whitewashed shutters on either side of the several windows. Even from this distance, running and scared witless, Owen could tell the shutters were purely decorative.

He wondered what the house was. He didn't remember hearing

about it or seeing it before. Maybe it was the servants' quarters, he thought. He opened his mouth to tell Jessica to head for it but she was on the same wavelength as him and quickly angled across the grass and up to the front door. Without a glance back or hesitating at all she threw the door open and ran inside.

Owen threw a look over his shoulder, saw the first of the creatures break through the trees onto the path. It was at least fifty yards away but it spotted them and rushed forward with a scream. Owen's mind yelled a curse that his lips were too exhausted to form. He ran through the threshold of the house with only a single thought riding his heels.

How are we going to defend this place?

10

The air inside the house was several degrees cooler than the forest they had just been in, and Owen felt a rush of cold as his skin broke into gooseflesh. His soaked shirt became a cold rag pressed to his torso.

As soon as they were across the threshold and he could tell that there was no immediate threat waiting for them in the large room, he spun and slammed the door shut. He engaged the deadbolt lock and the handle locks but knew that they would be a pitiful line of defense against the two groups of creatures. He turned back to the room, searching for something to push against the door.

The room looked like a lobby for a luxury hotel. There were half a dozen plush leather couches and an equal number of high backed chairs throughout the room. He saw at least three low, dark wood coffee tables and several smaller but equally thick and heavy looking end tables. The tables were tastefully decorated with lamps or magazines or hardbound books. A few had glass ashtrays on them. Large curio cabinets dotted the walls, each containing various items that Owen couldn't make out.

Jessica stood several feet ahead of him, taking in the paintings on the walls and the darkened hallway that led out of the room to their front and right.

"Jess," Owen gasped. His mind threw a vision of the group of creatures approaching the building. She turned quickly at his voice, a look of alarm on her face as if she had forgotten she wasn't alone. "We have to barricade the door and these windows. Help me push some of the furniture." He pushed away from the door and hurried over to the nearest couch. The thick, soft leather cushions gave under his touch, inviting him to lay down, enjoy their comfort and forget his worries.

The couch was heavy, heavier than he would have guessed and it took everything he had to push it and hear the legs scrape across the polished hardwood floor. Jessica ran to help and together the two of them managed to position the couch firmly against the door. They then added a second couch and several chairs and tables. There were six tall windows in the room, two on either side of the door they had blockaded and two more on each of the walls. Thick, heavy curtains that were pulled back and cinched with gold tasseled ties framed the windows.

Owen untied the curtains and drew them across the windows. As each one fell shut, the room fell into gloom by several degrees. He paused after the last one, letting his eyes finish adjusting to the murky gloom. Jessica stood a few feet away, waiting for him to finish so they could together push the curio cabinets against the windows.

"Where are they?" she wondered. Her voice seemed to thicken as she spoke. "I mean, they were almost on us when we saw this place. As fast as they are, they should have been here by now."

Owen shook his head as he began to push the first cabinet against the window, having to pivot it back and forth on its legs to get it moving. "Don't know," he grunted. "I know one of them saw us just before we came in. Maybe," his voice thinned as he exerted himself to push the cabinet fully into place. It stopped flush against the wall, pinning the curtains flat and effectively blocking any entrance via the window. He breathed heavily and they started toward the next window and cabinet. "Maybe they don't know we're in here, like they lose us if they don't see us. Out of sight, out of mind or something."

Jessica didn't say anything in response, but Owen could tell as they moved the rest of the cabinets that she didn't really believe his theory. He didn't believe it much either, but it was all he had to go on. Otherwise, he reasoned, they would be under attack by now. The creatures would have begun to force their way into the room, battering down the defenses. Or, he thought coldly, they would have come in one of the other rooms in the house.

Together, he and Jessica hurried to finish moving the cabinets, and then they ran down the hallway to examine the other rooms. The rest of the house contained fifteen bedrooms, eight bathrooms, a modestly-sized kitchen and a stairwell that led down into what Owen guessed was a root and provisions cellar.

They used mattresses and night tables to blockade the windows in three of the bedrooms before entering the kitchen. There they used a heavy dining table stood on end, and slid the refrigerator against that. Then they paused. Both knew they had to rush to barricade the rest of the rooms before the creatures realized they were in the house and began to batter their way in, but as they slid the refrigerator into place, their exhaustion began to take the lead.

Jessica opened the refrigerator and peered inside. Inside the icebox she saw several items of food and bottles. A few were bottles of water, their blue labels declaring them to be the finest water to be found in the mountains of Colorado. She grabbed two of them and passed one to Owen. He looked at it skeptically, then ripped the top off and drank the entire contents in several heaving gulps. Jessica followed suit.

They cast the bottles aside and stood, panting. Then she grabbed two more and they drank them down. Before Owen could finish his, a thought occurred to him and he gagged, spitting up a mouthful of water. Jessica threw her empty container aside and looked at him. "What?" she asked.

"We shouldn't have drank them," he gasped. Panic had seized his chest and threatened to squeeze all the breath out of him.

"Why the hell not?"

"Don't you remember Dixon? He drank water and turned into one of them."

Jessica looked at the discarded bottles on the floor as if they had contained an alien strain of Ebola. Then her features relaxed slightly. "Those were unopened and from Colorado. Dixon drank from a stream that was here on the island. If it was the water that changed him, I'm not sure it was the same as what was in those."

Owen started to protest but a crash and the sound of glass shattering deeper in the house stole all words from him. The sounds of the creatures growling and fighting with one another to enter the building pulsed down the hallways like a rushing tide. Shit, Owen thought, we should have waited until we had boarded up everything until we raided the fridge. Resounding thumps and crashes began to sound all around them as the creatures who were as of yet unaware of the open windows began to hurl themselves at the doors and blocked glass. The entire house took on the din of a drum heavy rock concert, with shattering glass and maniacal howls as the accent notes instead of guitars.

"What now?" Jessica asked. Owen threw his gaze around the room, looking for anything that could help them. There was nothing. He rushed forward to a nearby counter and pulled two knives from a block. Jessica equipped herself and together they stood in the center of the kitchen, ready to fight.

"What is it about us and kitchens?" she wondered. Owen ignored the remark, his full attention turned to the sounds around him. He strained to hear through the screams and banging behind them. The creatures had to have gotten inside by now, he thought. One of the bedrooms in the back of the dwelling. If they were at every window, then at least twelve windows have been breached. He felt he had to consider the worst case. How the hell were they going to get out?

Then it hit him. Without giving it a second thought, he nudged Jessica with his elbow. "Come on." He ran for the doorway, feeling her close behind. When he entered the hallway, he threw a glance to the right, toward the living room they had entered. He saw no movement in the shadows and turned thankfully to the left.

The creature screamed in his face and swiped a paw at him. The blow knocked him backwards and had it not been for Jessica, he would have gone down. He felt the claws rake his already cut flesh and he grunted in both surprise and pain. As he tried to recover from the suddenness of the attack the creature stepped forward. Owen saw the mottled discolor of its skin, the servant's uniform hanging in tatters on its body. It shrieked again and the breath that it expelled reeked of rotted fish.

Owen, his balance regained, stepped toward the beast and at the same time brought both knives up. One thudded hard into the creature's rib cage. Owen felt the knife blade wrench in his hand as it passed over the bones and into the deeper tissue of the lungs. The other slammed into the monster's abdomen. He pushed the blade fully to the hilt, until his thumb was pressed firmly against the hard, cold skin. Blood poured over his hands and the creature stopped its forward motion as if it had hit a brick wall. Its black and dirty yellow eyes bulged in surprise, pain and exertion. The jaws worked slowly as if even as it died it were trying to chew on him.

Owen pulled the knives free quickly and then shoved the creature backwards. As it fell he noticed other shapes entering the hallway at the far end. Not taking a moment to consider any other course of action he stepped over the body and pushed open a door to the left. The shadows pooled around the stairs after a few feet and Owen had the sensation of getting ready to walk into black waters at night.

"Whatever you're doing, let's go," Jessica said quickly behind him. Her voice told him all he needed to know. The creatures were inside and coming fast. He started down the stairs, not bothering to turn on the lights. Five steps down he stopped and waited for Jessica to enter behind him and close the door. Her hand went automatically to the handle and searched for a locking mechanism. "There's no lock," she said.

Owen brushed past her and raised one of his knives. He placed the blade between the door and the jamb and then pressed hard, wedging it in tightly. "That'll have to do. Won't hold them long, but maybe long enough for us to get the hell out." He flipped the light switches and they continued down the stairs.

The stairs deposited them in a cellar with shelves lining all the walls. The shelves contained canned foods, bottles of alcohol and other stores. To the right a central air conditioning unit hummed. The silver ducts that fed air to the rest of the house branched off like nickel-plated insect legs.

There were no other doors or windows. Above them, the creatures had found the body of their companion. Their feral growls and screams were a clear indication of their rage. Moments later they began pounding on the door. Owen could hear the wood vibrating under the onslaught of their fury.

Desperate, he moved further into the room. There had to be something here, some way out. He moved from wall to wall, shifting items and peering behind everything. Dust coated many of the items and when he slide them aside to look behind them he was rewarded with a cloud of dirt that stung his eyes and made him cough. Jessica took a cue from him and quickly began searching the other spaces in the cellar. The pounding above them drowned the sounds of their frantic breathing and the scrapes of items being moved.

Owen reached the end of the wall he had been searching, having moved boxes and old pieces of furniture. Nothing useful had been found other than a couple of tennis rackets. He had held them, waved them through the air and decided that their effectiveness would be worth nothing. *So that's it*, he thought. *I brought us down here to die. Pretty soon those things are going to muscle down the door and then it'll be all over. We can probably kill one or two of them, but they'll overpower us and that will be that. I'll die feeling my body being eaten and torn apart.*

"Owen!"

Owen wheeled around, bringing up the knife he had, his heart in his throat. Jessica stood by the air conditioning unit, looking in the small space behind it.

"There's a door here!" He moved quickly to her, having to step over several boxes to cross the room. When he reached her, she stepped aside to let him see. Sure enough, obscured by the air conditioning unit was a small wooden door. It reminded Owen of the access door to his parents house when he was a child, the door that let people into the crawl space below the house. This door was small enough that both he and Jessica would have to crawl through it.

"Where do you think it leads?"

"I have no idea." Jessica reached to open the door. It had a thin black metal handle. She pushed it and it swung in, revealing a low but fairly wide tunnel. Owen backed up and ran to the far side of the room, hurtling boxes. "What are you doing?" Jessica called after him as he searched the shelves, pushing items aside recklessly.

"Flashlight," he answered. Moments later he found it. It turned on, and he ran back to the doorway and shone the light inside. The tunnel ran further than the beam of light could penetrate. "What do you think?" he asked her, peering into the crawlspace.

Jessica leaned forward. "It could lead anywhere. Could lead out of here, could lead to another room with no escape. But either way, I think it's better than sitting here waiting for them to break down that door."

As if to punctuate her sentiment, a splintering crack ripped through the air. "Okay," Owen said, "we go. If it leads to nothing, then we'll just wait until we feel it's safe to come out."

Jessica leaned back on her haunches. She looked around the room. "Was there nothing over there for us to use?"

"Weapons? No. There was some food, but it was mostly really crappy canned food and we don't have a can opener. Alcohol, but I don't feel much like getting drunk, tell you the truth."

She sighed. "I wish we could start a fire down here, burn the fuckers up or something."

Owen considered this. "We could, yeah. But if this tunnel leads to another room and we have to wait until its safe to come back out, we'll be coming back to this basement. It could still be on fire, or the building could have collapsed and we'd be trapped in the tunnel."

"Right, I didn't think about that." She turned back to the small door. "Give me the flashlight and I'll go first. That way if they find the door and follow us, you'll be back there with the knives and can fight them off."

"Thanks for the sexist duty," Owen grumbled as he handed her the flashlight and took the cutter blade in return.

She smiled, leaned forward and kissed him quickly on the lips. "It's not sexist. It's chivalrous." Then she turned and squeezed into the hole, having to angle around the air conditioning unit. As her feet passed into the tunnel, Owen heard the door above them splinter and crack, followed by the howls of triumph from the creatures. He began to crawl into the tunnel as the sound of their footsteps thudded on the stairs leading down into the cellar.

The door shut behind him, and Owen paused behind it, praying silently that he had managed to close it in time and quietly enough. As he waited, he heard the sounds of the creatures tearing through the contents of the cellar, items being flung across the room as they ravaged the space in search of their prey. Not wanting to wait any longer, he turned and followed the dark outline of Jessica into the tunnel.

The space was wide enough for the both of them to crawl side by side but to minimize feelings of claustrophobia and to maintain a defensive presence Owen stayed in the rear. He stayed within a few feet of Jessica, pausing every few seconds to look behind him into the blackness and listen for sounds of pursuit.

The ground was dirt, soft and void of rocks or other detritus, and his fingers sank into the soil as he crawled. The air, as they traveled, became more humid and the scent of minerals tickled his nose. The sounds of their passage were muted by the softness of the earth.

After what Owen guessed was probably twenty minutes of traveling, the ground beneath them became firmer, rockier. Owen paused again, looking back over his shoulder once more and straining to hear any signs of pursuit. He had never heard the door open or the creatures enter and felt certain that he would have heard at least their growls as they moved down the tunnel toward them.

"There's an opening ahead," Jessica said. Her voice had a soft echo to it. Owen turned to her and put all thoughts of pursuit aside.

"Can you see what's on the other side?"

"Looks like a bigger room, but it's hard to tell. We're still about fifty feet away from it. Flashlight's good, but not that good." She began crawling toward the opening and Owen followed. Wherever it led, it was better than where they had been.

They reached the opening and stopped, catching their breath and looking through. The opening was literally that, a hole in larger rocks. The tunnel ended in what was basically a rock wall with a hole in it. It reminded Owen of pictures he had seen of the insides of ships, where the bulkhead had a ledge all around it through which you had to step to reach the next section of corridor.

The room beyond was a large cavern. The flashlight beam showed rock walls. Flecks of crystal in the rock winked back at them like millions of tiny flashbulbs. Jessica directed the light downward and in the thin spear of the beam Owen could see that the floor of the room was only a foot or so below them.

When they entered the cavern, Owen went first. He thought about making her pay him another kiss for the deed, but decided against it and crawled through the hole. He dropped down to the floor and almost slipped on the slick rock.

"Careful when you come down," he warned. He heard scuffling behind him as Jessica started through the hole.

"Mind if you give me some light?" she asked. Owen turned the beam to assist her and she finished the climb and stood next to him. "Where the hell is this?" she whispered. Her voice, although soft next to him, echoed off the walls.

Owen shrugged, then when he realized she couldn't see his gesture, spoke. "Don't know. Obviously an underground cavern." He took her hand and stepped forward, sweeping the flashlight before them as he walked. The floor was smooth stone and reflected back wetly at them.

"I smell water," Jessica said. Owen agreed. The soft, metallic scent of water was definitely present in the space. They continued forward, pausing every few seconds to sweep the flashlight beam from side to side. Owen guessed that the chamber was probably eighty feet wide and forty feet tall. As they moved forward, the scent of water became more and more pronounced. After a matter of moments, they found the source.

The underground spring was large, roughly a hundred feet across. The water was placid, a black obelisk set into the stone floor. Owen moved the flashlight over the water. The beam penetrated only inches, giving them a glance of murky, dark green water.

"Don't get too close," Jessica whispered.

"Why not?"

He felt her shudder next to him. "Remember Dixon? What if the water he drank came out of this?"

Owen turned to her. "Are you really suggesting that he turned into one of those things just by drinking the water from a river?" She pulled her eyes away from the dark water and looked up at him. He could see the fear that filled her gaze.

"What else could it be?"

"I don't know, maybe he got infected from some wound. Maybe whatever turned them is some kind of virus and when they clawed him during a fight the virus was transferred into him. It just took a while to affect him."

"Then why haven't you or I turned? We've both been wounded. Besides, you seemed pretty convinced upstairs that it was the water."

Owen considered this. "But if it were that bottled water, we would have turned instantly, just like he did after drinking. It can't be the water. But a virus makes sense to me. Maybe it reacts differently based on the physical composition of the body it's infecting. Maybe there was something about Dixon's physiological makeup that caused the virus to work a little more quickly than it has with us."

"So if you're right, we're both fucked and we're going to turn into those things. It's only a matter of who is going to turn first and kill the other? Hell, if that's the case, let's get out of here back up that tunnel and give ourselves to those things. Because if living means I have to become one, then I'd rather be food." She turned and walked carefully several feet away, then sat down and wrapped her arms around her legs.

Owen stood where he was for a moment, considering the water. Could that be possible? Could it be the water that turned all those people into the mutants? If it were a virus, how did the first person get infected? Owen found it hard to believe that a virus like this was just waiting around on the surface of some rock and a person tripped and scraped themselves on the rock, thereby infecting themselves. No, it had to be something else. What if it were a government conspiracy, or some corporate thing? Wee Lad Toys was a leader in the industry. Donovan certainly had plenty of enemies with lots of money. One of them could have learned of this island and paid some terrorist organization or stolen some experimental virus from a government lab and injected it into someone before they got here.

He stopped, amazed at how ridiculous that theory sounded. "I just don't get it, though," he said.

"What?"

Owen sighed and sat next to Jessica. "I just don't get how the virus or whatever it is got into the water. And how it managed to make its way to the resort. I may have gotten completely trashed that first night, but I don't remember seeing any streams or anything running through either the buildings or the grounds where we were."

"The resort has a water supply that pulls from the island. I bet that if we were able to see around the entire spring here we'd probably find a pipe somewhere leading out of it. Or maybe the pipes are buried beneath the water. I don't know. But the resort pulls its water from this island and I'm pretty sure it's not from the ocean then filtered. That would be too complex of a logistical issue."

"Donovan didn't seem to have any problems spending money on everything else."

"Still. Don't you think that if it were something in the ocean water, we would have turned already? Or don't you remember jumping into the ocean to save me last night?"

Owen stared at the murkiness that was the spring. "It still doesn't make sense. We were at the party. We drank, right?"

"You only drank liquor, and I was drinking Tequila Sunrises all night. Neither of our drinks had water in them. I'm like you; I don't put ice in my drink. Dixon was drinking bottled beer that Donovan had shipped from America. Everyone else had to be drinking something that either had water in it or had ice in it. And the others that weren't drinking at all, well, we've come across their bodies since all this started.

"I know it doesn't make sense. There's still the question of how did whatever it is get into the springs. Is it something that was man made and put into the springs? Or was it always there, part of the natural environment? How long has it been there?"

Something pulled at Owen's memory and he sat up straight. "Dixon." When he noticed Jessica's curious look he said, "Dixon was telling me on the plane ride over here that this island has been a source of mystery and legend for a long time. He was telling me that recently rumrunners and drug smugglers used it. But before that he said that the Spanish had been here, as part of their New World exploration. He said that he'd read a diary of some Spanish captain who claimed that his men refused to go ashore, that they used to see torches on the beach and hear screams of men, but the screams weren't pain."

"They were creatures screaming because they were hungry," Jessica said. Owen nodded.

"Had to be. Which means that either the creatures had an unnaturally long life span or were the mutated forms of explorers that had arrived on the island before this captain did."

"So what happened? Did the guy ever go ashore?"

"No. According to Dixon, the diary said that the captain had to force a crew of men at sword point to go to the island and see what was going on. I can't remember if they were there to rescue a group or if they were after something specific or why they had even come to the island, but when he sent that group, he never saw them again. Finally he gave up because it became apparent to him that his men would rather be run through with a sword than have to set foot on this island. That's why it's named Bezeten. Bezeten means possessed."

"Fuck me," Jessica breathed. "So we came to a party on an island that has a history soaked in blood and these murderous fucking things."

"Looks like it." They sat in silence for a while, resting and each pouring over their own thoughts. Owen thought briefly of Michelle, wondering what she was doing at that moment. He realized he had no idea what time it was, or even what day it was. The more he thought about it, the harder it became to figure out.

Finally, he became restless and couldn't sit any longer. "Come on," he said and stood up. "Let's figure out how to get out of here." He helped Jessica up and together they began slowly exploring the rest of the cavern. They found a wall and began to follow it, hoping for some opening or crack or tunnel that would give them a passage out to the forest.

It was Jessica who found the helmet. As they explored, the only sounds were their soft breathing and the even softer scuff of their feet on the stone. Then a loud metallic clang erupted in the space, the noise bouncing off the walls. Jessica screamed and Owen cried out despite himself. He whipped the beam of the flashlight around and saw the source of the noise. An old, rusted helmet lay a few feet away from them. It had a curved dome with an equally curved brim that tapered to a point on either end. It looked just like all the ones he'd seen in textbooks as a kid.

"It's Spanish," he said and went to pick it up. The helmet was heavy, much heavier than he would have imagined. He wondered what kind of strength it took to wear it and still function. Battling in it must have been horrible. He turned it over in his hands, marveling at the relic. It seemed so impossible that he would find something so old. "Dixon was right again," he whispered, remembering the man's excitement about the prospect of finding artifacts and selling them on the internet.

His hands moved over the rusted steel until they found a series of uneven, jagged grooves. Turning the flashlight to them, he felt his breath catch. "Hey, I found more stuff," Jessica said. Owen looked and saw her standing only a couple of feet away, looking at something on the ground. The flashlight's beam provided a circle of light that grew weaker at the fringes. It was in these fringes that she stood, bent over and looking at something. Owen directed the light to what she saw.

"It's a breastplate," she said. "I remember seeing these in school and on TV. It's like armor that explorers used to wear. And look," she pointed, "there's a few more and some helmets too. A broken sword and, oh my God, that's an old musket." Owen walked over to her. He looked down at the breastplate, his eyes pouring over the rusted steel shell. It looked like a smooth turtle shell, he thought, but with less of a dome and more defined arches for the arms and neck. Then he saw the grooves in its steel as well. There were four of them, all parallel to one another. The ones on the breastplate cut clear through the steel and allowed glimpses of the rock beneath.

Claw marks.

11

They reached the forest an hour later. After leaving the ruined and rusted Spanish equipment behind at the cavern —Owen had really wanted to take it, not for protection rather more to honor Dixon's memory, but Jessica had insisted it would only slow them down—they had managed to find another tunnel on the opposite side of the spring. This tunnel was large enough to allow them to walk upright, and after a while they had emerged from a crevice in some rocks covered with vegetation. When they were back in the forest among the sunlight, Owen had realized they were close to the stream that Dixon had drank from. The thought that they had spent time so close to the water that had infected their friend made him shudder.

Now they traveled slowly, cautiously. Neither Owen nor Jessica knew exactly where or how far away the creatures were. There was no telling what had transpired in the house after they disappeared down the tunnel. Had the creatures ransacked the place looking for them? Well, that much Owen was certain of. But had they stuck around after realizing their quarry had vanished? Had they gone out hunting for the humans? And if they didn't stay at the house or organize into hunting parties and begin a search, where did they go?

What do they do all day? An absurd picture of the creatures lounging on the beach in wooden chairs, sunglasses and straw hats adorning their heads while they sipped drinks with umbrellas danced before his mind.

Owen was too tired to smile at the thought. Instead he pushed aside a low branch of a tree and held it until Jessica had caught up and taken it. They moved slowly and they moved quietly, angling for the beach again and the boat they had gotten so close to. Around them the forest was a silent entity; a leafy tomb. High above him the trees whispered as they swayed in a breeze that couldn't be felt on the ground. Owen plodded on, ignoring his wounds, refusing to acknowledge the pulsing and throbbing of the cuts to his body.

They arrived at the beach as the light around them began to dim. The sun was sinking, draping shadows on the ground and painting the sky purple and orange. Owen crouched at the edge of the forest and the beach and looked to his left, where the sun was positioned. He couldn't see the orb itself but knew that it would be there, a blazing orange pit nestled in clouds that burned with color. Beside him, Jessica yawned.

"Where the hell are we going to sleep tonight?" she asked.

Owen stared across the sand at the white boat moored to the dock. The front of the boat seemed lower in the water than he remembered but he knew that could easily be due to the tides. "If we can maintain a tiny shred of luck for a little while longer, we'll be sleeping on that yacht out there." He looked from the smaller speedboat to the larger yacht. It remained in the same spot in the water, moving slowly with the undulating water. The hull was a dull white, and reflected mutely the colors from the sunset. He could see the sun's reflection in the windows of the pilot box. A sudden weariness overtook him as he thought about the comforts and safety within that yacht.

Just got to make it to the boat, then get the boat across the shallows and shark-infested water to the yacht. After that, we're home free. "You ready?" he asked Jessica.

"No. I just remembered I don't have my purse. I'm not leaving without it."

Owen looked at her as if she were an alien. "Are you shitting me?"

Jessica turned her face to his. Her expression was mute for a long moment then slowly a smile split her lips. "Of course I am. Now get off your ass and let's get off this piece of shit island." Owen stared at her a second longer, then shook his head.

"Remind me to whoop your ass good when we get to the yacht." Then he stood and began to walk onto the sand. His head turned immediately to the right where the corpse of the band member lay atop the large rock. In the dying light he could see that no creatures stood around it. The beach was deserted.

A soft rustling of leaves told him that Jessica had left the relative safety of the forest and was now on the beach behind him. He didn't turn to look at her and instead kept his gaze shifting from the boat to the beach and forest on his right, then back to the boat then off to the beach and forest on his left. When they had made it halfway across the sand, Owen kept his vision locked on the boat. *Don't take your eyes off the prize, man,* he thought and fought the urge to run.

The wood of the pier felt like heaven under his feet and he walked as quickly as he could to where the boat pulled at its moorings. He turned his head slightly when Jessica stepped onto the pier. It wasn't until she gasped that he saw it.

The port bow of the boat had a large hole in it. The wood was splintered and even in the dusky light Owen could see the claw marks in the wood surrounding the hole. The boat had sunk until it rested on the sand, which explained why it had appeared low in the water. A glance at the ignition switch next to the steering wheel confirmed that there were no keys.

"Why?" Jessica asked in a thin voice. "Why does this shit have to keep happening to us?"

Owen sat back on the pier and stared at the boat. Could they still use it? "You know how to hotwire a boat?" he asked.

"Shit no. Earlier I was hoping that either you or Dixon knew. But it doesn't matter, fucking thing won't float."

"I was just thinking that it doesn't have to float far. If we could figure out how to hotwire it, we could turn it toward the yacht and just gun the engine. Let that push us as far as we can get before it starts to sink. It'll either get us all the way, or close. If we get as far as we can in it, then we could swim the rest of the way."

"At night, through shark filled water; are you fucking kidding me?"

"Do you have a better idea? Because if you do, I'd love to hear it." Owen's rage boiled.

Jessica started to reply, her cheeks flushed and her eyes angry. "I don't even know how to hotwire the damn thing, so it wouldn't matter. Unless you have a set of keys up your ass, or know where we can get another boat, we're pretty much fucked. We can't row the damn thing, it would sink with both of us in it moving that slowly."

Owen groaned and lay back on the pier. The wood was still warm from the day and it soaked into his body. "There has to be another boat on this goddamn island. I can't believe that Donovan would have this place and not have a boat. It just doesn't make sense. Hell, this piece of shit isn't even Donovan's. So he has to have something else here." He turned his head and looked at Jessica. "Think. You were here before me. I don't remember Dixon saying anything about another boat, and I don't remember much anything because of the party. Did you ever hear anyone say anything about another boat?"

Jessica stared at the useless vessel. Her features were slack, as if she had finally resigned herself to being trapped. Slowly she shook her head, the movement almost imperceptible in the fading light. Owen was finding it more and more difficult to see her as the sun dropped more rapidly now. Around them the night closed in and the only sound accompanying it was the soft, gentle lapping of waves against the shore. Owen thought he could sleep right there, on the pier. He blinked and sat up.

"No," Jessica said. "I don't remember anything about another boat. But I agree with you. It doesn't make sense that Donovan would have this place and not have his own boat. Or several boats."

"But where could they be? I don't remember seeing any at the resort."

"You weren't really in the frame of mind the other night to see or remember boats, and we haven't spent a lot of time exploring the entire resort," Jessica reminded him.

"And the way things are spaced out on this island, with the cart paths leading everywhere, the boats could be anywhere." He looked at the speedboat. It was now a flat grey shadow in the water. "We need to figure out the lay of this place better, so we don't just wander aimlessly looking for a boat. That's looking for a needle in a stack of needles."

"We could just walk the beaches until we circle the island. At some point, we're going to come across the boat."

"Yeah, but unless you suddenly become infused with the clarity of how to hotwire a boat, we're still going to need keys. And I'm willing to bet that the keys to any boats are going to be somewhere in the main house."

"I don't know," she said, doubtful.

Owen felt his anger rising again, fought to temper it down. "You got any better ideas? Do you think we'll circle the island, find a boat and the keys will just be hanging in the ignition? Maybe ... maybe they'll have some sandwiches and beer set up for us too. Or maybe you'll find a manual on how to hotwire a boat somewhere along the beach. Wait. Don't tell me. You had one, but dropped it when you fell in the fucking water last night. Is that it?"

Jessica stared at him, but in the darkness Owen couldn't tell her expression. She made no sound. He was about to apologize when she said, "Fine. Come on. You want to go back into that fucking meat grinder of a main house, then we'll go." She spun on her heel and walked quickly down the pier to the beach.

"Jess, wait," Owen whispered after her. She ignored him. "Shit," he mumbled and got up and followed her.

He caught up with her just before she reached the tree line. He grabbed one of her arms and spun her to face him. "Hey, look, I'm sorry. What I said came out wrong. I'm just exhausted, I'm hurting like a son of a bitch and I could really use a cheeseburger." Jessica said nothing, only looked at the sand. "Jessica," Owen lowered his voice, "please don't be pissed. We need to keep our heads straight if we're going to get out of here."

"I'm not mad." Owen could tell she was lying.

"Okay. Well, I'm sorry. Really. Before we go, shouldn't we look through that boat and see if there's anything we can take with us?" Without raising her head, Jessica nodded then pushed past him and walked to the pier.

In a rear compartment of the boat they found another flashlight, three handheld flares and a section of rope. Owen didn't know what they'd use everything for but felt that they should take all of it. Owen searched the boat for paddles but found nothing, thinking that if they could find even one, they could row out to the yacht. Finding none, his last hope of leaving the island via that boat slipped away.

The forest, when they finally entered, was a vast, dark, alien world. Unlike the previous evening when they ran blindly through it, propelled by their terror and the close pursuit of the creatures, now the trees loomed above them like something out of a dark forest from a Tolkien novel. They held hands as they moved forward. Owen had the rope looped over his head and one shoulder, draped diagonally across his chest. In his back pocket he had placed two of the three flares. Jessica carried the other flare and the flashlight.

The black, still space between the trees and knee high brush seemed even more terrifying with the absence of wildlife. Having grown up in Alabama, Owen was accustomed to hearing crickets at dusk, even the rare bird or owl call. Sitting on his parents' back porch during summer nights he could listen to the symphony of the night insects punctuated by the quick scurrying of rabbits or raccoons.

But here, there was nothing. Only the sound of the ocean and soon not even that. Moonlight fell in thick patches between the trees and they used it to pick their way. After several minutes and two instances where Owen had gotten his feet tangled in the thickets, resulting in him on hands and knees cursing, they found the cart path. They paused at the edge of the concrete trail, catching their breath. Owen wanted to look at the wounds he had suffered in the servants' house but knew that to do that would require him taking off his shirt and turning on the flashlight, neither of which were appealing. Taking off his shirt would be a long and painful process and once it was off, he knew it wouldn't come back on.

They sat, silent except for their breathing for several minutes. Then Jessica signaled the rest was over by standing up and holding out her hand for him. Owen gripped it and stood, then together they stepped onto the path and began walking.

Twice they had to pause at intersections. Owen cursed Donovan for not having placed signs along the paths to indicate what structure was in which direction. The first time, they decided to continue straight, the second time Jessica insisted that the path they needed was to the right, while Owen maintained that it was directly in front of them. Without waiting or attempting further discussion, Jessica began to walk down the right hand path, which angled away from them slightly on a downhill slope. Owen didn't wait long before hurrying to catch up.

He also didn't wait long to apologize when it turned out to be the right path. They approached the main house from the rear, just as they had the night before. In the moonlight the structure looked almost perfect, the quintessential island retreat.

The lights were still on, dim amber filling the small windows on the backside of the house. Owen searched the lawn and the corners of the building, let his eyes play over the steep roof. In the silver lighting from above, he couldn't see any sign of any of the creatures. "Where do you think the keys would be?" he asked.

"Don't know. I hope like hell they aren't in the kitchen." Owen nodded, remembering the three creatures they had fought and killed in the room.

"What do you remember about the place? There are the hallways that open to the guest rooms, there's that large courtyard type place, and there's the lobby or lounge area where I met you ..."

"I bet they're going to be near that room. Unless there's some maintenance closet or something." She fell silent for a long moment.

"Fuck. They could be anywhere." In that moment, Owen felt her entire demeanor change. She dropped the courage she had used as armor for so long, and melted into a tired, hurt and frightened person. "I don't want to go in there, Owen. I don't."

He reached over and placed a hand on her shoulder. "I know. Believe me, I don't either. But if we're going to find keys to another boat—"

"That's assuming there even is another boat."

"Right, but it only makes sense. It's not like Donovan brought us here with no means of getting off the island. He wasn't planning on getting us here and killing us."

"He's doing a fucking great job of it so far."

Owen sighed. She was right. There was no guarantee that there was another boat on the island. Yet he felt positive that there had to be something. It didn't make any sense that the owner of Wee Lad Toys would buy an island, build a massive resort like this and not keep at least a boat or jet ski or something around for his guests. If not for entertainment, then he had to have something to transport people in the event of an emergency. Unless he built a hospital that we haven't seen, he reminded himself.

"Look, we'll go in just like we did the other day. See? The window we climbed in is just over there." He pointed and hoped she could see what he was talking about. "We'll get in, and start looking. We'll go fast, but we'll be thorough. Of course we have no idea how many of them are in there, but I think ..." His voice trailed off. "I'd rather know than stay out here running from place to place and not know. I can't take not knowing if there's another way off the island, if there are keys in there. It shouldn't be too hard to find. There's going to be something, some room or closet and it'll most likely be labeled." He looked at her, a dark lump crouched next to him. "Trust me."

They entered through the same window. Owen gave Jessica a boost, then climbed up himself. As he settled to the floor he found himself looking back to the window as if he expected Dixon to slide through right behind him, the man's usual wry smile etched on his face.

But there was nothing other than warm air tinged with the soft, briny smell of the ocean. It danced around Owen's head, tickling his nose and rubbing playfully at his hair as if to beckon him to come swim, come luxuriate in the surf.

They were in the same guest room as before, but to Owen, the air seemed to be charged, electrified with a nervous energy. He felt his hair standing on end along the nape of his neck, and small shivers washed across him as he crouched and tried to control his breathing. He turned and lowered the window, leaving it cracked slightly.

When he returned his attention to the room he found Jessica staring at the bed. "What is it?"

Her gaze didn't shift. "I just want to lay down. That's all. Just lay down, cover up and forget about all of this for just a little while." Finally she looked at him. Her face was slack and he could clearly see the exhaustion and the sadness that she had certainly been fighting for quite some time now. Owen sighed softly and walked to her, wrapped his arms around her. Jessica let herself be enveloped and placed her forehead against Owen's chest.

"I know," he whispered. He kissed the top of her head. "But we only have to go a little further. We find those keys, I will personally tuck you into the largest bed on that yacht." He pulled back from her, cradled her face in his hands. He could see the tears massing as the dam of her emotions weakened. "But we have to get there first. And to do that, I need you. I need you alert and ready."

A single tear rolled down her cheek. Jessica sighed and nodded. "I know. I am." She wiped the tear away and turned toward the door, rotating her body so that the bed passed behind her. She walked to the door, placed a hand on the knob and leaned close to the wood, listening. Owen stood perfectly still, afraid that even shifting his weight on the carpet would mask some crucial sound from the hallway. After several moments of agonizing silence, Jessica leaned back from the door and shook her head. "Nothing out there."

Without waiting for Owen's reaction, she turned the knob, moving it slowly as to minimize the sound of the mechanisms inside rotating. The door opened a couple of inches and she leaned forward once more, this time applying her eye to the search process. She was motionless for a while, and Owen began to feel an increasing nervousness well up within him. He began to imagine Jessica pulling away from the doorway, screaming, half of her face ripped away as the creatures mauled their way into the room.

When she looked back at him, her face was unharmed. She nodded to him, and then slipped into the hallway. Owen took a deep breath and followed her.

They moved slowly and quietly down the corridor, Jessica in the lead with Owen throwing cautious glances over his shoulder every few steps. The hallway behind them, while shrouded in gloom, was empty.

Doors passed by on their right, rooms that had recently held happy, successful people. Owen wondered at what point they mutated. Did the change happen when they were asleep, passed out from drinking too much? Did it happen the next morning when they took showers? Did it hurt, the shifting of their bodies tearing not only their flesh but their minds as well?

Jessica paused at the end of the hallway. Owen knew that ahead of them was the large foyer. To the left was the front door that led down to the beach. To the right was the dining area and kitchen and, beyond, the large courtyard. Christ, he wondered as a flash of hot panic washed over him, how many of those things are in here looking for us? He remembered hiding in the trees and brush in the courtyard and then in the ice chest as creatures stalked him. They were stupid to come back in here.

Jessica looked back at him. She stepped close, leaned into him and whispered, "I don't hear anything. Nothing seems to be moving. Any ideas where these things may be? The keys, I mean."

Owen shook his head and tried to think of where keys to boats would be. Frustration enveloped his thoughts and threatened to silence all ideas. He looked past Jessica, staring into the darkened hallway across the foyer. In his mind, he pictured his flight down that very hallway, running past the painted walls and the artwork that adorned them. He saw himself crash almost blindly into the garden-like courtyard and hiding from one of the creatures in the vegetation before rushing down another corridor.

Then it came to him. He remembered stopping in the entertainment room, confused at the sounds of civilized conversation amidst the bloody carnage around him. Conversation that, as it turned out, had come from a large television along one wall. But what stretched his memory, what pulled his mind's eye away from the television and the ice chest he had hidden in for what seemed like eternity, was the pegboard hanging next to the television.

He shifted his eyes and focused on Jessica. "In the entertainment room." When she furrowed her brow in confusion he said, "Where you and I met. I clubbed one of them on the head with a bottle." Seeing that she remembered, Owen continued more quickly, the words almost spilling on top of each other in their eagerness to get out and be heard. "Next to the bar was a pegboard on the wall. I remember seeing keys hanging on the board. Some of them had those little yellow float things that boat keys have."

Jessica thought about it. "Only one way to find out," she said and pulled the knife out of her belt before turning toward the foyer. They waited for what seemed an hour, Owen's need for action winding his nerves like a piano wire. Just when he thought he would scream or push Jessica forward, she stepped into the foyer. Instantly they heard the telltale noises of creatures to their right, in the direction of the dining room. Owen and Jessica froze, each in mid stride, their backs arched slightly as if they were doing a comical tiptoe across the area. From the dining room there was the scrape and thump of something on the large formal table. Owen's mind offered up images of a human buffet, members of the band laid out on the tabletop, their torso's ripped open to display the soft, wet entrails within.

Soft grunts interspersed with feral growls filled the air and Owen could tell that there were more than two of the creatures in the room, the open doorway of which stood gaping at them no more than ten feet away. Suddenly Owen wished he had withdrawn one of his knives before they had started across the floor. His hand began moving toward the wooden handle but he stopped it, fearful that the sounds of extracting the item would reach the mutant's ears. Instead he looked at Jessica, who seemed positively terrified and incapable of movement. He reached forward and touched her shoulder. When she looked at him, he mouthed, "Go!"

She looked back at the doorway and Owen saw her flinch and press her lips together tightly. He followed her gaze and saw a rivulet of blood running along the floor into the open space of the doorway. In the dining room, the growls were increasing and he could see shifting shadows on the wall as the activity ramped up. Careful of every step, Owen started forward, continuing down their original path.

He reached Jessica, placed both hands on her arm and pushed gently. She resisted at first, the lack of movement feeling to Owen as if she were truly rooted to the floor. Finally, after increasing his pressure on her, she lifted her foot and began to stumble down the hallway and away from the noises.

The hallway, saturated in shadows, gave the feeling of walking through a vacuum. The air was cooler, and after a few steps the sounds of the activity in the dining room behind them had been silenced. Owen wouldn't allow himself to think that the creatures had stopped and moved away. He knew that they were still back there, engaged in whatever bloody activity had produced the large pool on the floor.

Focusing all his energy on the hallway before them, Owen pressed on, keeping Jessica in front of him. Now that she had gained some distance from the dining room, she seemed to have snapped free of her fugue. They reached the courtyard within seconds and paused once again at the doorway. The room beyond their position was still as warm as Owen had remembered it being. The sound of the fountain in the center of the room was a constant high pitched roar, the frenzied babblings of a thousand watery demons. The din filled the room, echoing off of the walls. Owen and Jessica scoured the room, their eyes taking in every minute detail of foliage, every shadowy nook of rock or furniture.

Satisfied that there were no creatures in the immediate area, they crept forward. Owen had wanted to keep to the stone path that led around the garden but Jessica, without looking back at him, plunged into the brush. Owen opened his mouth to protest but realized quickly that his words, whispered, would have been lost under the fountain.

As he moved through the garden, the fountain's noise seemed to shift, undulating with the thickness of the brush around him. Owen's heart was a frantic drum solo in his chest. His eyes matched his heart's rhythm, darting everywhere at once to try to see any hiding creatures.

They passed the fountain, neither of them looking down at the soggy, shredded remains of the staff worker that lay near the water. Jessica paused at one point and looked curiously at Owen. After a second's pause, Owen understood what she wanted. He craned his neck slightly and spotted the corridor that would lead them to the entertainment room. He pointed, Jessica saw the right path, and they moved again.

Owen didn't know they were under attack until he was on his back, the creature's teeth deep in his arm. The pain ripped through him in a jagged, white-hot streak. He tried to scream but under the roar of the fountain and his attacker, he couldn't tell if the sound made it out of his mouth. The creature on top of him bit harder and raked its claws along the length of his body, the heavy points reopening old wounds and drawing fresh ones. Owen pounded the creature's body, a solid mass covered in wet rags that had at one point been a pair of men's pajamas.

Reacting, not thinking, Owen brought his knee upward hard and fast and felt it connect with the soft genitalia. He felt a satisfying pop, then heat on his knee. The creature stiffened, released its grip and Owen took advantage of the moment, shoving it off of him. He had no time to focus on the beast before Jessica fell on its head, her knife held before her, and drove the point deep into the side of its face. The creature spasmed, its limbs pinwheeling on the dirty floor. Twice a clawed foot connected with Owen's shin before he backed away out of range.

Jessica was over him immediately, her hands roaming his body, fingers probing his wounds. He saw her grimace then quickly swallow the emotion away. "You're fine," she said. Owen could hear the lie in her voice as certainly as he could hear the fountain behind them. He nodded anyway and let her help him to his feet. Once standing, he took a moment to find his balance. The pain in his chest and shoulder was a solid throbbing mass. It seemed to pulse with all the fervor of a heavy metal drummer on speed.

"Can you walk?" Jessica asked, keeping one arm around him. Owen winced at a fresh wave of pain and nodded.

"We get those keys and I'll fucking dance all the way to the boat." They started forward again.

The entertainment room looked just as it had when Owen was in it days prior. The only difference was the absence of the body of the creature he had hit with a liquor bottle. Owen regarded the spot on the carpet where the creature had fallen. There was no blood. He must not have hit it as hard as he had hoped. It was out there somewhere, hunting them.

"Here," Jessica whispered. Her voice sounded like a shotgun blast in the silence of the room. Owen turned sluggishly to face her. She stood near the pegboard, staring at the keys. Owen saw the yellow floating devices that marked the boat keys. "Which one?"

"Just take them all," he said. "We'll sort it out later."

Jessica's hand reached for the keys but never made it. Owen stared at it, her fingers trembling in space inches away from the patterned metal that would be their salvation.

Behind him, to both sides of him, he heard the growls and hungry keening of several creatures as they walked slowly into the room from both exits.

12

Owen's eyes raced from doorway to doorway, taking in the sight of the creatures as they advanced. They moved slowly, fanning out as they cleared the doorframes, approaching like African predators stalking their prey. In their demonic gaze he could see the hunger, the anticipation and the effort it took for them all to hold back, to not leap forward and attack immediately. They were savoring the moment, enjoying it the way someone would the first sip of wine.

Jessica's breathing seemed to drown out the creatures, her breath coming and going in rapid, deep pulses. Owen reached for her, placed a hand on her shoulder. He was afraid that if she didn't try to center herself she'd hyperventilate. He also needed her focused, in case an opportunity to escape arose.

Then again, he thought as he watched the groups approaching—there were five coming from their front and three from behind them—maybe it would be better if she were in a state of emotional and physical shock when the attack came. Because their deaths wouldn't be immediate; the creatures would pull them apart, ripping muscles from bone and tearing the tongues from their mouths. Maybe it would be better for Jessica not to feel anything, to simply retreat into a closet in her mind while her world ended.

The knife in his belt pressed uncomfortably against him, and he felt the sharp edges of the two flares he had stuffed into his front pocket. Keeping focused on the group in front of him, he began to move his hand slowly toward his pocket, hoping to be able to draw his knife first, then with his free hand pull out at least one of the flares. The creatures saw his motions and seemed to understand his intentions. They darted forward.

Their hands gripped him and his arms felt as if he were being compacted in a vice. He cried out, more of fear than pain. His wounds reacted to his yell and began thumping a steady rhythm through his body. The knife was pulled from his belt and tossed across the room. He felt the presence of the creatures behind him, their breath hot on his neck, rancid and thick. He saw the group in front of him disarming Jessica. Their hands roamed her body, finding her weapons tucked away and pulling them free. She stood stoic against the manhandling. Once she threw a glance back at Owen and in her eyes he could see the resignation; she had given up, had decided that any further struggling was useless.

"Jessica." She flinched at the sound of her name, and one of the mutants behind Owen growled and jabbed him with a finger as a warning to keep quiet. Owen felt a small trickle of blood run down his back from where the creature's claw pierced his skin. What the hell were they doing? he wondered. Why hadn't they attacked, ripped our throats out and begun to eat us like they have with all the other people?

"Jessica," he said again and this time one of the creatures in front of him stepped toward him and hit him across the face. The blow was open handed, but had packed enough power that Owen saw blackness interspersed with explosions of bright lights and fell to one knee. He stayed kneeling, trying to gather his wits. He heard a soft sound and looked up. Jessica was crying, her final defenses destroyed. Her shoulders jerked with her sobs. For a faint, fleeting moment Owen wanted to go to her, to comfort her. Then the moment passed and he sank back down. The creatures stood around her, watching her intently. Owen could see what little remained of their human features, the cheeks, nose and ears, the placement of the eyes; these things were still there, still in their normal places, but had been twisted and altered with the mutation.

That they still retained human features, that they had once been people who only hours ago had been friendly and accommodating, rich or poor with families and friends and hobbies, wrenched Owen's emotions and threatened to twist his mind. Suddenly he felt everything fall away. His body became numb as his mind released the will to go on, to fight and survive. There was no way they were going to get out of there; no way they were going to be rescued. Nobody knew they were missing or in trouble, and wouldn't know for at least another week. They had been stupid to think that they were going to be able to escape the creatures and find a way off the island. He thought of the yacht, moored off the island, bobbing in the waves of the Caribbean ocean.

I'll never see the inside of that boat, he thought. I'll never feel the comfort of sheets around me or hot food in my stomach. I'll never see a car or an office building, a traffic light or coffee shop. I'll never see Michelle. Owen let an image of Michelle float to the forefront of his mind. In the image she stood with her back to him, stocking shelves in the store. He approached and she turned, smiling. She was genuinely happy to see him, not because he was a co-worker or just a friend, but because he was Owen.

Never again. Before he realized what was happening, Owen leapt to his feet and charged the creatures in front of him. They were taken by surprise at the sudden rush of his attack, and he landed punches on two of them, knocking them to the floor before the others had a chance to react. Jessica didn't enter the fight, instead she stood where she was despite the absence of a mutant's restraining grip on her arms, and continued to cry. Owen kicked one of the creatures on the ground, felt something snap inside, and then brought his leg back for another blow.

Pain exploded in the side of his head. The room tilted to one side as if the resort house were on a sharply banking aircraft, then dimmed. As it dimmed, Owen felt his body falling and the wetness of his own blood dampening his neck. Then the world blinked out, and he knew no more.

Consciousness seeped over him like warm water spreading across the ground. It covered his skin and seeped down, burrowing deeper until it reached the depths of his mind and began to turn on switches, connecting synapses and bringing all his systems on line. Owen fought against it, his mind having been pulled from the nothingness into knowing and thinking, demanded that the unseen force leave him alone; that it let him sink back down into the unknowing bliss of the abyss. But the more he thought about it, the more he tried to will himself back asleep, the faster he rose toward waking. As he approached full awareness, the pain began to filter to him, as if it were a thermal layer just before breaking the surface of the waters of—

Awake. Owen opened his eyes, but kept them half lidded against the brightness overhead. He took stock of where he was. He lay on a bed, the mattress firm beneath him. The comforter and sheets were rumpled and one lump of them pressed uncomfortably against his left kidney. The pressure of it against him seemed to agitate his bladder and he felt the need to urinate like a heavy burning in his crotch. In an attempt to delay the need to piss, Owen turned his attention to the rest of his surroundings.

A stench filled the room, something that reminded Owen of a dead mouse that a friend of his had kept in a bottle once when they were kids. Gary Denote had found the dead rodent one day in the woods behind his house. The creature had been partially rotted or devoured by other animals, and Gary had forced it into a glass Coke bottle. He carried the thing around for weeks, forcing his buddies and the smaller kids of the neighborhood to smell it as it decomposed inside the small glass coffin.

Owen's arms were tied to the bed frame, thin white ropes connected his wrists to the headboard, and his feet were connected to the footboard. He tugged on the ropes and felt very little give. The knots didn't seem to loosen at all. After several minutes of struggling, Owen gave up and let his head fall back against the mattress. He looked to either side and saw that he was in one of the bedrooms of the resort's main house. However, this room was larger and much more lavishly decorated than his or any of the other guest rooms had been. It must have been one of the master suites, maybe even Donovan's room.

Rich wood furniture, lush plants and original paintings and statues adorned the room. To Owen's right was a larger room, a sitting room that contained two couches, a few chairs and a long bar. He could see the corner of a large flat screen television mounted on a wall, and a pair of French doors opened outward to what he assumed was the beach. From his vantage, Owen could only see the pale blue sky.

The stench in the room brought his attention back around. He lifted his head slightly and searched the surrounding area for the source. He saw nothing on any of the dressers or chairs in the sleeping area. The smell tickled his nose and made his throat constrict reflexively. Owen swallowed hard against the feeling of rising bile. Tied to a bed, the last thing he wanted was to vomit. To keep his attention away from the sickening smell in the room, he focused on the restraints. There had to be, he knew, some way out of the ropes. He twisted his head around so that he could study the knots that held his wrists. They were simple knots, but based strictly on their appearance, they were tied tightly. He followed the rope to where it was anchored on the headboard.

The headboard was a large piece, with solid blocks of wood on both the extreme left and right. However, next to those blocks were small, thin pegs that ran vertically. They provided a break in the solid piece of the headboard. Owen counted four of them before the large solid center, then four of the pegs and finally the outer block of wood. He smiled at his fortune when he saw that the ropes were anchored on one of these small pegs. Guess they didn't have enough to wrap around the larger posts, he thought. He glanced at his feet and saw that the ropes were, in fact, tied to the larger posts on the footboard.

Owen inched himself upward toward the headboard as much as he could then wrapped his hands around the ropes and began to pull. His wounds seemed to wake up and begin to scream in agony at the sudden exertion, but Owen set his jaw against the pain and continued to pull.

Nothing happened. He tried jerking the ropes in short, powerful motions, then tried to bring his hands together to combine and center his strength. The ropes weren't long enough to allow his hands to come more than a foot apart. After several minutes of struggling, he collapsed, exhausted. He lay there panting, staring at the white ceiling and wondering about Jessica. Where was she? Had they put her in a similar room? Was she trying to figure a way out of her bonds just like he was?

The thought of the beautiful woman laying on a bed and doing the same thing he was doing at the same time stirred something within him. He sighed and tried to control his breathing as he remembered their kisses in the jungle, the way her lips had felt on his, her tongue in his mouth. He thought about her breath hot in his ear, the feeling of her flat belly, firm legs and breasts under his hand.

Never thought that would be possible again, did you? He mused. Not after Heather. So what, another part of his mind countered; people have those kinds of moments in situations of extreme stress. It's normal. They need some kind of grounding, something set in a reality they know and can understand as well as the release of stress that comes with an orgasm.

Buddy, you know that's not all true. You don't hear about people trapped in an elevator on the brink of plummeting to their death ripping off clothes and having at it, do you? You aren't going to sit there and think that any of the people in those buildings on September 11 found themselves in a corner office having a gang bang to deal with the unreality of their impending deaths, are you?

Owen blinked. Still, the kissing and fooling around he had done with Jessica seemed proof that maybe there was still a life out there to be had. A life that he could claim if he could only find a way out of here and off the island. A life with Jessica, maybe.

Owen's foot began to itch and he rubbed at it with his other foot. The itching subsided but something had turned on in his brain. He lifted his head and looked down at the ropes on his ankles. He looked beyond that at his feet. The skin was dirty and streaked with mud and cuts.

Owen began to twist his foot, pulling against the rope and using his other foot as an added surface. The rope didn't move, didn't slide forward toward his ankle or heel. He then hooked the big toe of one foot under the rope on his left foot. Ignoring the pain in his toe, he strained to stretch the rope while he worked to slip his foot free.

Ten minutes later, his left foot was free. He repeated the process with his right foot. It took longer, because with the promise of freedom so close, Owen had become paranoid. He paused every few seconds to listen for sounds of the creatures approaching. He knew that in movies, it was at this point that a random guard happened by and saw the hero escaping.

When both feet were free of their bonds, he turned his attention to the ropes on his hands. He managed to squat on the mattress, but couldn't stand because of the length of the ropes. He pushed his legs beneath and behind him, laying flat, and placing his feet on the cool wood of the headboard. Again he wrapped his hands around the ropes to increase his advantage. Then he pushed away from the headboard, using his legs and arms to increase the pressure on the vertical pegs.

Within moments they had cracked and his ropes had slipped free. Owen lay on the bed panting, his hands dangling next to him, for several moments. He knew he needed to get up and leave, but his body needed the time to recover.

The stench in his room, somewhere beyond the bed he lay on, brought him back around. He blinked, then pushed up off the bed and began to work on the ropes around his wrists. The knots resisted at first, clinging to their twists and coils, but once he broke them free, the rope unraveled easily. He took a moment to massage his wrists. The effort of pulling on the ropes to free himself had left him with deep grooves in his skin. His hands tingled slightly as the blood flow regained strength.

The stench seemed to swell as he paused to asses his situation, the fetid air increasing its horribleness in a final attempt to sicken him. Owen breathed hard through his mouth and shut his eyes against the desire to throw up. His thoughts clear enough, he stood and walked away from the bed into the larger sitting room.

The source of the stench lay on the couch. It was a human, one of the staff, he judged by the tatters of white shirt and the few small remaining patches of darkened skin. The cadaver had been ripped apart, large pieces of the flesh torn away violently leaving ragged, bloody tears in the tissue that remained. Owen turned away from the carnage, away from the maggots that squirmed in the abdominal cavity of the corpse, and hurried to the French doors. Through them he could see the beach bathed in early morning light, an unobstructed view of the sand and surf beyond. He saw a volleyball net off to one side and little else.

His hands closed around the gold handle and began to turn when a woman's scream, muffled by the walls, reached him. He paused, closed his eyes and rested his head on the door. He had to go find her; he had to try to save her. When he opened his eyes, the beach and water seemed to call him, a siren song of freedom.

She's probably already too far gone, you know, a voice whispered. She's probably being eaten right now, and if you go in there or try to find her, you'll die too. Go out the doors, get to the beach and find a way off the island. That yacht isn't too far away. You could swim it. The sharks aren't that bad.

"She could be alive. She needs my help," he whispered.

She's most likely alive, but not for long. It's hard to live without your guts. Just ask that poor son of a bitch behind you. He'll tell you. He'll spill his ...

Owen turned away from the doors and walked quickly across the room, refusing to look down at the dead man on the couch. Before he reached the main door to leave the suite, something caught his eye. The bar that he had seen earlier drew his attention and he walked to it. Several bottles of liquor stood, waiting patiently. He picked two of them up and hefted them, debating on whether or not to use them as a club. He placed them back down and picked up instead a long, silver handled ice pick. The pick wasn't a long knife like he had used earlier, but certainly was better than his bare hands or the blunt edge of a bottle. He began to turn away from the bar when something on a label caught his eye. He snatched a small pint sized bottle of rum and jammed it in his back pocket.

Owen returned to the main door and hesitated before going through. He took deep breaths, gathering his resolve before taking the plunge into the nightmare world again. Then, before the voice could start again, Owen twisted the knob and slipped into the hallway.

The hall was quiet and looked very much like all the other halls he had been in so far. Deep red carpet ran the length of the corridor, and plants on stands dotted the walls. The hall ran for several yards to his right before ending in a solid wall, and to his left it stopped after only fifteen feet or so. Beyond that he could see the courtyard he had traveled through so many times. No other doors lay between him and the courtyard, so he knew that Jessica would be in one of the other rooms along the hall.

He tightened his grip on the ice pick and moved along the carpet. He assumed she would be in a room close to the one he had just exited; otherwise he may not have been able to hear her scream. There were four doors in the hallway, all of them on the same side as the room he had been in. Based on that, he assumed they were all similar, executive type suites with a bedroom and living room, designed for Donovan and his high-level cronies, while all the lower echelon workers were relegated to the simple single room guest suites.

The first door was locked, and after pressing his ear to the door and hearing nothing, Owen moved on. The second room was unlocked, yet no sounds issued from within. Owen glanced over his shoulder at the courtyard. Nothing stirred other than the large fountain, sending a fine spray of moisture through the air. He twisted the knob and slipped inside, closing the door noiselessly behind him.

The growl seemed to reach down into his chest and squeeze his heart. Owen saw the creature move from around the corner where the room's bathroom was located just behind one of the large leather sofas. It approached, wearing the tatters of a pair of women's khaki shorts and nothing else. Stringy black hair hung in wet clumps and from where he stood, Owen could see clumps of something unidentifiable in its hair. He couldn't tell what they were, but deep down he knew they were pieces of flesh. Her teeth and chin were stained a deep red as if she had been eating fresh berries with no regard to the juice running down her lips. The bloodstains extended to her small but sagging breasts and even a few drops dotted her flabby stomach.

Owen tried to place her, which board member or storeowner she was, but couldn't. He didn't remember most of the people who had been here and her appearance had altered so horribly in her mutation that any semblance to her former existence ended at the basic humanoid form she maintained.

The creature seemed taken aback slightly by his sudden appearance, and he assumed that she had expected another one of her kind. However, her shock quickly melted away and she wasted no time in rushing him. Her hands reached for him, claws slicing through the air as she mewled like a feral beast.

His legs seemed to move of their own volition, pushing him toward the oncoming creature and then instantly away as she sped past him. He brought the ice pick up and around in an instinctual reaction. The creature howled in pain as the metal blade bit deep into her upper arm. Owen could see the tip of it exposed on the opposite side of her arm. He pulled it free and stabbed again, this time moving under his own free will. He drove the blade into the creature's throat, just above her breastbone as he pushed his body weight into her, driving her back against the door.

The creature hissed at him, its breath sickening and ragged from the damage to its windpipe. Her claws raked at him weakly but still did damage to the tiny areas of his shoulders and back that hadn't been cut or scraped yet. Owen felt his blood running down his back as he pressed harder on the ice pick and watched the life seep out of the gaze of the creature's eyes.

When he was certain it was dead, he stepped back and pulled the bloody ice pick from the creature's neck and then turned to the rest of the room. To his right the bed was unoccupied. To his left he could see most of the sofas and a quick few steps confirmed that the rest of the furniture was devoid of either creatures or Jessica.

He knew she had to be in here. Hearing her scream so clearly and the presence of this creature almost mandated that she be in here, he reasoned. But where? He took several steps and crossed the living room, angling for the bathroom the creature had emerged from.

What he saw inside made him finally vomit. Quickly he turned to the sink and expelled what little of the fruit he had eaten hours before. Jessica was in the tub, tied to the shower nozzle. Her head hung down, her hair covering her face and breasts. Her arms were raised above her.

Strips of her flesh had been peeled away. Owen saw large portions of her legs, those beautiful legs that had at one point been wrapped around him, seeming to pull him closer to her waiting sex. Not only skin had been removed, but also muscle and tissue all the way down to the bone on one thigh. Her calf muscles were gone, having been cut away viciously. Patches of skin and meat had been torn away from her ribs, and he could see the whiteness of the bones staring out at him. The creatures hadn't attacked the soft flesh of her abdomen yet.

"Oh Christ," he moaned and backed up a step until he connected with the sink. "Oh dear sweet God, what did they do to her?"

Jessica's head stirred and Owen thought he would die of fright. A brilliant flash of terror exploded in his chest and raced through his body as she lifted her head and looked over at him. Her face hung slack, her eyes mirrored the unimaginable pain and fear she felt. When she focused on him, her mouth fell open.

"Owen," she whispered and the sound of his name brought tears to his eyes. He took a step toward her.

"Jessica, what did they do to you?" he restrained himself from reaching out to her.

"Owen," she whispered again, and Owen began to understand. She was delirious with pain. "They're eating us," she said. Her voice was a weak tremble.

"Eating?"

"Saving us. Saving you. For later. For dessert."

Owen looked at her ravaged body. "They're keeping you so they can eat you slowly?" Jessica's head bobbled almost imperceptibly. Instantly what he was seeing made sense. Why they had tied him up in the other room instead of killing them both out rightly in the lounge made sense. They were planning on keeping the two of them around as extra meat. Jessica had drawn the unfortunate luck of being the first. It could have just as easily been me, he thought.

"Owen."

Owen blinked and looked at her. "Yes, baby? What do you need?"

"Kill me." Owen felt his breath catch. Kill her? No, there was no way he could do that.

"No. I can't do that. I'm going to get you out of here. I can undo those ties and we can get out of here, get to the boat and get you some help. You're going to be alright, I swear." As he spoke, tears ran down his cheeks and his words began to mingle with soft sobs.

"Owen. I'm. Dead. Already. It hurts. So. Much. Please. Kill. Me."

His resolve died as he stood there looking at her, the woman who could have been his salvation, his lifeline out of the depression and hell on earth he had been suffering through since Heather's death. She looked up at him, her eyes pleading. "Please."

"I don't know if I can do it, Jess."

"Stronger than you know."

Owen squeezed his eyes shut and stepped toward her. He felt her hair brush against his cheeks. When he looked at her again she was staring straight at him. They said nothing for a long moment, only staring at one another. Then he leaned forward and kissed her. She kissed back, but only weakly. Their lips were still touching when he drove the pick into her chest. Jessica's body bucked and she gasped for air, but the pick had found her heart and within seconds her jerking and thumping in the tub ceased.

Owen turned and started to leave the bathroom, tears streaming down his cheeks, the feeling of her lips still lingering on his own. Through the tears, something on the floor caught his eye. He blinked and bent to pick it up, shoving it into a pocket.

When he stood and rounded the corner near the door, three creatures stood inside the doorway, staring down at their fallen companion. As Owen approached, they looked up simultaneously as if their heads were attached to a single string and controlled by a master puppeteer. Owen threw a look over one shoulder, saw the double doors that led to the beach. When he looked back at the creatures, they were moving toward him, staying close to one another as they gained on their prey. Owen began to back toward the door, deciding that he would crash through it if he needed to, cuts and damages to his body be dammed at this point. His mind was still numb after having to kill Jessica.

He bumped into the back of one of the sofas, and the contact drew his attention to the bottle of rum in his pocket. Part of his mind turned back on, pushing aside the shock of Jessica's death. He considered the bottle, thought about his options. As he slid along the back of the ˙h, never taking his eyes off of the trio before him, something ught his thoughts. He cleared the couch and stopped, ˙es were within five feet of him and when he hey. They remained crouched, ready to pounce on o pieces. Owen reached into his back pocket and e. He showed it to them, and they regarded it ubconscious part of them knew what it was er comprehend and translate what they were e they could act further, Owen threw the bottle as s he could at the center creature. It—a man in its former life —threw up its clawed hands in defense. The bottle shattered, glass and rum exploding outward and covering the three. Owen felt more than a few drops of rum hitting him, one landing on an exposed wound and stinging as the alcohol mingled with his raw flesh.

He pushed that pain aside and held up his other hand, which had reached deep into his pocket as he had tossed the bottle. He popped the cap off of the flare he had found on the floor, igniting it as he did. The flame sputtered then caught and burned hard, a short red flame that hissed and coughed, smoke pouring upward in the small space. Owen looked at it briefly and then tossed it at the creatures. They shrieked at the sight of the flare approaching, and their shrieks turned to screams of outright pain as the rum ignited and the flames engulfed them. Owen turned quickly from the creatures that began to run blindly through the room, setting pieces of furniture ablaze as they did.

He ran to the doors, pulled them open and dashed out onto the sand.

13

The sand was hot on Owen's legs as it sprayed against his skin when he ran across it. The sunlight glared and he squinted in the sudden onslaught of brightness, his gait staggering as he adjusted. Behind him he could hear the continued screams of the creatures, but they seemed lessened; perhaps only one of them remained able to cry out. He heard the pops of wood catching fire, the steady crackling of the flames as they reached desperately for new fuel.

A breeze flew in his face, heavy with the tantalizing odor of the ocean. It seemed to call to him, to beg him to come play, swim and let the undulating waves wash away his worries. He ran toward it, not thinking, unsure of a direction in which he needed to go. He stopped when his feet were covered to the ankles by the foaming surf. He felt the sand wash away beneath him, his feet sinking deeper as it receded.

A crashing of glass brought him out of his reverie. Owen turned and looked at the house. Black smoke poured from the windows and the open door through which he had escaped. The glass of the second door had shattered outward; the smoking and still burning body of one of the creatures lay in the center of the frame. Owen stared at it, the fear that had consumed him during his flight out of the building subsiding and giving way to anger fueled by the sight of the creature and the memory of Jessica hanging in the shower, the flesh stripped from her body.

Before he knew what he was doing, Owen walked quickly across the sand toward the creature. The smoke that poured from the room stung his face and the flames inside seemed to push him away with their heat, but he moved right next to the creature. It laid face down, one hand stretched above its head, the other still inside the doorframe. Its clothing was smoldering, and most of the hair had burned away from the skull, leaving only a black and red blistered head. It was dead, Owen knew, but still he drew his foot up and slammed it down as hard as he could on the creature's head. His foot slipped off as the skin sloughed away.

Satisfied, he turned away and moved back toward the beach. Before he broke cover past the brush that lined the edge of the building he paused, debating his next move. The screaming behind him had ended, he noticed, but now there were new sounds, others moving in the house. The other creatures left inside would be aware of the fire, would be either coming to investigate or trying to flee. He wondered if they retained enough of their humanity to be able to fight the flames and prevent them from consuming the entire building.

Owen flinched as something heavy passed through the air close to his head, the wind from it ruffling his hair. As he recovered from the shock, he looked up to see a splash in the surf from the object's impact. He twisted around to see a single creature—a woman from the resort staff—bringing her arm back to throw another rock.

Owen turned and sprinted down the beach, keeping the water to his right and the rock wielding creature to his back. Moments after he began running, he heard her cry out in anger and begin pursuit. Gambling that she wouldn't be able to throw the rock either effectively or accurately while running, Owen didn't swerve his pattern, instead he continued in a straight line, following the water.

As he ran he threw quick glances back over his shoulder. For several dozen yards as he raced down the increasingly rocky shoreline, the creature was alone. But soon one, then three more of her kind joined her. Owen's panic began to rise, threatening to overtake his thoughts, to shut down his body. Tears clouded his eyes and he blinked them away, willing down the surge of hopelessness he felt welling within. Instead, he tried to sharpen his thoughts, to plan ahead while he still had distance between his pursuers and himself. The jungle continued thickly to his left, but to reach it he would have to cross the thick sand that would severely slow him.

To his right was the water, the ocean that had for years terrified him. He pictured himself swimming away from shore, leaving the creatures on the sand howling their rage after him, but quickly dismissed the thoughts. There was no place for him to swim. No boat waited in the deeper waters on this side of the island, and he wasn't quick enough of a swimmer to fight the waves and the undertow so as to outpace the creatures on land. All they would have to do is walk, conserving their energy while they waited for him to dispense all of his. Eventually he or the waves would carry his body back to shore and they would have him.

Not much of a choice, he thought. Something in the trees to his left caught his eye. A flash of bone white at the base of a large palm tree drew his attention. It was the cart path, but the white came from the rear bumper of an overturned golf cart. Owen knew that it would be impossible to cross the sand, reach and upright the cart before the creatures were upon him.

But, he thought, once I hit the path, I can increase my speed, put some distance between us.

No, jackass, you increase your speed on the path, so do they. And you've seen how fast those fuckers can move when they have good ground beneath them.

A rock hit him in the right shoulder blade, sending him stumbling forward, pain burning across his back and down the length of his arm. Owen managed to regain his balance, and before the creatures could rearm themselves and hurl another missile, turned sharply to his left and ran with everything he had toward the cart path.

Halfway across the beach, his gait desperately slowed by the deep sand Owen heard the creatures snarling as they changed course to intercept him. Their growls sounded like the gleeful chuckling that a large man makes when presented with an all you can eat buffet. The chords resounded deep in his mind, sending a fresh burst of adrenaline through his body, his chest tickling at the rush. In response, his legs churned faster and before he realized it, he was on the path and moving quickly along it.

The woods were as dark and deep as ever, trees and brush blurring past him as he raced for his life. Inside the forest, Owen lost all sound of his attackers and the silence, save for his deep breaths and the slapping of his feet on the pavement, gave his fear the fuel it needed to continue in its attempts to cripple him.

It wasn't until he had ran for what had felt like half a mile that he realized he had no direction, no plan to get off the island or away. He had no key to any boat; the keys had been dropped and lost in the attack in the house. Throwing a glance over his shoulder he saw nothing behind him. He didn't believe his eyes and continued to run several dozen more yards before looking again. Again, there was nothing behind him. Owen slowed without thinking about it, keeping his vision locked on the trail he had just run along. He held his breath and strained to hear anything. There was nothing. The silence that enveloped the forest around him was all encompassing, unbroken by even the soft breeze or the sound of what he knew had to be a blazing inferno by now at the main house.

The creatures were gone, it seemed. Owen wasn't sure if he could believe that; it seemed impossible that a group that large would have abandoned their pursuit of him after so long. Where had they gone? What had called them away from the chase? Or, he wondered as he turned his head slowly, had they disbursed to the woods, and were even now creeping closer under the cover and concealment of the brush and trees?

It didn't matter, he decided. They weren't chasing him, weren't immediately in his vision and for that he was thankful. He let out his breath slowly, not wanting a loud sigh to reveal himself. On his subsequent inhale, for the first time he detected the faint oily stench of smoke in the air.

His shoulder throbbed where the rock had impacted him, and a wave of nausea passed over him. He had lost blood, he knew, a good bit. He had no idea how much exactly, or how much it took to render him a sack of meat on the ground. No figure floated to his mind out of the swamp of his memory, nothing learned in a YMCA class or high school health class, nothing gleaned from a Trivial Pursuit card. All Owen could do was continue on as if he were fully healthy and hope that he didn't suddenly pass out.

He began walking slowly down the path in the direction he had been running. As he moved, he tried to control his breathing, to steady his heartbeat which would not only help calm him but would also lessen his blood loss and the throbbing pain from his multitude of wounds. He tried to speculate on the creatures that had been chasing him, wondering if they had decided to return to the house and help tend to the fire, or if they still were after him only split up and creeping through the woods instead of racing along the path. After only a few seconds, he realized that continuing to wonder about it only distracted him from the immediate issue of escape and he turned his mind away from it.

But the thoughts wouldn't go away, and with each passing step his stress increased. Finally he decided to take action to prove or disprove the multitudes of theories in his mind. He turned off the path at a random spot, walked a dozen feet into the woods and found a large tree with a twisted trunk. The folds and grooves of the trunk formed a deep but short alcove in which Owen could crawl. Once inside, he could see only a small portion of the trail, but felt comforted in what he could see, and that if he couldn't see it, then anything on the trail couldn't see him.

He sighed and waited, feeling hundreds of beads of sweat tickling their way down his cheeks and nose, chest and ribs. To pass the time he tried to think of a plan of action. He realized he had no keys to the boat, if another boat was even present on the island, and had no idea how to get a key. The more he tried to think about a course of action, the harder it became to focus on one. His thoughts were continually interrupted by images of Jessica, her body ravaged by the creatures as they kept her alive while they used her as food. He saw her slender fingers dangling above the showerhead where she had been tied, the abject pain and fear etched on her beautiful face. He remembered the deep wounds on her body; her sobs and pleas for death echoed in his mind, each one a painful punch to his soul.

A sound ripped him from his ruminations. Owen squinted through the leaves and felt his breath catch. All four creatures moved in front of him. At least one was in the woods between the path and where Owen crouched in the tree. He could see the heads of the others and guessed that they were all on the path. They hadn't given up their quarry, had only been delayed by either caution or something else—what, Owen could not guess.

For the second time, Owen held his breath. As he did, he became aware of the pounding of his heart and closed his eyes, wishing it to calm. He steadied his breath, focusing on letting each one out through his barely parted lips so as to minimize noise. As he worked to relax his body, he listened to the soft sounds of the creatures moving through the woods. Their passage was so quiet that if he hadn't known differently, he would have sworn that no creature more harmful than a chipmunk prowled before him.

He opened his eyes, feeling slightly more relaxed than he had moments before, and immediately felt his breath catch. The creature that had been nearest him had now moved even closer and stood hunched with its back facing Owen. He could see its torso moving rhythmically as it breathed, could see the clawed hands opening and closing as it scanned the forest.

Go on you piece of shit, he thought, sending every ounce of energy he had into the mental barb, wishing that the mere thought would strike the creature dead. The former staff member wasn't killed and instead turned to face the tree Owen crouched within. Under the gaze of his pursuer, Owen felt as vulnerable as a wounded field mouse under the watchful eye of a hungry hawk.

One leg began to spasm, as if it were suddenly desperate to move, to drive his body up and out of his hiding place and begin his sprint along the path again. Owen clutched it with his hands and begged it to stop. Slowly, as he stared at the creature's searching face, his leg relaxed and fell still.

The creature took a tentative step toward Owen but found its attention drawn away from its undiscovered quarry by the grunts of its fellow hunters. It turned away and moved back toward the path, making slightly more noise than it had when first approaching the area. The group congregated at the path and for a brief moment Owen thought they were huddling and discussing their next move. He wondered if they actually spoke or if it were more a series of gestures. The foliage obscured his vision and made their movements hard to discern. Finally they began down the path, continuing in their original line of pursuit, moving off to Owen's right. Again they moved noiselessly. Owen watched them go, watched them melt into the forest like shadows into the murky depths of an ocean.

When they were gone, he relaxed more and leaned back against the roughness of the tree. He stared into the woods in the direction the creatures had vanished. They move so goddamn quietly, he thought. He had never noticed that before, all his encounters with the creatures having been blind rushes away from them, or quick violent moments in close quarters in the guesthouses.

He took a deep breath and tried to think of how many creatures were left. However, the more he focused on the number of guests and tried to guess at the amount of staff Donovan would have employed for the week then subtract the bodies he knew of both victims and dead creatures, the more he became confused. After several long minutes of frustrating math, Owen was left with one conclusion. There were a hell of a lot more of them and only one of him. There was no way he was going to escape them forever. Only one way to go about this, he thought.

He needed the keys to a boat. That was imperative. If he couldn't get keys then there was absolutely no point in attempting an escape unless he could manage to keep the speedboat afloat long enough to paddle it out. Of course, that was only based on the chance that there was a paddle still in the boat, and he didn't remember seeing one. If there was another boat on the island, without a key Owen knew he lacked the strength to paddle it from it's mooring all the way around to the yacht.

Swimming to the yacht was already an impossibility because of the sharks just beyond the sandbar. It was a gamble, he thought. Just because they're known to hang around that sandbar doesn't mean that they'll definitely be there when he tried to swim the distance. But he knew the hard reality. His seeping wounds would leak blood into the water and that coupled with the frenzied, spastic and tired motions of his exhausted limbs as he swam would be literally ringing a dinner bell for the sharks. Plus, the last thing he needed was to get within an arm's length of the boat only to have at that moment the feeling of teeth wrapping around his leg, jerking him under as others closed in on his arms and torso.

No, it was better to deal with the creatures here on the land that he could see and had a better chance against. If he could find the keys in the room, he would be all right to search for another boat. Owen thought back and decided that the keys had to have been knocked free when he and Jessica were first found in the entertainment room. They would be there.

Yet, as he opened his eyes and looked again at the forest in the direction the creatures had traveled, he understood once again the sheer numbers he faced. He couldn't outrun them anymore. He couldn't outfight them. When he went back to the main house to get the keys, he was going to be going back into their midst. There was no escaping that. His only choice was to get in as quickly and quietly as he could and pray that he could do so without being found.

He had absolutely no hope that it would happen that way. When he stood his knees popped and he froze, one hand on the tree the other dangling near his knee. To his tired ears, the joint popping had sounded like a shotgun blast. However after several moments he realized that the sound couldn't have traveled beyond his immediate hearing range. He started forward slowly, testing his legs. They were shaky and uncoordinated for having ran such a distance and then crouched for so long in the tree.

The cart path was reached and Owen's legs felt better when he stood on the solid asphalt. He looked the length of it, saw no creatures in either direction, then stepped off of it again and into the woods on the other side. He began walking in a direction he thought would take him close to the main house, deciding that when he got within range he would circle around until he found the same window he and Jessica had entered through.

After that, he thought, it would be pure luck. But as he walked slowly through the trees, his mind began to work, and with each step he devised a plan that would either ensure his survival or end everything in one fell stroke.

His lips mumbled a quiet prayer that it would be the former.

Owen wiped a hand across his face for what seemed to be the hundredth time in ten minutes, and drew away the sweat that had coated his skin, more instantly replacing it. His throat ached, in dire need of something to drink and he promised himself that once he got inside the yacht, he would drink and eat until his stomach ruptured.

The trees ahead began to thin and he knew he was nearing the grounds of the main house. The air was filled with a thin grey smoke that stung his nostrils when he inhaled. He paused, kneeling near a thicket of bushes and looked around. The trip through the woods from the cart path had been uneventful, but long and slow. Owen had moved carefully, certain that at any moment he would be spotted.

Now he peered through the gently moving leaves and stared at the small patches of the house that he could see. From his vantage point, it seemed that the fire had been put out and he wondered again if the creatures had managed to band together and fight it or if maybe Donovan had a sprinkler system installed, recessed into the ceilings of the houses and that was what had killed the flames. Either way, he thought, the good thing is that the house is still standing. If the fire didn't spread widely through it, the entertainment room should still be fine.

Nothing moved around the house other than tiny wisps of smoke trailing upward into the sky. Owen watched for a moment longer and determined he was near the window that they had used before to enter. He stood and began moving, angling slightly deeper into the woods away from the house as he moved to the right, in the direction of the window.

After traveling several yards, Owen changed direction and walked straight toward the house, certain of his location. He kept his eyes constantly shifting, moving from the approaching grass and building to the trees around him and the woods behind him. Nothing stirred, nothing moved and no sound reached his ears. In the absence of everything signifying life, Owen found himself growing more and more tense, his muscles knotting painfully as he expected an attack.

When the attack did come, it came from his rear and left. Owen realized the creatures were there when he heard the sudden snapping of twigs and rustling of leaves. The mutants made no other noise, no growls or cries. He spun and saw five of them rushing through the woods, closing to within several dozen feet of him. Owen sprinted toward the house and as he broke free of the woods he heard other creatures take up the pursuit. They emerged slightly ahead of him, coming out of the trees like ants flooding from their tunnels.

Owen changed direction, turning to the house itself and searching for a door or open window. There was nothing; he was on the backside of the building. Without thinking, he increased his speed and raced along the wall of the house, keeping one eye on the lead creature approaching him from the front. It was angling in from his right, its claws already poised for a sweeping blow. Owen waited until it was almost on him then quickly stopped running and cut in toward the creature. The mutant swiped at him as it passed, unable to stop for its momentum and Owen ducked. He felt the wind of the claws' passage rustle his hair and then he was running again, ahead of all of the creatures and turning a corner of the house.

Luckily the ground on the other side of the house was devoid of threats and he continued to run as he searched for a way in. Ahead of him was a small covered boardwalk that led from the house down to the beach. Logic told Owen that a door would be there, so he turned toward it.

The door was there, a heavy wood and glass door with painted designs on the glass. Owen didn't dare look behind him; he could hear the creatures as they closed the distance to him. He prayed that the door was unlocked, knowing that if it weren't he would have to crash through the glass and risk further wounds.

The door opened easily and Owen whipped around and slammed it shut, not seeing a locking mechanism, then raced down the hallway. Doors on either side of him passed unnoticed. He didn't have time to enter one, and the creatures were too close to him to be fooled by such a disappearing ruse. Just as he neared the end of the hallway, he heard the glass shatter as the first creature connected with it. Owen didn't look back and turned right at the end of the hall.

He found himself in the atrium with the fountain. A small surge of hope dared flare in his thoughts and he plunged into the greenery, raced past the water and then down the corridor that would take him to the entertainment room. The air in the atrium was thick with a grey haze from the fire, and the smoke burned Owen's nostrils and lungs as he ran. Over the roar of the fountain he couldn't hear the pursuit, but knew it was still there. Having him in such small quarters, the creatures wouldn't abandon their chase. They would hunt him to the end now, and when they caught him they would take him to one of the rooms and use him as a food source for as long as the meat would last.

Despite the pain in his body and the burning in his lungs, Owen redoubled his effort as he ran down the hallway and burst into the entertainment room. He slowed then stopped as his foot kicked something, sending it clattering across the floor. He looked down and saw one of the red flares that had been knocked free during their capture. He grabbed it then turned to find the keys.

He spotted them on the floor, the yellow floats catching his eyes. Just as his fingers closed on them, he heard the growls behind him and knew the creatures had found him.

Refusing to look at them, Owen held the keys tightly and sprinted toward the exit, taking the doorway and hall that he and Jessica had used after first meeting. The creatures were after him in an instant. Owen ran for his life, and when he reached the exit door he plowed through it, sending the door slamming into the wall and then rebounding back closed. Owen searched the landscape, and tried to remember which direction he needed to take. He ran through the sandy tunnel created by the hedges on either side of him and then turned sharply right at the end, angling toward the beach and back to the house rather than deeper into the woods and the direction of the abandoned boat.

Can't believe I'm actually going to do this, he thought as he ran. The beach angled lower than the house for a short distance and he looked up at it as he traveled the length, expecting to see the creatures leaping from windows. He heard his pursuers banging through the door and wondered if he would have a few seconds to clear the beach and get back to the house before they realized which direction he had gone. A wooden staircase led up from the sand to the house and he took the steps two at a time.

He approached the front of the main house for the first time. On the porch, a wide wooden structure with only two steps leading up to it, he paused to catch his breath. He could hear the creatures' howls but couldn't tell which direction they came from. Not wanting to be caught resting when they finally discovered he had doubled back to the house, Owen stood and entered through the front door.

A low growling greeted him as he closed the door behind him. He looked up and saw coming across the entryway was Dixon, his eyes glinting in the dull light of the room. Owen darted a glance to the hallway beyond the thing that had been his friend and confirmed that his goal lay along it.

Dixon leapt, his claws extended and hooked. Owen charged low and caught Dixon around the upper thighs. He felt the creature's claws rake across his lower back, the pain searing. Owen lifted and thrust upwards, throwing Dixon over his shoulders. The mutant crashed to the floor with a sickening crunch and howled in pain. Owen twisted around and kicked the thing hard in the ribs. One of Dixon's arms was broken, the hand hanging down as if attached by a second wrist joint.

Despite the wound, Dixon started to climb to his feet and Owen planted another kick in his gut, then dropped to his knees atop the creature. Blind fury drove him, images of Jessica being ripped apart, the band members being tortured and stripped of their flesh while still alive. Owen punched Dixon hard in the face, scraping his hand across the creature's razor sharp teeth. Dixon flailed at Owen with his free claw, beating and scraping against Owen's body with a fury born of survival instinct.

Owen plunged his thumbs into Dixon's eyes and pressed, squeezing as hard as he could against the demonic orbs. Dixon howled in pain, the scream rising in pitch and volume as Owen increased his pressure. Finally Owen felt the orbs pop, his thumbs sliding further into the ocular cavities as blood and fluid oozed around his hands. Owen pushed until he couldn't push any further. Beneath him, Dixon thrashed and roared, his body bucking and spasming. After several seconds he lay still, and Owen kept his thumbs deep inside the creature's skull for several moments more until he was certain that the stillness wasn't a ruse, that the creature was, in fact, dead.

When he climbed off the body, Owen swooned with nausea, turned away and vomited on the floor. He heaved until there was nothing left, then choked and gagged. When he had regained his composure, he wiped his hands on Dixon's ragged clothing and stood. He staggered down the hallway, leaving the body behind.

Owen passed once more into the dining room, then into the kitchen. The bodies of the three creatures he, Jessica and Dixon had killed still lay in twisted heaps on the cold floor. Owen passed over them, refusing to look too closely at them.

Instead, he pushed deeper into the kitchen to the set of four large stoves. The units were huge, the kind anyone would expect to see in a restaurant kitchen, clearly suited for cooking vast amounts of food for a large contingent of guests. Despite his pain and thrumming heartbeat, Owen grinned.

The stoves were all gas.

He quickly twisted the dials on all the surface units, turning them so that the gas hissed out yet the igniters did not engage. He slammed open the ovens and turned their dials to the same setting.

The hissing filled the room as the gas flooded the air. Owen coughed as the gas tickled his throat, and he rushed out of the kitchen, propping the door open with one of the dining room chairs as he left. He paused in the dining room, bent over, one hand on the table as he caught his breath, but his reprieve was short lived as the smell of the gas flowed out of the kitchen carried by the air currents of the central air system. Owen stood and moved on.

As he approached the front door, he heard the crashing sounds of other creatures entering the house, closing the distance toward him. Owen reached the massive door, placed on hand on the large handle and waited.

He listened to the sounds of the creatures approaching. They arrived from the hallway that led to the atrium. At the sight of their quarry, the creatures bellowed in rage and hunger and charged for him, oblivious to the gas that hung in the air. Owen stood and backed quickly to the open door, waited only a fraction of a second longer as the first creature reached within twenty feet of him, then popped the cap off of the flare and ignited it. The red flame was still sputtering to life as the flare flew through the air, angling toward the dining room.

Owen turned and ran harder and faster than he had ever ran in his entire life. The explosion came not as a thunderous roar but rather as a single, heavy blast that seemed to suck all the air inward like a giant taking a deep breath. The roar sounded as the giant exhaled, a hard, heavy and fast hot wind that pushed Owen to the ground. He felt the heat all across his body and twisted around to his back, fearing that his clothes had caught fire.

The house was engulfed in flames, pieces of the structure flying through the air. Wood and concrete fell all around, thudding into the brush nearby. Owen scrambled to his feet and began running deeper into the woods as he tried to avoid being killed by falling debris.

He was certain that several of the creatures had died in the blast, but had no idea how many. As he ran, he wiped his hands on his clothing almost obsessively in an attempt to clean them from the blood that had come from Dixon's head.

The woods passed by him almost as if the trees were curious spectators rushing to the scene of the explosion. Owen ran almost blindly, stumbling through the brush as he fought back tears. He turned and angled to his right. After a distance, his legs buckled and he crashed to the forest floor. He stayed there, on his hands and knees, sucking in huge breaths of air, tears and snot and sweat pouring from his face.

Eventually he regained control of his breathing. He had to decide where to go, where a boat could be that would match up to one of the keys he had. He tried to picture the island and locations he had already visited, but couldn't think where else a boat or other craft would be housed. A thought occurred to him and he dug in his pocket for the keys, hoping one of them would have some label on it to give him a clue.

His pockets were empty.

Owen stared at his empty hands, disbelieving. Frantically he dug through his pants, even reaching down into the crotch, feeling desperately for the keys. They were gone. A fresh round of tears came as he realized that the keys must have been knocked free when Dixon attacked him. Fear and sadness overwhelmed him then, and Owen buried his face in his hands and cried, hard and long for his predicament.

Eventually, through a great force of will he managed to calm himself, to steady his breath. He snorted loudly, spat out a wad of phlegm and wiped his face with his hands. Okay, he thought, it's the band's boat or nothing. He would find something to paddle with, and if there was nothing, he would swim to the yacht, wounds and sharks or none. His time on this island was over.

Owen picked himself up, spat one more time and then looked around to gauge his surroundings. Then he started jogging. Somewhere through the dense forest, waiting patiently was the boat. Owen only hoped that the hole that was in it hadn't let in so much water that it was useless.

14

Smoke moved in quickly, filled the air, overtaking him despite the distance he had put between himself and the house. The smoke was thick and it burned his throat and lungs. It was everywhere, unavoidable and oppressive. Owen ran stumbling through it, coughing loudly, barely able to see for the thick haze and the tears in his burning eyes.

He ran with his arms outstretched, hands gripping and pushing aside trees to avoid colliding bodily with them. Limbs and large leaves slapped at him, raking across his forearms and occasionally landing a blow to the side of his face.

Owen stopped for a moment, holding onto a large tree and bent forward coughing. "Christ, why did I blow up the house?" he grumbled between fits. He turned his head upward and saw, in the direction from which he had come, a thick column of black smoke rising into the air. The whole place was on fire now, he realized. It occurred to him briefly that smoke of that magnitude would have to attract attention from other people, someone on the main island and that if he could make it to the beach, it would only be a matter of time before they came to investigate.

But, he rationalized, while that was most likely true, it would mean staying on the island with no food or water for an unknown period of time with an unknown number of creatures still on the island. While he was certain that he had killed several of them with the initial blast, and was hopeful a few more died in the ensuing inferno, he was realistic enough to count on their survival.

As if in direct response to his thoughts, a tortured scream tore through the haze. Others joined it, further in the distance. Owen spit on the ground. "Fuck," he whispered, then started running again through the grey haze. This time when he ran, he moved with more of a purpose, a sense of direction. His mind calculated where he was in relation to the main house and where the band's yacht had docked. His legs carried him through the brush, up and down small peaks and valleys.

He was three steps past the stream before he realized he had run into and out of it. Owen skidded to a halt, his legs and feet soaked and dripping water. His heart lurched at the prospect of what had just happened and he felt his chest constrict with fear. "Oh fuck me." He stared helplessly at his legs and feet. He closed his eyes and waited for the change, imagining it to be horrendous, painful ripping and twisting of his joints and muscles.

Nothing happened. Owen looked back at the stream. Had he managed to find the only stream on the island not infected with whatever virus had turned the other people on the resort into killing machines, twisting their minds as well as their bodies? No, based on what he and Jessica had found underground, he knew that wasn't possible. It had to be that the only way the water affected you is if you ingested it. That was why Dixon had changed, and why the others had changed. They had been drinking the water, either mixed in their drinks or as the ice cubes. Since Owen and Jessica both had been drinking with no ice, they hadn't changed.

Later, he told himself. He'd consider it all later, when he was on the yacht, miles from the island and drinking a beer watching the sunset. He took another deep breath, coughed and started again, picking up speed as he passed through the trees.

As he neared the beach, the smoke began to thin and the air grew lighter. Having heard no sounds of pursuit despite the earlier screams, Owen slowed to a walk and approached the end of the trees slowly. He scanned the surrounding woods and the short patch of sand that was visible from where he stood. The memory of the ambush at the main house was still fresh in his mind, so he walked with caution.

He stopped at the edge of the forest and crouched at the base of a palm tree. He took several deep breaths to help clear his lungs. The smoke thinned completely out on the beach, and was visible only as a faint haze high up near the tops of the trees. Owen turned his attention to the stretch of sand and the water beyond. To his right was the rock the creatures had used to kill the band members, and almost directly in line with him was the pier with the boat still attached. The boat still sat low in the water, but from where he observed, Owen couldn't tell if it had sunk any more since he had last looked at it.

Waves lapped steadily at the shore, the noise normally a calming sound, now gave a feeling of dread. Owen knew what was going to happen. He was going to actually have to get back into the ocean again, a task that brought him a great deal of fear despite his leap into the rough waters the night before to save Jessica. Confront your fears is what the popular consensus was, but confronting them just one time generally wasn't enough to overcome them. He stared past the boat to the deeper blue of the ocean and knew he was going to have to get back into it.

And this time, there were sharks.

He ran through the plan again in his mind. He would untie the boat and push it out away from the dock. He would then climb in, find something to use as a paddle, and then propel the boat as fast and as hard as he could straight for the yacht. At some point, whether that was before or after the sandbar he wouldn't know, the boat would most likely give in to its wounds and sink. At that point, Owen would be forced to abandon ship and swim the rest of the way.

His eyes shifted upward slightly, and focused on the pale green water dozens of yards off shore where the sandbar was. He remembered the band's boat having no problems crossing over it when they arrived, so it made sense that he may be able to do the same if the boat now held up.

The sound of the waves seemed to swell in his ears, as if the water was beckoning him, begging him to jump in. To Owen it sounded as hungry for his flesh as the creatures had been. He felt a breeze at his back, smelled a renewal of the smoke in the air and coughed. He thought for a moment that the island itself was trying to push him into the waiting maw of the ocean. All at once, so close to his potential salvation from the terrors he had endured, Owen wanted nothing more than to collapse onto the sand and sleep, to let the pains simply drain away as he fell into sleep. He looked down at the sand, the mixture of pearl white granules with the darker flecks of soil from the forest. It would be so easy, just to lie down for a moment, to close his eyes and relax. He nodded dumbly, yes, that's all; just lie down and rest for a few minutes and then get up and try the boat.

His eyes were pulled away from the sand by a thrashing sound several yards to his right. He reacted slowly, as if he were just waking. The sound of leaves tearing and limbs snapping seemed to have no effect on his daze. It took Owen several seconds to realize that what had caused the commotion—what he was looking at—were three creatures who had torn through the forest and spilled out onto the sand in an escape from the fire and smoke. One of them, he could see, was badly burned, the mottled skin now black and charred, broken apart by jagged cracks of bright pink and red where the flesh beneath had blistered and now shone through. The burned creature made mewling noises as it crawled across the sand toward the ocean. Its companions raced forward toward the water as well, though neither of them seemed burned.

None of them had noticed Owen, crouched on the edge of the forest. However, as they approached the water, Owen's mind seemed to click on and he shrunk even lower. His heartbeat sped as he realized that even this last task of getting off the island wouldn't be met easily. Not that getting past the sharks would be a picnic, he reminded himself.

The creatures plunged into the ocean on the opposite side of the pier from the capsized boat. Owen watched them rolling around in the surf, heard the agonized screams of the wounded one as the salt water bashed against his burns, and estimated that they were probably twenty or thirty feet from the pier. It would be close, he thought, and turned his attention back to the boat. It was still moored to the pier, but he believed that if he could get to the water, he could put the boat and pier between himself and the creatures, and then somehow free the lines that held the boat fast.

Of course, if there was no paddle, or if once moving the boat wouldn't travel more than a few feet before fully succumbing to its wounds, nothing would really matter. The creatures would most likely see him. If he couldn't get at least several yards offshore, he had no chance at all. Of course, that's assuming the fuckers can't swim, he thought. He watched them for a moment longer, then stood and ran in a low crouch as if he were a soldier advancing under intense fire, toward the ocean.

The water was warm against his skin, but burned when it lapped against his dozens of cuts. Owen crouched low in the surf against the boat and grimaced against the pain. His entire body felt as if it had been caught on fire, the salt water invading the open wounds. The pain made him dizzy and he shook his head to clear away the nausea. Later, he thought, later I can get sick and vomit and pass out and all that. He focused on the boat in front of him. The rope that held the boat steady was on the pier side, attached to a cleat on the port bow. Owen searched for an easy way to board. There was none, so he settled on pushing himself up and sliding over the side of the boat.

It took a massive effort to board the vessel, and he lay for a few seconds on the floor of the boat, in several inches of water, and attempted to catch his breath. When he felt sufficiently less winded, he rolled over and began looking for a paddle in the sides of the boat, in the floor.

His hands pushed past various debris, cigarette boxes, a beer can, pieces of paper, but he found no paddle. He was about to give up, turning to look behind the pilot's seat, when his fingers brushed across something under the water. Initially he pulled back his hand in fear, but something in his brain recognized what he had touched. He reached forward one more time then closed his fingers around the object and pulled it free of the water. In his hand was a silver key attached to a small, bent key ring. Owen nearly screamed in relief, clamping his mouth shut only at the last minute and stifling the noise. The key must have fallen from the ignition switch or from the pilot's hands when the creatures attacked the band. Owen gripped the key tightly as if needing to feel it digging into his palm in order to maintain its reality.

Carefully he crawled to the cleat on the pier and began working on the rope. The mooring line was soaked and difficult to manipulate. It took several seconds for Owen to realize that he wasn't battling a knot, but instead a rope that was simply wrapped around the cleat. He pulled on the rope, forcing the boat closer to the pier. Once there was slack in the line, he quickly unraveled its criss-crossed layers.

As he worked, his eyes moved constantly from the rope to the creatures thrashing about in the surf. The one that had been burned had retreated from the water and collapsed into a shuddering, whimpering mass on the sand. The others continued to beat at the water as if it were attacking them. Owen couldn't figure out what about the water bothered them, or if that weren't the case, what on their bodies had they not cleansed yet. He returned his attention to the rope, deciding that it was impossible to discern the behavior patterns of things that had once been human but now had completely devolved to basic murderous animals.

How that was any different from "normal" humans, he mused and gave a sarcastic chuckle. The laughter surprised him and he paused in his work and blinked several times in response.

The rope came free and he lowered it quietly to the water. He doubted the sound of it tapping against the pier as he let go would be heard over the waves and the noises the creatures made, but he decided that at this point he would not push his luck. Instead he rolled over and crawled to the pilot's seat. He slowly inserted the ignition key into the slot. He was about to turn it, his jaw clenched tightly in anticipation, when he paused and looked up.

The bow of the boat faced the beach. If he cranked the boat and it fired, he risked the motor pushing the unsecured boat into the sand. At that point everything would be over. He had to turn the boat around. Moving as quietly as he could, Owen slid back into the water and pulled the boat away from the pier, turning it out to sea.

The sound of the motor hitting the wood of the pier sounded like a gunshot to him. He froze, his heart pounding. Had they heard it? He strained to hear over the thrumming of his heart and the waves around him. He couldn't tell if the creatures were still in the surf or not. Quickly he worked to finish the turn, and within seconds the boat was facing out to sea. There was a soft sucking sound as the hole in the frame began to take in more water and Owen knew he wouldn't have much time.

The boat rocked in the waves and he once again climbed over the side and into the boat. It was then that he heard the growling of the creatures. He looked up and saw that the boat had drifted a few feet from the pier, but now the two healthy creatures stood on the wood planks staring down at him. Owen maintained eye contact with them, staring deep into their horrible eyes as he moved to the pilot's seat and gripped the wheel and key. With each movement he made, the creatures seemed to shift in response, crouching low and preparing to leap to the boat. Owen swallowed hard, a thick knot lowering in his throat.

He twisted the key. The engine coughed, coughed, fired. A thick plume of purple-grey smoke drifted up and between the boat and pier and in that moment Owen pushed the throttle forward. The creatures leapt as he did that and Owen fell backward into the chair as the boat thrust out into the ocean. As it moved forward, its progress was sluggish and Owen knew instantly that he wouldn't make it too far.

The boat rocked violently as one of the creatures landed on the stern. Owen looked back and saw the second thrashing in the water where it had landed, having missed the boat. However, the other one moved quickly to him, its claws open and mouth gaping to tear him apart. Owen whipped the steering wheel back and forth and the boat responded with sickening thickness. However, it was enough to throw the creature off balance. To Owen's disappointment, the creature didn't go overboard, but rather fell to its knees. It began to stand when Owen grabbed the nearest object, the fire extinguisher, and threw it at the beast. The extinguisher caught its target in the chest and the creature gripped it as if it were a football being handed off, just before toppling over the motor and into the white wake.

Owen looked for a moment longer, hoping to see red froth in the water indicating that the creature had come in contact with the propeller, but saw none. Before he saw the beast's head rise above the water, he turned his attention back to steering the boat. The controls had become much more difficult as the hole in the frame admitted more water. The wheel began to shake in his hands, and he could tell the front of the boat had begun to nose lower to the water.

Ahead of him, approaching quickly, was the pale green water that marked the sandbar. Owen steered directly for the yacht that was anchored roughly twenty or thirty yards away from the far edge of the sandbar. He pushed the throttle as far as it would go and felt the boat lurch in response. With the increased speed, the steering wheel became violent and Owen had to hold it with both hands to manage it. Even then, his control was tenuous at best.

The nose of the boat passed over the front edge of the sandbar and Owen let out a yell of triumph. He had a chance here, he realized. He hadn't bottomed out and the boat hadn't sunk low enough from the water intake to force him out. If he could keep up the momentum for only a few more yards—

The impact of the motor on the sandbar jarred him. The boat stopped instantly and Owen was thrown forward into the steering wheel. The wheel hit his chest and knocked all the wind from him. The impact felt like being hit by a baseball bat wielded by a major leaguer. Stars swam before Owen's vision and the edges of the world became black and fuzzy. He blinked hard and shook his head. Slowly, both his vision and his breath came back to him. With them came the pain. His chest seared with pain every time he drew in a deep breath, forcing him to take short shallow ones. The crash had reopened some of his wounds. Blood flowed down his arms and torso.

He sat back in the seat and tried to collect himself. The boat shifted beneath him and he looked up to see the front of it dropping slowly into the water. Ocean water streamed over the sides and filled the boat like marauding soldiers storming a castle whose last defenses had gone down. With a curse, Owen stood and climbed over the side of the boat, dropping down into the warm ocean water.

Immediately fear claimed him like a cold blanket wrapped about his body. He was in the ocean again. The other night when he had jumped in to save Jessica, he hadn't been able to see the water much, hadn't been aware of what was going on because of the storm and his sudden need to save her. In fact, after it was over, Owen found he didn't remember much after his initial leap into the water.

But now, he stood in chest high water, clearly able to see everything. The boat behind him, the blurry sand beneath his feet, the water all around him. To his left, where the yacht was, the water turned a much deeper blue. To his right it deepened for only a short distance before becoming light again as it washed against the shore. He could see the burnt creature lying on the sand, unmoving. One of the other two—the one that had missed its leap onto the boat, he assumed—had managed to climb back onto the beach and stood watching him. Its companion was nowhere to be seen, and Owen could only hope that it had drowned and was now at the bottom of the ocean.

Something tickled his calf, then the shins of both legs. Owen yelled—then winced immediately as his chest reminded him not to make noises—and looked down into the water. He could see everything relatively clearly and watched as tiny fish, no more than three inches long darted at his legs. "Go on, bastards," he wheezed. "I'm not your damned dinner."

He looked at the yacht. Twenty or thirty yards. Not far. From where he stood, it looked like a mile. And with the wounds on his body seeping blood into the water, it would be the longest distance of his entire existence. Owen tried to muster courage, tried to manage a thought of someone who may have endured worse than he was about to attempt, but all he could come up with was people storming the beaches at Normandy. Well, he thought, if they could do that, I can do this.

"Fuck I don't want to, though," he said. He turned back and looked at the creature still on the island. He saw the billowing black smoke rising from the woods, a tall and thick tower of it thrust into the air like a fist. He lowered his gaze to the creature, raised his arm and extended his middle finger. Then, despite his chest pains, he yelled, "Fuck you!" The creature yelled in response, and Owen kept his finger raised defiantly for several seconds.

Then he turned and plunged forward into the deeper water. The feeling of nothing beneath his feet took him immediately and he almost panicked. Then he began swimming, moving in steady strokes and trying desperately not to splash the surface. He had read somewhere that sharks, in addition to blood, would be attracted to splashing.

The distance to the yacht diminished slowly, and Owen maintained steady eye contact on the boat. He didn't want to look away from it, afraid that if he did, it would disappear for ever and he'd be stranded in the ocean with no way to get out.

He felt the first shark pass beneath him, a thick and solid mass in the water. The ocean seemed to push him up slightly as the bulk of the fish moved under him. Owen kept his pace, continued to move his arms and legs, kept his head above the water and eyes locked on the prize.

Movement to his right caught his peripheral vision and he risked a glance over. The tip of a slate grey tail fin sliced the water half a dozen yards away, then dipped below the surface. Still, Owen continued to swim. He was now three quarters of the way to the yacht. He could see the silver ladder on the side of the boat where he would have to climb up.

Something big and alive bumped against his thigh, pushed him several feet to the left. Owen yelled, tasted seawater and spit it out immediately. Fuck, fuck, fuck, what was I thinking? This is insane.

I'm going to die out here, a few feet from the boat. One of those big bastards is going to come up and drag me under like that chick in Jaws. I may have a moment where I pop back up and breathe quickly and panicky, but most likely I'll just go down, down, down while it chews on me.

He felt something hit his left foot, pain immediate and intense. Owen screamed and kicked with his right foot and connected with something solid. He could feel the burning pain in his left foot as he continued to kick. He knew he had been bitten, but how severe would have to wait. Owen kicked and swam with everything he had, forgetting about the no splashing theory.

When his hand touched the hard surface of the yacht, he cried out again, thinking he had placed his hand on the body of a giant shark waiting to eat him. He looked up, saw the boat and lunged forward to catch the bottom rung of the ladder. His fingers gripped it, but another large body bumped into him and he fell free of the rung. He bobbed and twisted in the bloody water, searching for the next attack. Seeing no fins and deciding that it would come from beneath when it did come, he lunged for the ladder again.

After two tries he caught it and pulled with every ounce of his being. He brought his feet to the side of the boat and pushed, using them as extra leverage. His left foot flared in white-hot pain and he had to let it dangle as he pushed with his right and pulled with both hands. After several slow, agonizing seconds, he managed to get high enough to grip the second rung. From there he pulled to the third with shaking arms. His shoulders felt as if they would erupt from the strain but after the third rung he was able to hook his right leg onto the ladder and begin to climb up.

The deck, when he reached it and fell down, gasping and crying with relief, had never felt so good.

15

Owen lay on the deck of the yacht, feeling the rough surface of the boat against his skin. He held his eyes closed and focused on breathing, on slowing his heartbeat. Beneath the pounding of his blood in his ears, he could hear the faint sloshing of water against the boat's hull and—even more faintly—the whisper of waves on the island.

The wounds on his foot, chest and shoulders burned and throbbed with every pulse of his heart, and he knew he had to tend to them soon, but for the moment Owen couldn't move. He needed to take the moment to center himself, to breathe for a few minutes after what he had just been through.

Get your ass up, his mind seemed to bark at him. You can rest later. You can sleep all you want after we're under way, several miles out and this island is nothing more than a miniscule speck on the horizon and several hundred thousand dollars of therapy in your future. Get the fuck up.

Owen opened his eyes, squinted in the harsh light of the cloudless sky, and struggled to sit. The very act was a feat of unimaginable strength, and his left foot screamed in protest the entire time. Once upright, he tucked his right foot beneath his left leg and bent forward to inspect the shark bites.

Under the blood coating his foot he saw in a faint semi-circle pattern a series of five half inch long black gashes where the animal's teeth had punctured his skin. They didn't seem to be too deep, and he pictured the shark simply finding his foot in its maw, and just before the animal could bite down fully to see what it had gotten, Owen's foot had slipped free.

Owen turned his attention from the bloody appendage and looked at the boat around him. He had boarded near the rear of the boat. The aft deck was a large space with a bench and deck mounted chairs along the section of the boat where Owen was accustomed to seeing motors mounted. A small wooden table sat between the chairs and the bench, and held three green beer bottles. A silver railing ran around the edges of the boat and around a corner, encircling the entire craft, he assumed. To his right was a large sliding glass door with tinted, reflective glass that led into the main cabin area. Owen could tell there was a second level to the boat, and assumed the entrance to that would be found inside.

Never having been on a yacht, Owen didn't know much about them, other than they were usually furnished with the latest technology as well as whatever other amenities their spoiled, rich owners insisted upon. However, he felt confident that there would be a first aid kit found aboard somewhere. If a band either owned or rented this, their manager would insist on having medical supplies around for when they drunkenly damaged their bodies.

He staggered to his feet, pulling himself up using the silver railing, and balanced as best he could on the gently swaying ship. He then hobbled toward the sliding glass door, hoping that the crew and band had left it unlocked when they had made that fateful trip to shore. As he reached the door, he wondered if anyone was left aboard, but thought back to the crew he had seen accompanying the band and felt certain that all aboard had gone to the island. As computerized as these boats were, it wouldn't take more than one or two people to operate it.

Before he entered the cabin, he turned and threw a look across the water to the island. The beach was deserted save for the one creature that had been burned. It lay in the same crumpled heap it had been in when he left shore, and Owen assumed it was dead. The other creature who had watched him swim to the yacht had disappeared, and for a moment Owen had a horrifying thought that it had returned to the main house for keys to a jet ski craft or other smaller boat, that it had retained enough of its human thought processes to remember where a craft could be found.

But the thick wall of black smoke pouring up from the trees told him that the houses were destroyed, there would be no going into them for anyone. He inhaled deeply and was surprised that he could smell the smoke, oily and dark.

The tinted glass door slid open with hardly a whisper of sound, and Owen stepped inside the cabin. He was several steps away from the door when he stopped abruptly, his eyes going wide in shock. He looked back at the door, and then down at the thick red pools of blood he had tracked along the plush white carpet. It took him a moment to realize that it didn't matter if the carpet got ruined; he had more important things to be concerned with. He chuckled at his reaction and continued through the quarters.

The room he had entered was a living room of sorts. Thick white carpet lined the floor, deep rosewood cabinets and walls surrounded him. Recliners and couches that were probably more expensive than his car were arranged to his left. To the right of where he limped was a bar, littered with bottles of hard liquor and beer. Most of the bottles were empty, several lay on their sides. He noticed one bottle of Vodka had fallen over and lay on the carpet, resting against the wood of the bar. A musky thickness in the air told him that the band members had smoked within the confines of the cabin.

Ahead of him stood a spiral staircase, also made of the deep colored wood. Owen paused at the base of it and looked around. He saw more empty alcohol bottles in the space occupied by the couches and recliners, a large flat screen television recessed into one wall to the right of the door he had entered through, but nowhere did he see anything that would indicate a first aid kit.

Upstairs he found himself standing in a large kitchen with hardwood floors and deep green granite countertops. A massive stainless steel refrigerator seemed to dominate one wall near the stove. Owen's stomach grumbled at the sight of it. He licked his dry lips and promised himself that as soon as his foot and other wounds were tended to, he would destroy whatever food could be found in the large box.

Beyond the kitchen was a bathroom. In the drawers to either side of the sink, he found a box of Band-Aid's, a roll of gauze and antiseptic cream. He stared at them, then—brushing the two empty beer bottles that stood sentry to the left of the sink into the trash can—he placed his wounded foot onto the counter and studied it. No, he thought, Band-Aid's won't cut it here. Got to find a needle and thread. His heart lurched at the thought of the pain to come when he sutured his wounds, but Owen swallowed hard and continued his search.

In one of the bedrooms, he found a small roll of red thread. It was buried in a drawer filled with various odds and ends. It took him several minutes longer to find a needle. He gathered them, along with a cigarette lighter that he found on a bedside table in one of the four bedrooms, and returned to the bathroom. The lighting overhead was recessed, but bright enough to illuminate his wounded foot substantially. He cleaned it with warm water, wincing at the sting. Next he threaded the needle and sterilized it with the lighter, running the flame along the metal barb for several seconds. A bottle of Advil produced three brown pills. He swallowed them with a handful of water from the sink.

Then, taking a deep breath and praying that he wouldn't pass out, he inserted the needle into the skin of his foot and began to sew himself up.

The control deck of the yacht looked like a perfect blend of rich comfort and alien technology. The white carpet continued through the space as did the rich wood paneling. Owen walked slowly into the room, wincing with each step. The sutures seemed to hold, and while it hurt him worse than anything he'd ever experienced in his life, Owen had managed to finish cleaning all of his wounds. There were two gashes on his upper body, one on his left shoulder and one across his chest that needed to be sewn up, and he had tended to them as well.

Now he stood just inside the doorway of the control room, clutching an oversized T-shirt that he had found along with a pair of blue jeans slightly too large for his body. He stared at the controls across from him. Mounted on the floor in front of the controls were two leather bound captain's chairs on swivel poles. The controls themselves seemed to be mostly computer screens, all of them glowing a soft blue. From where he stood he could make out icons and writing on the screens but couldn't read any of it with clarity. The chair on the left was positioned in front of a small steering wheel, and he assumed that was the main pilot's chair.

Owen sniffed and walked slowly across the floor and sat in one of the leather seats. He let his eyes drag across the screens, the dials and buttons set within the mahogany dash. One hand rose and rubbed absentmindedly across his chin. The screens seemed to be simple LCD displays of the various controls used to power and steer the ship as well as manipulate various features throughout.

A large screen mounted into the control panel just on the other side of the steering wheel glowed green instead of blue. Owen looked at it closely and saw that it was a radar screen. Images, jagged blurry lines, stretched in different directions from the center point. He assumed that the information displayed was differences in the ocean floor. He saw a large mass on the left side of the screen that looked like the island.

Another screen to the left of the wheel was divided into quadrants and showed different angles of the exterior of the boat. He saw the rear deck and the water beyond in one square, his left and right flanks in two others. The fourth quadrant gave a view that was difficult to discern, the screen dim and murky. It took him several seconds of staring at it to realize he was looking at a camera shot beneath the boat. He let out a soft breath, a chuckle and shook his head, then turned back to the main controls. To the right of the wheel were two silver handles with black grips. They were mounted side by side and he took them to be the throttles for the dual engines. He wondered briefly where the engines were located, since they weren't mounted to the rear of the vessel like normal boats.

Must be mounted within, and extend below the water or something, like a jet propulsion thing, he thought and let his fingers trace lightly over the black grips of the throttles. It seemed odd that everything was on within the boat but the motors didn't make any indication that they were on. He looked to the right of the throttles and saw a third screen, this one displaying a blue operating system page. He saw icons for power management, systems, navigation and several others that made no sense to him. However, around the screen there were no buttons or levers, no dials or switches. He couldn't see anything that would activate anything. Tentatively he reached out and touched the screen on the icon labeled Power Management. The screen flashed and changed displays to show animated diagrams of the two engines, one on each side of the monitor.

Owen looked at the diagrams and came to the conclusion that they provided power information on each engine when the engines were running. That way the crew could monitor heat levels or fuel flow or things of that nature as they passed through the water.

He gripped the throttles again and pushed them forward slightly, anticipating the sudden movement of the boat. Nothing happened. The levers moved smoothly forward, but the yacht didn't respond. He returned the throttles to their original position and looked back at the screen showing the engines. There was nothing on it to indicate how to power on the motors, and he couldn't figure out—no matter how many times and in what areas he tapped the screen—how to return to the starting screen.

Owen turned his attention to the rest of the dash, searching for anything that would indicate a power switch, a key ignition, anything. He found a door mounted in the ceiling that opened to reveal a black radio. Turning it on, he tried speaking into the small hand held microphone several times as he switched frequencies. He paused after every transmission but heard nothing. Finally, frustrated and exhausted, he let the microphone drop and dangle by its cord. He slumped into the chair and stared out through the angled glass over the bow of the ship and to the blue-green water beyond. He saw the island to the left but no creatures on the small patch of sand visible to him.

His eyes drifted to the video screens. Everything was still and quiet, as if he were looking at camera views of an alien landscape in the vacuum of space. "Nothing out there," he mumbled. He stepped down from the chair and moved toward the door. His steps dragged the floor as weariness settled on him. The exhaustion was heavy on his frame and as he passed through the door he had begun to hold onto every surface as he stepped forward.

He moved through the yacht and down to the deck. The salty air that pushed across and around the boat ruffled his hair and cooled his skin. Owen stood on the aft deck, feeling the wind tug at his baggy shirt and stared at the island. The motorboat he had used to escape the land was completely submerged, but even from where he stood he could see the dull grey of it against the lighter sand and water.

The island beyond was as still as if it were a painting of some tropical paradise. Paradise that continued to belch black smoke, he noticed and smiled. He took another long, steady look at the land, his eyes focusing on the crumpled heap of the dead burnt creature, the pier and the forest beyond. Nothing moved. After a while, he sighed deeply and turned back to the cabin. He needed food and rest. He knew he had to get the boat operational and get farther out to sea, but reasoned that the creatures most likely couldn't or wouldn't swim, and if they did, the sharks would have a field day with them. Despite being so close to such a horrible place, Owen knew that if he didn't eat and sleep soon, he would be unable to function at all at the controls of the boat. The last thing he needed to worry about was getting the engines started only to misdirect the boat and steer it toward the island, grounding it on the sandbar and damaging it beyond repair.

He climbed the spiral staircase, thinking of the anchor. He could pull it up and let the boat drift out to sea. But he reasoned that the anchor would be powered electronically. He had no clue which switch or button would operate it, and knew that there was no way he could manage to lift it manually. No, the anchor would have to wait a few more hours.

Owen reached the top of the stairs, shuffled through the kitchen and stopped at the large refrigerator. Inside he found more beer than he had consumed in any twelve-month period of his entire life, and a veritable cornucopia of food. He pulled out a plastic container of spaghetti, grabbed a beer and walked out of the kitchen to the closest bedroom.

He raked the empty bottles and ashtrays from the nightstand, and placed his food and beer on it. He looked around for an alarm clock, anything to set a timer so that he didn't sleep for an entire day, but found nothing. In the end, he settled for turning on the flat screen television mounted near the low ceiling. He hoped that at some point, the noise from it would rouse him from sleep.

The boat had satellite cable and Owen stared at the screen as he switched channels. The mere fact that he was able to watch such a multitude of stations, the normalcy of it all compared to what he had just experienced, seemed surreal to him. Almost at random he stopped changing the channels, stopping on a grainy, black and white episode of The Andy Griffith Show. He took a long drink from the beer and coughed immediately, spilling some of it down his chest. He slowed and drank again, then opened the container of food. Still standing, he began to eat, shoveling each bite into his mouth until it became difficult to chew. He forced himself to slow down, to take his time.

Once he got his emotions under control, Owen found that he filled up quickly. He put the half finished spaghetti on the nightstand and pulled back the covers to the bed. He pulled off his pants, then his shirt, wincing at the tenderness of his wounds. The stitches seemed to be holding well, and he climbed into bed.

In all his life, Owen had never felt anything as comforting, as good as the mattress beneath him and the sheets around him. He lay there for a moment, stretched out and basking in the coolness of the soft blankets. Then he began to cry as the images of Jessica and Dixon floated before him. They had gotten so close, and that they weren't there with him, Jessica especially, to feel such wonderful comfort pained him worse than the wounds he had suffered. Owen rolled to his side and cradled the extra pillow against his chest, buried his face in it and sobbed.

After a while, he slept.

A scream jerked Owen from sleep, and he sat up quickly, his heart racing, adrenaline tasting sour in his mouth. The scream was followed by a crash and another yell, then the sound of cheering. Owen's head moved around as he searched frantically for the source of the noise. He imagined a shattered flowerpot on a wooden table outside his door, and he felt his mouth go dry at the thought.

The screaming continued and Owen's eyes tracked upward to the television. The Jerry Springer show flickered across the large screen, and despite his recognition of the program, it took Owen several moments to realize that the source of the screams were the two women fighting on the stage. They seemed to be obsessed over the same man, a behemoth of a human too large for any single chair. Owen pulled his sight away and grabbed the remote and flicked off the set.

Complete dark settled over the room. Once again he felt a nervous creeping sensation, as if the blackness was alive and creeping along his skin, prickling the hairs on his arms as it moved in search for a way inside his body. To combat it he turned on the bedside lamp. Though not completely dispelled, the shadows were pushed to the far corners of the room where they crouched, waiting and hungry. Owen swung his legs out of bed and sat on the edge of the mattress for several seconds, breathing evenly and waiting for his heart to slow. He rubbed his eyes, yawned and forced himself to stand, despite the siren song of the warm covers and mattress to his back.

Shambling across the floor like a recently animated corpse, Owen made his way out of the room and toward the bathroom. When he was finished, he hesitated outside the doorway, wondering what to do next. He wondered what time it was, and rather than searching the boat for a functioning clock, he walked toward the spiral staircase. Down on the first floor, he moved to the deck, already aware of the general time of day despite the dark tinting on the glass. He slid the door open and stepped out into the warm night. This time the breeze was cool on his bare skin and the moonlight reflected off the water making the surface of the ocean look like diamonds scattered across black velvet.

The waves in the distance were louder than normal, and he assumed that meant the tide had come in. The knowledge still didn't tell him exactly what time it was, but he had gone for several days now without knowing the exact time, only reacting off of the position of the sun and the amount of light by which he could see.

He inhaled deeply and winced when his nose detected the faint scent of the fire on the island, the smoke still in the air. It was less now, and he assumed that the blaze had all but burnt out, clearly not spreading to the jungle surrounding the houses. He walked to the railing and stood to the right of the ladder. The silver rail was cool in his hands as he leaned forward, the water below inky blackness.

In the distance he could make out the pale thumbnail of the beach, the hulking dark shape of the forest beyond it. The moonlight illuminated the whitecaps of the waves as they boomed against the shore. In that moment Owen realized it was difficult to imagine the unspeakable horrors that had taken place on the shore, the lives lost, the people bent and twisted in mind and spirit and body as they had mutated. Now, standing on the safety of the yacht, knowing that he was to leave soon and would be able to return to the comfort of the large bed upstairs, Owen felt rage course through his body at the thought of the blood and destroyed lives he had managed to wade through.

The island, a tropical paradise, a lush escape from the so perceived horrors of the real world back home. He thought of the people there, scurrying about their lives, desperate to make a dollar or to get home in time to watch American Idol. People so concerned with whether or not their coffee has lactose-free creamer and not even remotely interested in the fact that all the while, Death hovers among them, flitting about through their ranks on the currents of the very air they breathe.

He blinked out of his reverie, looked down and realized how tightly he was gripping the railing. He relaxed his hands and thought, they don't know, they will never know. But I'll never take it for granted. He swallowed anger at himself when he thought back to his own considerations of suicide only a few days ago. Owen shook his head and began to turn back from the railing when something caught his eye.

He looked out over the water, leaning over the railing and squinting into the night. The object, whatever it had been, was gone, faded back into obscurity. If, he thought it had even been there to begin with. Despite being convinced that he had been imagining things, that his exhaustion was playing tricks with both his eyes and mind, Owen remained at his post, staring out across the water toward the island.

He turned his head from side to side, trying to catch a glimpse of the object out of his periphery. At times he thought he could just barely make it out, something low and wide in the water. Quickly he turned away from the railing and walked back to the sliding door of the cabin. Just inside, along the wall was a row of light switches. He flipped them all on, then quickly flipped one off as the lights in the cabin illuminated as well as the exterior lights of the ship. Once again he returned to the railing and found that he could really see no better, the lights of the ship penetrating the blackness only a few short yards.

Before he left the railing again, he looked down and noticed the green water lit from below as lights on the hull burned in their mounts. He walked back into the living area of the cabin and began rifling through cabinets. Finally he found a large, red, hand-held spotlight. He thumbed the switch on and marveled at the intense brightness of the beam that reached out and struck the far wall. Satisfied that the flashlight worked, he returned to the deck railing. He looked again without the aid of the spotlight, and was again rewarded with no definite visible sign of the object.

He took a breath and flipped on the light. The beam speared across the expanse of the water, a white arm punching through the abyss around him. It ended on the water, and Owen shifted his hand, bringing the light upward to bear on the object he had until that moment been unable to see fully.

As the strength drained from his body and the light's beam began to quiver, Owen stared at the motorless rowboat manned by three creatures, and wished that he had never been able to see it.

16

In the brilliant whiteness of the spotlight, the creatures looked pale, albino-like. Their eyes glowed as they crouched in the boat, holding onto the sides with clawed hands. One of the mutants operated the oars, her powerful arms sending the boat forward in bursts as it struggled to break past the sandbar.

Owen stared numbly at them, only barely wondering where they had found the boat. The boat sliced through the black water, the light from Owen's flashlight wavering on them like a pearly white tractor beam from a spacecraft. A soft chuckle of disbelief slipped past his lips and Owen felt himself teetering on the edge of madness. How could they? His mind reeled at the question and the dozens of potential answers.

Slowly the realization of what he was seeing, the reality of it, began to sink into his mind and spread outward through his thoughts. He felt his body coming alive, turning away from the approaching craft. The flashlight clicked off and the rowboat was immediately lost from view. Owen started toward the sliding door that he had left open. As he moved, he looked upwards at the sky. The velvety expanse was clear, broken apart only by the cold, watchful eyes of the stars. He thought that a horrendous thunderstorm should be breaking right now, so intense was the energy around him. If this were a movie or book, he thought, that's what would be happening. Lightning would be slicing apart the sky, the waves throwing everything off balance as he struggled to survive one last battle with the mutants.

The sky showed no hint of clouds though, and the seas remained calm. Owen hurried into the cabin. When he reached the spiral stairs, he was moving at a jog. He wondered how long he would have before they reached the boat. Then it occurred to him: they may get hung up on the sandbar, if their boat hit the sunken speedboat that he had abandoned, their progress may be slowed, if not thwarted altogether.

Fat chance, he thought, and continued his scramble for the pilot room. He slid into the chair mounted in front of the wheel and scanned the controls. His eyes slid over each dial and button several times before he realized that he was panicking, and, because so, giving his brain no time to focus. He blinked, took a deep breath and forced himself to slow down and inspect each control.

To his right, the screen still displayed the icons for power management and other functions. Owen licked his lips and leaned close to it, taking his time to read each icon. On the left hand side of the screen, very small and colored blue, he saw a tiny image of an anchor. He pressed it and the screen flickered, bringing up a new menu. He sighed with relief when he read the words, Anchor Utilization Menu across the top of the screen. There were varying controls for the anchor; too many, he thought. It seemed there were several things a person could do with the anchor other than simply raising and lowering it. It took him several seconds of scanning to find the "Raise Anchor" option. He pressed it and immediately felt a soft humming through the floor as the weight drew itself up into the hull of the ship.

"Now we're cooking with Crisco," he mumbled and looked around for a power button for the engines. He saw none, but knew there had to be something. Turning back to the screen he chose the Exit option and the monitor returned to the main screen. Owen took a moment away from the menu to look at the monitor that provided camera views. The one that pointed in the direction of the creatures was still dark, but he saw no evidence of the rowboat in any of the available camera angles. Afraid that they had reached the yacht at an angle not covered by the cameras, Owen had to fight an urge to run from the controls and look back over the aft deck. No, he commanded himself. Stay here. Get the boat moving. Once it's powered and away from the island, you can go check it out and see if you left them behind or not.

He turned back to the screen. Once again he went into Power Management, since a careful examination showed nothing else that could possibly be a command to turn on the engines. The last time he had looked at the screen he had been starving, dehydrated and exhausted. Now, fed and somewhat rested, his eyes were able to see the icon for Engine Power. He pressed it and was told to please wait, the engines needed time to power up and for any water that may have found its way inside to be bilged out.

Owen sat back in the chair, nervously chewing his lower lip as he stared at the camera views. He stood up and looked out a window, saw only blackness beyond. There was no telling where the creatures were. Again, he had to fight off the need to run downstairs and look for them. This time, just as he was losing the battle and beginning to slide out of the chair, a soft chime sounded and he looked to the monitor. The power management screen now displayed that the engines were properly functioning and powered up. Owen gripped the throttles and in his fear and excitement almost slammed them down at max power.

Instead he eased them forward and felt the boat respond all at once, like a massive elephant being commanded to move forward. He turned the steering wheel to the right several inches and increased the power, feeling the heaviness of the yacht moving forward effortlessly. In front of him, the ocean was as dark as pitch, the sky equally so.

Owen began another search of the controls, looking for anything that would power external lights. On a console overhead, just above the glass of the windshield, he found a row of silver switches. He flipped them, desperate to try anything and cried out with joy when the ocean in front of him lit up brilliantly.

He slapped the steering wheel happily and reached for the throttle. His hand faltered and stopped, fingertips touching the black grip of the levers. His smile died like a cancer patient withering away. Standing on the bow of the yacht, facing the windshield, was one of the three creatures.

Owen stared at the beast and it seemed to stare back at him, its eyes glowing with hunger in the brightness of the ship's lights. With the stunning quickness that the creatures had demonstrated on the island, the mutant darted toward the main cabin, ducking out of Owen's line of sight. Owen cursed and brought the throttles back to stop. The yacht continued to drift forward in the water. Certain that nothing lay ahead in the water that could cause damage to the boat, Owen turned from the controls and dashed out of the room.

He moved quickly, not wanting to sprint for fear that his momentum would take him into a room or around a corner occupied by one of the creatures and he would have no time to react. He passed bedrooms as he moved along the corridor, his eyes darting across each open doorway. Seeing nothing inside the rooms—but knowing that he should slow to make a more thorough inspection—Owen entered the kitchen. He paused next to the refrigerator and listened, straining his ears. From the floor below he heard the soft thumps of movement, and tried to determine how many creatures he was hearing.

Eventually he gave up on the attempts and stepped quickly to the counter where he plucked several gleaming knives from a magnetic rack. He began to tuck them into his waistband, but then realized he was wearing no pants. For several seconds he stared at his nude body, uncomprehending. How the fuck had he managed to lose his pants? For the life of him, he couldn't remember what had happened to the pants he had found on the boat. Then reasoning kicked in and he recalled stripping them off to sleep. Stepping quickly and quietly,

Owen darted back down to the master bedroom and slipped on his clothes.

Dressed, he tucked the knives into the belt of the pants and brandished a blade in each hand. Now that he felt suitably armed, he began moving along the hallway again, hunting. He stepped slowly, careful not to make any sudden motions. He felt fortunate that the boat was an expensive luxury yacht, for the floor made no squeaks or groans as he passed along its surface.

The kitchen opened before him again. He scanned it, ensuring that no creature had crept into it as he had dressed. The room was empty so Owen turned his attention to the spiral staircase. He stared at it, debating the best course of action. He thought that he would be able to descend without detection if he crouched and moved slowly. The handrails were not open, but rather solid wood that, when ascending or descending properly, would come to about his hips.

In his hands, the knives felt slippery and unstable. He quickly wiped his hands on his pants and reestablished a grip on the weapons, then crouched and began moving down the stairs. Three steps down was the first bend, the stairs angling sharply to the left. Owen tried to control his breathing as he wiggled down each step, keeping his legs close to his chest.

On the floor below him, the grunts and sounds of the creatures moving through the room continued. He heard glass breaking as they knocked empty beer bottles aside or threw objects across the room. He wondered why they would be spending so much time inspecting the room when it was clearly devoid of their quarry. Did they think there were others on the boat, possibly hiding in one of the cabinets or behind a piece of furniture? Owen closed his eyes and tried to picture the room. He couldn't remember seeing any other doors leading out of the space, but also knew that his mind hadn't been focusing on things entirely well since arriving on the yacht.

The scent of fetid breath pushed up the stairs and washed over his face. He opened his eyes and recoiled at the stench. His body tense, he waited. When the creature turned the corner, Owen was ready for it. The thing, he could no longer tell if it were a former employee or one of the guests of the island, the clothes had long ago ripped free, stood upright as it climbed the stairs. Owen surged forward and drove both knives deep into its body, sinking one in its chest and the other in its fleshy abdomen. The creature uttered a surprised grunt, and then toppled back and down the stairs.

The noise brought resounding growls from its companions, and Owen heard them moving toward the stairs. They pushed aside furniture as they moved, the chairs thudding dully on the floor. Owen turned and dashed back up the stairs, continuing to crouch. He wanted to keep himself as invisible as possible for as long as possible, to give him any extra edge. Behind and below him there was a commotion; heavy bangs and growls from the creatures as they tried to hurriedly negotiate over and around the body of their fallen comrade.

Owen reached the kitchen, pulled two more of the knives from his belt and turned left, moving along the hallway toward the pilot room. His mind raced, trying to push through his fear and exhaustion and formulate a plan. To either side of him were the bedrooms. They all had windows overlooking the ocean, but Owen didn't know if they opened or not. He didn't want to inspect them either, for fear of being trapped in one of the small rooms when the other two creatures entered.

Lacking any other options, he hurried to the control room. Just as he spun to shut the door, he saw two creatures in the kitchen, their twisted features scanning the room. One saw his movement at the end of the hall and shrieked. Both of the beasts sprinted the length of the hallway, their footsteps resounding through the small space like shotgun blasts. Owen slammed the door shut and threw the latch, then quickly backed away from the door. It began to shake in its frame as the creatures threw their bodies against it.

There was nothing in the room that he could see that would lend extra security to the door. Instead he turned his attention to finding an escape route. As he had feared, the windows in the room were all solid, secured in place and unable to be opened. The sounds of the creatures trying to break in grew in intensity and Owen thought he heard the sharp cracks of wood splintering intermingled with the thuds of flesh against door.

Moving quickly, he approached the radio compartment and grabbed the microphone as it dangled in the air from where he had left it. Again he twisted the knobs on the radio, saw the LED display light up. He grabbed the microphone and shouted into it.

"Mayday, mayday, is anyone there? I need help, if you can hear me!" The radio responded with silence just as it had before and Owen dropped the mic, letting it dangle on its cord. He spun around and scanned the far wall.

Something on the floor caught his eye. It looked like a raised impression on the floor, beneath the carpet. He hurried to it and dropped to a knee, feeling the flooring with his hands. His fingers found an edge in the carpet and pulled it back easily. The fabric revealed a trap door in the floor of the control room. He wondered briefly why it had been covered with carpet but found that he didn't care. It didn't matter to him if it was covered to hide it from sight of the rich people who traveled on the yacht or to hide it from prying eyes that may want its contents. What mattered is that it was there and possibly a way out of the room.

The butterfly latch twisted and he raised the door. Inside was a metal ladder secured to the wall. A cool breeze wafted upwards to him and on the faint current he could smell the greasy stench of oil and gasoline. As the door to the room behind him cracked even more loudly than before, Owen placed his knives back into his belt and then lowered himself onto the ladder. He paused a few rungs down and grabbed the door as well as the carpet. He pulled them both down, trying his best to keep the carpet smooth over the door so as to mask the presence of the door.

When the tunnel was sealed off, he continued down the ladder in complete darkness. As he descended, he heard above him the final explosion as the door to the control room gave in under the weight of the creatures' assault. Owen increased the rate of his descent as the thumps of feet overhead faded.

The air grew considerably cooler as he lowered himself, and

when he reached the bottom of the ladder he was standing in a short, narrow corridor that led toward the rear of the boat. Dim red lights mounted near the ceiling of the tunnel encased in wire sheaths provided enough visibility for Owen to proceed. He glanced once back up the dark shaft to where the trapdoor was. The space remained pitch black, and he turned away from it and began down the hallway.

He had to hunch forward as he moved, the ceiling being much lower than normal. Noise filled the air, increasing in its buzzing as he moved forward. The corridor ran for only a short distance before ending at a rounded, open doorway. Through the opening he could see the engine room, a large space made to look impossibly small and claustrophobic from all the pipes and mechanized parts.

He stepped through the doorway and onto a metal grating that served as the floor. The noise in the room intensified and he winced at the brashness of it. To either side of the room, two large engines dominated their spaces. Each one was long and cylindrical, sprouting pipes like twisted alien insect legs. Dials and LED monitors were everywhere in the room, providing constant detailed information on the status of various facets of the engines' performance.

The metal grating continued between the two engines, then ended at a T-junction to pass in front of the powerful motors. Owen noticed that at the far end, each engine's piping dropped down to the floor, where he assumed it snaked out to the ocean, where the thrust would come into play. Not knowing much of anything about engines of any sort, Owen searched for a way out of the room. Past the port side engine he found a ladder leading up to another hatchway. He climbed the ladder and hesitated at the door, wanting to listen for movement on the other side but knowing that the engines masked all sounds.

When the hatch swung inward on its hinges, he found himself looking out onto a small catwalk that encircled the exterior of the boat. A small spray of ocean water splashed up over the railing and peppered Owen's face. He leaned out and looked to either side, saw nothing along the path, then stepped fully out. He brought the door closed, but not fully, leaving it ajar just enough to ensure an easy escape should he need it later. A quick look over the railing confirmed that while the boat had indeed stopped moving, the ocean had become more and more choppy. Small waves slapped at the hull of the boat, sending more droplets of water toward him.

Owen wiped his face and pulled his knives free, then started along the catwalk, heading toward the front of the ship. As he moved, he kept a constant eye on the boat above him, expecting to see one of the creatures emerge from some doorway that he hadn't discovered yet. Aside from the ocean, the night was silent.

Approaching the bow of the ship, he remembered the first creature he had seen, the one that had stared at him before running out of sight. He had no way of knowing if that was the same one he had killed or if it were one of the two that had chased him into the control room.

As if his thoughts had been a summoning bell, Owen heard the bulkhead door clatter loudly against the inside of the engine room. He flinched and crouched as he spun to see both of the creatures from the control room emerge, their eyes glinting with animal-eye shine as they focused on him. The lead creature, upon seeing Owen, opened its mouth and hissed. Owen turned sideways, keeping the railing and ocean to his back, and began moving quickly along the catwalk to the front of the ship, needing to get into an area where he would have a chance to effectively fight.

He continued to move along the catwalk and found himself in the open space of the foredeck before he knew it. The deck was as he remembered from his vantage point at the pilot's chair. However, being on the deck, things seemed somewhat smaller and he felt much more exposed. The deck wasn't massive, and didn't contain too many places where a creature or human could hide. Owen moved to his right, keeping the creatures to his front, and gazed along the port side of the boat. He saw no movement along that catwalk, so he returned his attention to the walkway he had just emerged from.

Eyes glowed out at him from the dark, a pair on top of each other. It took Owen several seconds to realize that the lead creature had knelt and its companion was now standing behind it. Both paused at the edge of the walkway, just before entering the gray-white glow of the open deck. Owen stared at their shapes, and thought about hurling one of his knives at them. He had seen knife throwing enough times in movies, and a few times at local fairs, that he felt the task couldn't be very difficult. But his lack of experience and the gentle swaying of the boat discouraged such acts of movie heroics.

Instead, he crouched and waited for the creatures to advance.

When they did, they didn't charge directly at him. Instead, one continued toward him and the other separated, crossed the deck and positioned itself on Owen's flank. Owen threw a glance over his shoulder, then retreated several steps to the edge of the boat. He felt the safety rail against his thighs.

The creatures advanced slowly, pacing one another and approaching their quarry evenly, not giving him any chance to attack or defeat one before turning his attention to the other. Owen watched them come, his heart trying its best to break free of his chest and go careening down into the black water below.

With not much distance to cover, the creatures reached Owen within seconds. They didn't hesitate before attacking, gave him no advance warning before the first blow came. Instead they both swiped at him at the same time. Owen ducked one but felt the searing heat of the second's hit as it tore into his skin, ripping stitches loose and spilling blood down onto the painted white deck. Owen reacted instinctively, blind in his own panic. He lashed out with the knives, aiming before him and to his rear with each blade.

The knife in his left hand jarred as it landed a glancing blow on the creature's midriff. A scream of pain was Owen's greatest reward but he had no time to savor the brief victory. His second blade went short of the intended target and he suddenly found himself thrown off balance. Unable to stop himself, Owen fell forward to the deck, his face inches from the clawed foot of the creature. Above him, he heard the beasts growl with triumph and felt them both reach for him.

Without thinking, he rolled away, the safety rail brushing across his back and arm. Then he was on nothing, the only thing below him air and water. He snapped his hands up and gripped the rail, stopping his fall. The creatures paused, staring at him as if he were performing some intensely entertaining magic trick. Owen grunted and struggled to maintain his hold on the rail despite the slickness of his palms and the searing pain in his body as gravity's pull strained his muscles.

With an effort that he thought himself incapable of, Owen began to move along the side of the yacht, using the railing as a mode of transportation. His arms burned with the movements and he stopped after several feet. He cast a glance at the creatures. They remained rooted to the spot, staring at him with quiet amusement. Of course they were, he realized. Where the fuck was he going? The worst that they figured could happen would be him falling into the ocean and drowning or being killed by a shark, thus depriving them of the opportunity of eating him. They knew he was trapped, a dog beaten and backed into a corner. It was only a matter of time before he realized it too and surrendered.

Something boiled in Owen's mind as he stared at the creatures. A hot rage railed against the cage within Owen's emotions it was kept. Owen's gaze narrowed and in an instant he opened the cage within himself. His rage came screaming out, tearing and clawing at the fabric of his mind. Owen vocalized it, screeching his hatred for the creatures, for the situation he was in, for those he had lost.

Before he realized what had happened, he was over the railing and back on the deck. He had the faint, fuzzy knowledge that he was still screaming as he found his footing on the deck and charged the dumbfounded creatures. Owen collided with the closest one, sending it over the railing with the ease of knocking an empty bottle over. Owen heard its shocked cry and was only distantly aware of the splash as it hit the water, then he was on the other one.

The second creature was more prepared, having witnessed its companion's demise. It accepted Owen's attack with only half readiness, however. The two combatants went sprawling to the deck, Owen grunting in pain as the rough surface scraped harsh against his skin and wounds. He pushed the pain aside and attacked the creature with a fury that scared even himself. His fists beat down on the creature's head and torso as the creature mounted a weak defense, placing its own hands up in a halfhearted attempt to block. It screeched in pain and anger, confusion and fear. Owen didn't relent. He hit with every ounce of himself, aiming for any part of the mutant's body. Gashes appeared on its face when he was able to penetrate the defenses, and blood slicked his knuckles.

His hands became numb and yet he continued to hit. The creature went slack, its arms dropping to the deck and the bloody mess that was its head lolling to one side. Owen didn't know if it was dead or unconscious but he did know that he wouldn't be satisfied, wouldn't be free of the horror, until he knew. He gripped its head and slammed the skull over and over again onto the hard surface of the boat.

He didn't stop until long after the skull had begun to flatten and the deck was slick with gore.

17

Owen sat back and took in a deep lungful of air. The warm ocean wind slowly began to clear his mind, drain some of his tension. He looked down at the dead creature that he sat on, studied the ruined skin and flattened head..

As he stared at it, his rage depleted, having fled out of his body, and Owen felt a new emotion fill the void. The tears came sudden and immediate and he did nothing to hide them. He looked up at the sky and screamed his anguish at the cold stars that stared down at him like aliens observing an ant farm. Owen yelled and cried until his throat was raw and his voice broke like waves on rocks. Exhausted, he slid off of the corpse and lay on his side, panting on the deck.

He drifted then, slipping into unconsciousness with the ease of drawing a breath, then tumbling into wakefulness just as easily. Back and forth, back and forth he swayed between the land of pain and suffering and the land of silent oblivion and unknowing.

When at last he did manage to pull himself fully into reality, it was with a sluggishness that refused to let his body function correctly. The entire boat seemed to rock violently as if a new rage of waves attacked the craft. Owen managed to get his knees beneath him, then spent several long minutes bent over with his head resting on the deck, his ass in the air and arms splayed wide to balance himself.

He got to his feet and staggered away from the bow of the yacht. He moved to his right, toward the port side of the ship. When he reached the base of the main cabin, he paused with both hands on the cabin wall. He looked back over his shoulder at the corpse and thought he should go back and dump it into the water, but he lacked both the physical and mental strength to make the journey across the foredeck. Instead he continued along the catwalk until he reached the aft deck. There he turned and entered the ruined living room.

He moved ghost like through the carnage, past the destroyed sofas and shattered glass. Glass and pieces of splintered wood crunched mutedly into the carpet beneath the oversized shoes he wore. Owen saw none of it, heard nothing. His sight was fixated on the spiral staircase and the corpse of the creature heaped three steps from the bottom, his knifes still protruding from its body.

He slipped only once stepping over the dead body, and then was climbing, rising higher into the ship's cabin. His eyes misted again with tears when he looked at the kitchen. The sight of something so normal seemed like a life vest to his drowning mind.

He remained rooted where he stood, tears flowing down his face as once again the enormity of what he had done, what had been done to him and others that he had become close to—however brief their time together—settled heavily on his thoughts. He wasn't sure if he'd ever fully recover. The therapy bills would be outrageous. Doctor Sturn would probably make the serious brown in his corduroys as soon as Owen started to relate everything to him. Those thoughts slowed the tears and brought a half smile to his face. The image of the normally conservative doctor, sitting on his expensive chair and jotting notes with his one hundred dollar pen as liquid shit oozed down his legs and over his patent leather shoes twisted Owen's smile into a gale of laughter.

He doubled over, holding onto the wall for support lest he fall into a giggling heap, unable to stand. The laughter wracked his body, his face and throat burned from the exertion; his abdomen clenched and grew sore. But still he continued, pausing only long enough to suck in huge breaths that were immediately let back out as he continued to laugh.

He didn't know how long he was incapacitated by his mirth. The fit slowed and stopped only when his body could no longer physically continue. Owen's throat was raw and scratchy, his chest felt as if he had sprinted a mile. Slowly he stood upright and swallowed, wincing against the irritation in his throat. Then, looking around the kitchen one last time, he began to walk.

The control room was in disarray, but not overly so. Several cabinets had been left opened, and the radio had been pulled out of its moorings and smashed on the floor. Something caught his eye and he turned and saw the hatch that he had used to escape. It was open, the carpet around it thrown back and torn from the effort of the creatures. Without even realizing it, Owen walked over and closed it with his foot. The door closed with a sharp crack and he flinched, turning to the main entrance with all his nerves on fire.

Nothing stood in the doorway. Owen remained still, frozen ready for action for several seconds. Then slowly he relaxed and walked to the control panel. He sat in the pilot's chair and looked across the display screens. Everything seemed to be running like it should, but he knew that he didn't know thing one about the boat's systems.

With a few touches he re-engaged the engines. As he increased the throttle he felt the yacht respond as it had earlier, like a sleek, powerful beast eager for motion yet completely subservient to its master's touch. Owen turned the steering wheel and watched out the front windshield as the beams of the yacht's forward lights poked into the blackness like twin fingers.

He steered as best as he could, keeping one eye on the green radar screen, the other on the dark horizon. The ocean and sky blended together into an inky mass and for a while he reduced his speed, afraid that he would run into something and become stranded, or worse, sink. But, he reminded himself, he was now in the open ocean, in water that was at the very least several hundred feet deep. When that thought took hold of him, he pushed the throttles forward again.

The pain from his wounds receded to a dull throb, noticeable only when he turned his attention to them. However, he found that as long as he focused on piloting the boat, he was able to ignore the pain throughout his body as well as the feeling of blood dribbling from his opened wounds.

He traveled for a while; what felt to him like an hour but he knew was most likely only a few minutes. Then, in the quiet of the cabin: "You're going to die out here if you don't find help soon." Owen didn't turn and look at his dead wife when she spoke to him, only nodded.

"I know."

He heard her shift in the leather chair next to him, a soft groaning of friction. "Why even bother? I mean, you were going to end it all anyway."

"Don't say that."

"Well, it's true. And you know it is. Come on baby; it'll be like going to sleep. And then we can be together forever. It won't hurt like if one of the things on that island had gotten you."

Owen closed his eyes. "I'm not going to die out here. I'm not going to kill myself either. If you came back to tell me that, then you can go fuck yourself. You're not my wife."

"What am I, then? Just some whore you liked to fuck? Some slut you showed off to people so that you'd feel better about yourself?"

Owen's head dipped slightly and his voice softened. "You're nothing more than my imagination. My wife was the greatest woman to live. She wouldn't say things like that."

He turned to face her, but the chair was empty. He returned his attention to the controls before him and the black abyss beyond the bow of the ship.

"But you can't help it," she said, this time from the hatch leading down to the engine room. Her voice was muffled as it traveled through the door and the carpet. "You're too tired, dehydrated, malnourished. You've lost too much blood; you're exhausted. Why don't you go take some pain pills and lay down? That would be so much better than the gun you were thinking about using the other day. Just go stretch out in that incredible bed and close your eyes. I'll be there. I'll make love to you again."

"You're not my wife!" Owen slammed the throttles all the way forward.

The boat reacted. Owen felt the entire yacht tilt, the bow rising up in the water as the engines employed all their thrust. He stared out, blinking the tears out of his eyes as the luxury yacht rocketed through the water. He didn't look down to see how fast he was going, didn't consult the radar. Instead he kept the steering wheel locked in place and let the vessel travel straight ahead.

His wife's voice had stopped. Or if she continued her suicide sales pitch, Owen didn't notice it. He didn't notice many things at that moment, the tingling in his arms and legs, the growing heaviness over his body, the tears that seemed to pour forth from some inexhaustible well within him.

He didn't notice the orange twinkling lights of the beachside town on the island a quarter mile in front of him. He didn't notice the piers, the beachside resorts or the sand itself. He didn't notice when the yacht plowed onto the beach, jerking to an immediate and violent stop, throwing him forward onto the control panel.

The face that filled his vision was blurry, as if it were being held under water or visible through a thick pane of frosted glass. Owen tried to blink it into focus and found that his eyelids responded slowly and heavily. He blinked for what felt like several hours and with each motion the face became more and more clear.

A young black nurse looked at him, her expression mute. I thought nurses were supposed to smile when their patient's woke up, he tried to say but found that his mouth didn't react properly to his brain's instructions. His lips moved, but even in his condition he could tell they moved on a fraction of an inch. The nurse reached forward and pried open his right eye more than it should have been. Bright white light flooded his vision and he tried to flinch away from her, but his reactions were slow and gummy.

She pulled back and turned her attention to something behind

Owen's head. When she was finished she looked at him again. "Can you hear me?" she asked in a soft yet commanding voice.

Owen tried to say yes but managed only to move his lower lip. He blinked again, remembering that was how people in movies communicated with the—

An idea cleaved through him, white hot with terror. That's how they communicate with people who have no arms or legs and who can't speak any more. That's how they talk to people who are going to be fed strained peas through a straw for the rest of their lives. He struggled to look down his body, to see and verify that his arms and legs were still attached. However, he could only move his head slightly, yet it was enough to see both of his feet peeking at him from his lowest extremity. He dropped his head back to the pillow and tried to nod as best as he could.

Unflinching, the nurse said: "You're in Princess Margaret Hospital in Nassau. You're all right, except for some serious cuts that will probably leave you with some scars to tell your friends about. We've got you on a high dose of pain killers because of your extensive bruising and the cracked ribs you suffered during the accident."

Accident? Owen stared at her face and tried to understand what she was talking about. What accident? How the hell had he gotten here? The last thing he remembered was ... He closed his eyes. He couldn't remember. His memories sprinted away into the murky depths of unknowing.

"You've been here for three days, and this is the first time you've been fully conscious and aware since they brought you in." She paused, her eyes darting to the item she had worked with behind his head. "I'm going to go get the doctor, let him know you're awake." She turned to go, then looked back at him again. "You have a visitor also. Been here all day. If the doctor clears you for a visit, I'll show her in."

Owen let out a sigh and stared at the white ceiling. A sudden feeling of dread crept over him, seeping down into his bones. He felt trapped, constricted within the boundaries of the bed as if the hospital staff had brought him here and tied him down so that he would be easy prey for—

He heard the growling, a wet, gurgling sound and knew immediately that he had been right. He was either still on the island or the creatures had managed to travel to this island with him. He mustered all his strength and tried to sit up, to raise his arms in some kind of defense. If this was going to be it, he thought—if he was going to be ripped apart while strapped to a bed and wearing a tissue thin gown with his bare ass stuck to the mattress, he was going to put up as much of a fight as he could muster.

The bubbly growling sound approached and Owen's pulse began to rocket. His eyes went wide and he clenched his fists, held them up slightly in a weak defensive gesture.

"What is he doing?" a man's voice asked.

The nurse stepped into Owen's sight and placed a hand on his right fist, lowered it gently to the mattress. From behind her came the gurgling growling. A tall, rail thin black man in a white doctor's coat moved forward, his hands steepled in front of his nose. He blew loudly into a handkerchief, producing the wet, growling sound again.

"I don't know," the nurse answered him. "I think he got scared of something."

The doctor checked the item behind Owen's head just as the nurse had, then bent over his patient. When he leaned close to Owen's face, Owen could smell the mucus still trapped in the man's nose, the greasy smell of it wafting out with every exhalation. Owen felt his gown lifted and hands probing his flesh, fingers feeling along the stitched wounds. He winced sharply when they touched his ribs.

"Responsive?"

"Not yet," the nurse said. "He's aware though; I can tell by the color in his face and the look in his eyes. When you speak to him, he focuses on you. He's with us, just not able to speak just yet because of his pain and the drugs."

The doctor studied Owen longer, shining a light into his eyes and asking him questions. Owen was able to answer only in a weak, raspy whisper. No, he didn't know how he got here. No he didn't remember crashing a boat onto a beach. No, he doesn't know who owned the boat or how he got the wounds that covered him. Finally the doctor stood back and returned his pen flashlight to the breast pocket of his jacket. "You said he has a visitor?"

"That's right."

Owen watched the man's face, trying to guess which way he'd answer. If what the doctor had asked about really happened, then the visitor was probably a local policeman, or at best a representative from the US Embassy there to take his statement.

"Five minutes. No longer."

"Right." The nurse left the room. The doctor jotted notes into a chart that he returned to the foot of Owen's bed, and then followed.

An uneasy silence settled over him as he waited. He listened to the muted sounds of the hospital around him, footsteps and muffled voices, dull thumps of doors shutting and soft chimes of phones.

Then, through all of it like a shining beacon, a choked sob and his name. "Oh God, Owen." He had no time to react before there was pain throughout his body as someone leaned across him and embraced him hard, their arms holding his body tight. Owen gasped from the pain and took in a heavy scent of lilac shampoo.

Michelle. He didn't know how she had gotten there but the solidness of her body against his, her hair and wet cheeks pressed against his own skin, the feeling of her arms enveloping him were proof enough that she was with him now.

Her voice mumbled something into his neck and Owen felt fresh tears spring to his eyes at the beauty of the sensation of her breath on his skin. When he didn't answer, she lifted up, pulled back from him. Her face was red, her cheeks flushed. Her eyes had bags under them and were bloodshot from crying. Her hair fell about her face in thick strings and what didn't hang was squeezed together in a bastard ponytail.

She was absolutely beautiful. She sniffed loudly then took his hand. "The nurse told me I only have five minutes with you here, and that you can't really talk right now. That's okay. Just lie there and listen. I don't know everything that happened to you. The hospital staff called me because I'm the only person you have contact info for. I'm still not sure how the cops figured out who you were; they said you didn't have any ID on you. I didn't ask. I got on the first plane I could get and I've been down here for two days. We didn't know if you were ever going to wake up. Well, they didn't, but I did. I just knew you would."

Owen blinked at her, trying to convey his heartfelt gratitude that she was there. He opened his mouth to whisper to her, but his throat closed up, his emotions overwhelming him. She saw his gesture and gasped a smile, then with trembling fingers wiped tears from her eyes. They sat silent, staring at each other for a while, and then there was a sound that drew Michelle's attention. She nodded and looked back at Owen.

"Alright, I have to go for now. I just had to come see you, make sure with my own eyes that you were safe." Owen had a flash of fear that she was going to go home now that she had seen him. Suddenly he desperately didn't want her to leave.

He held her hand, trying to hold it as tight as possible. She squeezed his fingers reassuringly. She coughed, wiped her face with her free hand and looked back down at him, her face now serious. "Listen to me and listen good. Starting right now, shit's going to change. From this moment on, you are not going to leave me alone like you did. You hear me? You're stuck with me. I'm not saying you're going to marry me, Owen. I'm not saying that at all. But you're going to have me around for a while. I almost lost you it seems, and that makes a girl think." She shook her head contemplatively. "Nope. You're stuck with me until I say so. And if you don't like it, I'll plant my foot squarely up your ass."

Owen squeezed her hand and stared into her eyes. Life was about starting over when things had reached a dead end. The only way you grow is to take steps forward in a new direction. After Heather and Jessica, after the island and everything that had happened, Owen knew that with the woman in front of him, he would be able to take those steps.

He squeezed her hand again and she leaned forward and kissed him, gently on the lips. When they parted, she locked eyes with him. "You're stuck with me until I say so, Owen Thompson."

Owen mustered every ounce of his strength and whispered, "Yes, ma'am."

The End

∽

Thank you for reading! If you enjoyed this book, please leave a short review. It doesn't have to be fancy. But, as I said at the front of this book, we authors live and die by reviews. They help me get more eyes on my work and I greatly appreciate every single one!

REVIEW ON AMAZON
REVIEW ON GOODREADS
REVIEW ON BOOKBUB

∽

Find me on the web where you can email me, learn about new things coming soon and even get a free story for signing up for my newsletter! www.byjonathandaniel.com

ALSO BY JONATHAN DANIEL

Blood Night

No reason. No remorse.

It's June, 1987, and with the single flip of a coin, Death has come to the quiet town of Elden Mills.

No one is safe; a flicker of movement or a sudden noise is all it takes to draw his attention. Lurking in the shadows behind a pale mask, he is driven by the need to fill the streets with blood and screams.

If he sees you, you're dead.

Morgan Bell fled Elden Mills and everyone who cared about her after a life-shattering assault. Now, after years of self-alienation, she returns to her hometown to pick up the pieces of her former existence. But Morgan's hopes of starting over are ripped away during a deadly encounter with the madman.

In her darkest moment, Morgan must confront both the painful memories of her own attack and the cold, unfeeling brutality behind the mask.

Will she find healing in the shadows, or add her voice to the chorus of screams?

"Evocative, hypnotic, and ruthless... Blood Night *is alarmingly engrossing from the dreary opening scene all the way to its breathtaking crescendo. Jonathan Daniel effortlessly paints a gorgeous, dark world through his masterful prose, and populates it with distinct and fascinating*

characters. The story drips with atmosphere, brims with dread, and bursts with thrilling flourishes sharp enough to ribbon the pages with readers' blood."

Felix Blackwell, bestselling author of "Stolen Tongues" and "The Church Beneath the Roots"

ALSO BY JONATHAN DANIEL

The Killing Tide

In the silence, doomsday whispers; in guilt, screams echo – who will survive the Killing Tide?

Colin Dowey can't forgive himself. Plagued with survivor's guilt for freezing up during a lethal workplace shooting, the bank teller pours his heavy heart into elaborate roleplaying games as the ultimate detective. But he lands one last chance to ease his conscience in real life when a deposit box's cryptic contents attract the attention of a psychotic assassin.

Desperate to stop the homicidal lunatic from gleefully torturing his loved ones, Colin takes the encoded info to the smartest pair of redneck preppers he knows. But when the wise-cracking brothers break the cypher, he's shocked to discover an obsessed billionaire with a gun aimed at the whole world's head.

Can he overcome his post-traumatic fears before his first live-action adventure triggers a deadly game over?

The Killing Tide is a fast-paced standalone thriller. If you like captivating protagonists, ethically driven villains, and hilarious sidekicks, then you'll love Jonathan Daniel's high-octane race for survival.

Printed in Great Britain
by Amazon